PARIS, ADRIFT

Juliana Series: Book 3
(1955)
LGBT Life in Paris

BY VANDA

Sans Merci Press

This is a work of fiction. Any resemblance my original characters have to a person, living or dead, is merely coincidental.

COPYRIGHT © 2018 VANDA
All rights reserved. This book or parts of it may not be reproduced in any form, except for short citations needed for articles or reviews.

Cover Design: Ann McMan

Edited by: Deborah Dove at Polgarus Studio

Formatting by: Polgarus Studio

Library of Congress Number: 2018902433

Want something for nothing?

Vanda is giving away

Why'd Ya Make Me Wear This, Joe?

her full-length play that inspired the Juliana series

Details can be found at the end of *Paris, Adrift*

Praise for *Olympus Nights on the Square*
Book 2 of the Juliana Series

"A tale not to be missed." (Indie Reader, Dec 6, 2017)

"The novel begins immediately after the war and is chock full of specific details that may not have made it into the history books . . . In every chapter, Vanda highlights the political climate of the times and brings forth a wealth of information describing the anti-Gay, anti-People of Color, anti-Communist, anti-Jew, and anti-Woman policies in New York City and America." (Chanticleer Book Reviews, 11/16/17)

"I pulled my first all-nighter since college reading this book at one setting." (Barbara Kahn, playwright, Theater for a New City, 11/8/17)

"Not only do we get a glimpse into the lives of post WWII characters, we also are reminded how tough it was to be a woman back then. I eagerly look forward to the next additions to the Juliana series. If you've read Juliana, read Olympus as well! If you haven't read Juliana, well, what are you doing with your life?" (Amanda Beilfuss, Amazon Customer, 1/1/18)

"A good story with good characters set in a realistically told dynamic time in the history of New York. Indeed, I would say (the author) makes NYC as much of a character as any of the animated ones in her book. You can feel the breath of life in NYC . . . But this is not a "gay" book any more than a novel set in a concentration camp is a Jewish book. This is a book about people dealing with oppression while they try to live large. That is of universal interest." (Amazon Customer, 10/19/17)

In 2018 *Olympus Nights on the Square* received an Indie Reader Approval Sticker

Praise for *Juliana*
(Book 1 of the Juliana Series)

"As World War II begins, Al and Juliana cross paths repeatedly and a complicated relationship develops. This romance provides a fascinating entry into New York's gay community during a rarely explored era." (Publishers Weekly, 6/4/16)

"Juliana is a masterful work of historical fiction that leads you through the early 1940s with substance and style. It is an LGBT coming of age story, a tale of sexual awakening. . .that really opened my eyes to some of the truth of gay history." (Amazon customer, 7/11/16)

In 2016 Juliana received an Indie Reader Approval Sticker and was shortlisted for the Goethe Historical Fiction Award presented by the Chanticleer International Awards.

DEDICATION

JAMES L. EVERS,

a Teacher

There are teachers and then there are TEACHERS.

Mr. Evers was a TEACHER.

He even got the boys to write poetry.

In his eighth grade class, I wrote my first poem and my first novel,
With the Dusk Came the Dawning

He would come in early, before school once a week to meet with me to discuss my novel. He took my work seriously. For a long time, it was only my little sister and Mr. Evers who did.

At the end of eighth grade he wrote in my junior high year book:

"My children will read your words."

His prediction came true. Now, he's my Facebook friend.

Isn't life weird?

WHY?

This history has to be known.

Sure, you can go and read a non-fiction text.

Lillian Faderman, George Chauncey and others have written terrific books.

I've used them to develop my own story, but watching people live through this history brings you into the heart of the pathos, the humor, the tragedy, the fear and the love all wrapped into one.

Check Out Receipt

Ithaca-Tompkins County Public Library
607-272-4557
http://tcpl.org

Thursday, December 19, 2019 9:56:53 AM
64689

Item: 200226206
Title: Paris, adrift : book three in the Juliana series
Due: 01/25/2020

Total items: 1

Upcoming closed days: Dec 24-26, Dec 31 & Jan 1. No items will be due between Dec 22 and Jan 2.

Give in joy instead of paying fines! Go to www.tcplfoundation.org/donate-now.

CHAPTER ONE

SEPTEMBER 1955

I leaned against Max's Packard staring up at the huge ship. The *SS United States* was the largest, most modern transatlantic ship the US had. It was faster even than England's *Queen Mary*. It was the only ship that could promise to get you from New York to Paris in five days!

When we'd climbed into Max's car a half hour ago, the air had been sticky warm, but down by the harbor the cool breezes flicked at the collar of my dress. I watched the ship's red, white, and blue smokestacks pour smoke high into the air, spreading out over the afternoon sky.

I could smell the salt of the Hudson and taste it on my bottom lip. I remembered that taste from the days Danny and I sat for hours at Huntington Harbor watching the sun slowly sink behind the tugboats. I could still hear their haunting sound in my mind. I remembered Danny and I before the war walking the docks in the West Village, a little more than a mile from here. We'd argued about whether we should go see Max's "nightclub singer" or not. I'd been against it. I thought Max was a charlatan and I hadn't been completely wrong. Even Max admitted that. But imagine if I had won that battle. How different my life would be now. That night changed everything. I went from the potato fields of Long Island to the chaos and bright lights of New York City, where I managed one of the most successful nightclub stars of the decade. And I had a whole lot to do with that success. And now this—the doctor had given me my typhoid shot and I was on my way to Paris on a luxury ocean liner. And soon, very soon I was going to spend five glorious days *and* four nights with Juliana in our own private stateroom. For the first time since we met fourteen years ago, we were going to be a couple. Of course, outside our stateroom we couldn't act like a couple. But behind closed doors. . .

Mercy drove up in her Studebaker and bounced out of the car. "Al! Al! This is so exciting," she squealed as she sprinted toward me. She wore a small, round, white hat that sat on the top of her head like a saucer, a green and white print dress with a bow at the waist, and a pair of short green gloves. She threw her arms around me. "Oh, Al, I'm green." She held up her gloves and laughed. "I really am."

I laughed too.

"Al, you're going to have such a wonderful time," she went on.

"Someday you and Shirl will go."

"I doubt that will ever happen with Shirl's heels dug in about what she wears."

Ever since '52 when Gladys Bentley, the Negro male impressionist, wrote the article about turning back into a woman by getting married and washing dishes, Shirl refused to wear a skirt for anyone under any circumstance. She didn't come to the docks because she didn't want to embarrass us or give us away. "Oh, but look at you," Mercy went on. "I always liked you in blue." She twirled me around. "The cut shows off your petite shape nicely. And the hat suits you."

"I don't look silly, awkward?"

"No. All right, I prefer you in a man's suit, but this dress keeps that basic idea. It's not frilly. You wouldn't look good in frilly."

"I guess Max knows what he's doing."

"Well, that's who I'd ask if I ever got a chance to go someplace nice. Who's the designer?"

"Designer? I forgot to ask Max. I just paid the bill."

"Oh, you." She grabbed at my collar. "Turn around. It should say in the back—Evan Piccone. Oh, that's lovely. You *are* lucky."

"Shirl has the money to get you dresses like this."

"You know how Shirl is about money. Besides, where would I wear it?" I detected some sadness in her voice. "Oh, no matter." She let it roll off her. "I've got something for you. From Shirl and me. Oh, hasn't this heat been awful? You're lucky to be getting away from it. And your ship even has air-conditioning! Let me go get your gift."

I watched her trot back toward her car through the crowds of people that were arriving. Max and Scott stood at the back of the car, talking. Max smoked a cigarette. I studied Scott. He looked okay. Healthy. During the last few months he'd seemed happy. Still, he scared me. I didn't like being responsible for someone who might do some impulsive harm to himself at any minute. I promised his grandma, Mattie, I'd keep an eye on him and make sure he kept playing the piano, which she was certain was his cure. From depression, not homosexuality. She was one of the few straight people I knew that didn't think he needed to be cured from that. I suspected my sudden hiring of Scott for this trip had more to do with Mattie than Scott. The days Mattie and I spent together visiting Scott in the hospital, going to shows, going to the lawyer's office, kind of made me feel like I *was* Scott's wife and Mattie was my mother-in-law. Not that I *wanted* to be his wife, but I liked having her as a mother. She made me forget the horror my real mother had been. It'd kill me if I let her down.

Big muscled longshoremen sweating into their T-shirts dashed down the gangplank of the ship to grab luggage, preparing it to be loaded. I saw Max giving the men a quick up and down look. I don't think Scott noticed. Even with all the love he felt for Scott—and I believed he did love him—he didn't seem able to stop himself from giving a quick look at other men. Maybe Scott didn't mind.

Juliana's colored driver, Sam, turned her Lincoln Premiere onto the lot. He hopped out of the car and quickly opened the door for her. She slid out, carrying an alligator hatbox along with her Chanel navy-blue quilted handbag, and leaned against the car, talking and laughing with him.

She wore a navy-blue suit with a wide-brimmed white hat and white gloves. Watching her with Sam, leaning against the car, was like seeing her for the first time. It was hard to believe I was thirty-two and she was thirty-eight. Was it possible that with age she'd grown even more . . . "She's so beautiful," I whispered to the salty air.

"Yes, she is," Max said, and I looked up to see him standing behind me smoking a cigarette. Scott was over by the car arguing with a longshoreman about how to load the musical instruments. I'd never seen Scott argue with anyone before. He was taking his musical director job seriously.

Mercy dashed up to us. "Here." She held a bottle of Dom Perignon with a ribbon tied around it. "It's from Shirl and me." She had a rectangular package wrapped in bon voyage paper and ribbon under her arm. She left it there, not saying a word about it.

I took the bottle in my hands. "Thank you, Mercy. This is nice of you. Be sure to thank Shirl."

"Well, kid," Max said, "you have yourself one terrific time and come back with lots of stories."

"Aren't you coming to our stateroom to drink this? We won't be leaving for hours. Mercy, you're coming, aren't you?"

"Shirl made me promise. Look what she sent along." Mercy reached into her purse and pulled out a fistful of colorful streamers. "When you leave, I'm going to throw these at you."

"See, Max? You've got to come on the ship. It wouldn't be fun without you. You have to say goodbye to Scott."

"I will. Here on the dock. I don't think Juliana would like being stuck in the same room drinking champagne with me."

Max and Juliana hadn't spoken since '39 or '40, after a horrendous fight. One story said it was because of sex, another story said it was because she married Richard, and still another said it was because she was trying to be heterosexual. It was impossible to tell which story was true, but their feud continued right into the fifties.

I turned to Max. "Well, *you're* my friend and I don't give a damn what Juliana—"

"You should watch your language, dear," Juliana said from behind me. "You never know who might be listening."

I turned toward her. "Uh, Juliana, I didn't mean . . . what I meant was, well . . ."

"You'd like Max to come help celebrate your bon voyage. I see no reason why he shouldn't. He's your friend. I would never want to stand in the way of friendship."

"Thank you," Max said to her with a gallant nod.

"Sorry Shirl couldn't join us, Mercy," Juliana said, not acknowledging Max. "But we're glad *you* came. Oh, look, people are boarding. Shall we?"

As we moved toward the ship, more people came up to us and collected around Juliana. They were fans and friends who'd come to see her off. They piled bouquets of roses and daisies in her arms. Scott and I gathered up the bottles of champagne they offered. Many of them followed us onto the ship as they chattered away in Juliana's ear. I wedged myself past a fat man who was making googly eyes at Juliana.

A thrill jumped into my stomach, embracing me, as we walked up the gangplank. I felt an urge to run, jump, and do somersaults up the length of it. But I reminded myself I was Juliana's manager and put on my stern face; still, a child's grin kept poking out.

As soon as we crossed the threshold into the ship, our shoes sinking into the plush carpeting, the crew—men dressed in blue uniforms and bright smiles on their faces—greeted us. They waved and shouted, "Welcome," and the thrill in me grew. One of the men gathered up our passports and took them to a desk where another man stamped them. The first guy came back and handed them all to Max. I guess they thought he was the father of the family.

A bellboy took some of the bottles I had in my arms, but he was a little guy and couldn't hold them all. He kept dropping them, so after a while he gave up and let Max and me take some of them as he led us toward a hallway that had a sign that read "First Class." *I* could afford first class. Wow. But where did the other people go? The ones who *couldn't* afford first class? I approached the bellboy, his arms filled, trying to lead us toward the elevator. "Where do the other people go?" I asked.

"Other people?"

He kept trying to push through the crowds to get to the elevator while at the same time answer my question. He had to please me because *I* was first class. "The other people who aren't first class."

"Oh. The cabin class people are beneath your staterooms and the tourist class people are way down where the ship shakes. They have their own dining rooms and public rooms, so you don't have to worry. Those types won't bother you. Each class is locked behind an iron gate, so you'll never see them." He hurried ahead of me.

"I'll never see any of them? Ever?" I asked, running beside him.

"Huh?" He was pretty preoccupied. "Oh. No, never," he said. "They won't bother you."

A chill ran through me. "Bother me? I'm one of them. *I* belong where the ship shakes." The elevator door opened. Still staring at that first-class sign, I followed our overworked bellboy and the others onto the conveyance that would take us to where the ship didn't shake.

We got out on the Promenade Deck, away from the ones who weren't as good as us. I wanted to be sick, but I had to push it away. I had a job to do. This was for Juliana. She would've had a fit if I'd stuck her down in tourist class. She didn't know how to be anything but first class.

The bellboy led the way down the hallway to our room. Other passengers were dashing about looking for their rooms, too. Some were raising glasses to each other and there were a few who were already pickled. Our bellboy got swallowed up in the crowd. We were in danger of being lost, but I happened to have a paper in my purse with our cabin number on it. I led the way down the hall, looking for our stateroom. As we moved deeper into the hallway, it became clogged with passengers moving back and forth. Bellboys and deck stewards dashed past us with arms filled with flowers, fruit baskets, ice buckets, and luggage.

Our group got shoved up against the wall as we searched the numbers on the doors. We slid along, moving closer to our own cabin. I wanted to hurry and get Juliana out of this cramped mess, but she, of course, was laughing at the absurdity of it all.

A young man in a tux, his tie hanging loose around his neck, his collar open, bumped into Juliana. He pressed his hips against hers, grinning, "Well, hello there, doll," he slurred, expelling his alcohol breath all over her. He put his hands on her waist and grinded himself against her. "Tight space, honey."

Juliana, her arms filled with flowers, her hatbox, and handbag, looked him right in his eyes. "Take your person off my person. Now." There was no hint of humor in her voice. "Or you will soon find *my* knee in your person."

Max yanked the guy back by his shoulders. "Get your hands off my wife, buddy."

"She's your wife? Gosh, you are one lucky son-of-a-gun."

"Yes, I am. Now get lost."

The guy staggered away to be swallowed up in the crowd.

"Your wife?" Juliana said with raised eyebrows.

"Well, it worked, didn't it? A little gratitude might be nice."

"You wouldn't know what to do with a wife."

"You see, Al? See how she talks to me?"

"Come on you two," I said. "Play nice." I guided our group as we slid along the wall past the crowds and found our door.

We entered the sitting room portion of our stateroom. I set the champagne bottles on the glass coffee table in front of the couch. A steward dashed in with vases for Juliana's flowers and those got placed around the room. More stewards arrived with more flowers and more bottles of champagne and baskets of fruit.

I ran to see the bedroom. It had two large double beds. Well, we won't need two of them, I thought.

"Well?" Juliana said from behind me.

"It's . . . well gee, Jule, it's magnificent."

"Come, look here." She went to the curtains and pulled them aside to reveal two portholes. I threw off my shoes, jumped on the bed, and looked through one of them. "You can see outside."

"Uh, huh. And there's another two under this curtain and three more in the other room."

I sat on the bed. "Juliana."

"Hmm?"

"Nothing. I wanted to say your name."

She smiled. "We better go out and entertain our guests."

Our guests? *Our* guests.

* * *

We had a few more hours of noisy people chattering and drinking in our stateroom before the ship took off. I couldn't wait for this part to be over, so I could be alone with her.

Juliana, of course, was the perfect hostess. The whole time she had a few men gathered around her flirting. She flirted back, but that was her job. I wanted her to do that.

Max was the life of the party, making pains to meet people who would be good for business. Both of us met lawyers and their wives, and art dealers, and their wives and financiers and their wives. Even the Baron and Baroness Kronecker of Belgium stopped by our stateroom. They were making their seventieth crossing and were trying to meet everyone. Scott got back from supervising the storage of the instruments and stood in the doorway. I had to coax him into the room. He was never comfortable at these types of gatherings, but he was looking more sullen than usual, and that made me worry.

When the time to leave drew near, I watched Max and Scott retreat from the others and light up cigarettes. They stood as close to each other as decorum would allow two men to stand. They restrained themselves from even the slightest, inconsequential touch. We all did that. It was automatic to turn off our true selves when in a room filled with straights. And this room was bulging with straights, so we were all on guard.

"Max," I said, going over to them. "You're not going to see Scott for five months. Why don't you go in the other room and give him a proper goodbye?"

"You think I should?" Max asked, looking hopefully at Scott.

"It's too risky," Scott said. "Someone could see us go in there and easily put two and two together."

"Everyone's too drunk to care," I said.

"No, Al. Thanks for the offer," Max said, "but I think Scott's right. It's too risky."

"And it could impact Juliana," Scott said. "If her public thought she hired, you know . . ."

"Damn," I sighed.

"Yeah, damn," Max said.

The ship's whistle blew and a voice over the loud speaker said, "All ashore who's going ashore."

Juliana and I stood by the door shaking hands and saying thank you as people said their goodbyes. Mercy handed Juliana the box she'd been carrying around with her. "Here. This is for both of you from Shirl and me. Enjoy, but open it when you're alone." Juliana put it on the table next to a fruit basket. Mercy hugged and kissed us. "Have a terrific time, and when you get home, I'll make a special dinner. You'll tell Shirl and me all about it."

When I turned, I saw Max and Scott through the full-length mirror that hung between the sitting room and the bedroom. They were shaking hands. "Juliana, it looks like everyone has left." I nodded over at Scott and Max.

"Yes." She looked at them quickly, and back at me. She said loudly, "Let's go out on deck. There's at least a half an hour before the ship leaves. This door locks automatically."

We closed the door behind us as we went.

Out on deck, we hung over the side and yelled down at the people on the pier. The stewards handed out streamers and we threw them at the crowds below. Mercy with her own personal bag of streamers was throwing them up at us.

The orchestra played rousing tunes as we cheered. Shortly, Scott joined us on deck while Max ran down the gangplank. He stood next to Mercy, waving from the pier.

The ship's baritone whistle penetrated through the cheers as it slowly rumbled away from the dock, kicking up a strong breeze.

I felt the vibrations under my feet. "We're moving, Juliana. We're going to Paris. We really are." I think I might've been jumping up and down by that time. The orchestra burst into, "Anchors Aweigh."

"Yes, Country Girl." Juliana smiled. "We're going to Paris because *you* planned it. Remember?"

Gosh, I wanted to kiss her right then.

CHAPTER TWO

"I can't do this. I can't. I can't." I threw down four of my hats and three single mismatched gloves.

"What's the matter?" Juliana asked, stepping into the bedroom.

"Look at you. You're dressed and beautiful. It was a piece of cake for you, but me? Look at me." I was still only in my bra and girdle. One stocking was hooked, while the other wilted around my ankle. I looked down at the mass of clothes I had spread over the two beds, the floor, and the vanity. "What's supposed to go with what? Do I have to do this *every* day?"

"Most nights, dinner will be formal. A cruise ship is a pretty formal place. I'll help you." She took off her gloves, dropped them on the vanity, and sorted through the mass of gowns that I'd thrown all over the place; she hung most of them in my trunk. Our trunks stood five feet tall and were pressed against the wall; they opened outward like closets. She pulled a gown from its hanger and gathered up a hat and a pair of gloves. Magically, every item matched the way it was supposed to. "I don't understand why this has you all upset," she said. "You've been to formal dinners before."

"Yes. And Max always told me which *one* dress went with which *one* hat and *one* pair of gloves. I've never had to deal with this many dresses all at the same time, along with all these gloves and hats. And shoes! I forgot shoes." I ran to the trunk, yanked open a few of the bottom drawers, and threw shoes into the middle of the room. "Which shoes? Which ones, Jule? I can't figure it out. There's something wrong with me." I plopped onto the bed with a thud.

She laughed. "There's nothing wrong with you. Here, put your gown on; I'll lay your gloves and your hat on the vanity, so you can find them. These shoes will go perfectly with this outfit. Lavender is a good color for you.

You'll look lovely. But hurry. Scott will be here soon."

"Let's open our present from Shirl and Mercy," I said, pulling a slip over my head.

"I don't think there's time. Scott will be here in a minute."

"So? He'll wait while we open it." I hooked up my second stocking.

"I have a feeling it's something we wouldn't want to open in front of Scott."

"No kidding?" I pulled my dress over my head and stepped into my shoes. "Then we definitely have to open it *now*."

"I don't know, Al."

"Oh, come on. How can you stand it?" I ran into the other room to get it.

"No. Let me," she said, following me into the other room. She picked up the package.

I sat beside her on the couch. "Do you know what it is?"

"I have a pretty good idea."

"What?"

She slipped off the ribbon and pushed a fingernail under the seal of the wrapping paper. I noticed that she'd let her nails grow long. That seemed strange since we were going to have lots of time together. Oh well, she'd file them later that night. Inside the box, the gift was covered with white tissue paper. Juliana turned away from me, looked in the box, and closed it again. "Yes. I was right. Stand up so I can see how you look."

"What is it?"

"Not something you'd be interested in."

"How do you know? Tell me what it is."

"A dildo. All right?"

"You mean one of those, uh, uh. . ." I made a gesture depicting a, well, you know, with my hand.

"Yes."

"What'd they give us that for?"

"What do you think?"

"Yeah, but we never. . ."

There was a knock at the door.

"That's Scott. Answer the door. I'll put this away."

"Can I see it?"

"Not now." She walked into the bedroom.

"Have *you* ever. . .?"

"Are you going to leave Scott standing in the hallway? That's rude."

I opened the door.

* * *

The dining room was quietly opulent with white columns and a two-story vaulted ceiling. The floor was a glistening polished black. Each table had three red roses in the center, along with highly polished silverware and folded linen napkins with the imprint of the ship's logo. A huge sculpture of four women who looked like they might be goddesses extended toward the high ceiling. I'd heard that the art work and the furnishings had all been designed by two women. Women! The thought made me proud. The orchestra in the balcony played softly in the background.

Our waiter guided us toward a table, but before we reached it, a few people hurried over to Juliana. "Oh, Juliana," one chubby woman in a pink gown that showed too much cleavage said. "When I heard you were going to be on this ship, I thought I'd perish, just perish. I told my husband, Oscar—oh well, you don't want to hear about him. Will you be singing on the ship?"

"No, I'm a passenger like everyone else, and right now I'm a hungry passenger, so if you'll excuse me. . ."

I tried to get between Juliana and the woman, but the woman's elbow somehow made its way to my stomach. "I must have your autograph," she oozed.

"Certainly," Juliana said. "Do you have something you want me to write on?"

"Of course," the woman giggled. "You'd need that, wouldn't you? Can't write on the air. But I don't seem to have . . . I left my purse back at the table with Oscar." She flapped her arms around. "Oh, there must be something, something . . . Yes!" She whisked a folded linen napkin from one of the tables. "This."

"Oh, uh, well, mightn't someone need that?" Juliana asked.

"Oh, poo, they can get another. When do I get a chance to have the *real* Juliana give me her autograph? Won't you, please?" She held the napkin toward Juliana.

"A pen?"

"Here you go," Scott said, taking one from his inside pocket. What a terrific idea inside pockets were.

Juliana quickly scribbled her name across the napkin, trying to stay calm when I knew she would've rather bopped the woman.

"I loved you at the Latin Quarter two years ago," the woman said, taking back the napkin.

"Thank you."

"And so did Oscar." She flexed her eyebrows up and down. "If you know what I mean. You gave us a such a nice night that night."

"Glad I could be of help," Juliana said. Scott took Juliana's arm and moved her away from the bottleneck of people who were beginning to gather.

We had almost made it to our table when the captain of the ship appeared. "Miss Juliana," he said, standing at attention. "I'm Commodore Jonathan Black." He was a slender man, not too tall, with gray hair. His uniform was an impossibly spotless white. "I wonder if you would do me the honor of joining me at my table tonight."

"Well, that'd be lovely," Juliana said, "but I'm here with . . ." She turned toward us.

"Sir," Commodore Black said, eye to eye with Scott. "Would you mind terribly if I borrowed Miss Juliana for a mere hour or two?"

"Uh, me?" Scott said, shrugging. "Sure. Why not?"

"Thank you, sir." He nodded at Scott and me and put out his arm for Juliana to take. "I saw you, my dear, at the Copa last year and I was whisked away." Then he whisked Juliana away.

"Why'd he ask *you*?" I said to Scott as we were about to take seats at our assigned table.

"Because I'm a man. Sit down. The waiter's waiting."

"But *I* hired *you*," I said as the waiter pulled out my chair for me. "Doesn't that make me *your* boss and Juliana's, too? Shouldn't *I* be deciding these things? She needs rest."

Scott shrugged his shoulders as he sat and opened his menu. "Technically my boss is Richard. Juliana's too. He's the one who signs the checks."

"But you know it's me who does the work."

"But Captain Black doesn't know that." He studied his menu.

"So, he *assumed* you, of course, were in charge."

"Of course."

"That makes me livid."

"Al, forget it. It's not a big deal."

"Not to you, it isn't. You're a man, but . . ."

"Calm down. You're going to burst something. Look at this delicious menu. It's just the way things are. You can't change it. Be glad you're on this beautiful ship with this wonderful air-conditioning and not sweating in New York."

The waiter still stood at our table, waiting—I guess waiting for us to take a breath. He turned toward Scott. "Would the lady and gentleman care for an aperitif?"

"You want something, Al?"

"Not now."

"No thanks," Scott said to the waiter. "We're going to look over your entrées."

"Very well, sir." He nodded his head and left us.

"The smoked Irish sturgeon might be a nice appetizer," Scott said. "What's important is that Juliana is getting noticed. Isn't that why you put this whole thing together? To rebuild Juliana's confidence and career?"

"Yes," I sighed, taking off my gloves. "You're right. That's what's important." I opened my menu. "What do you think about the braised smoked ox tongue?"

"It makes me want to be sick," Scott said.

"Well, that's not good."

"No. I'll stick with something I know like the salmon steak."

I watched Juliana flirting with all the men at the captain's table. I worried she wouldn't pay enough attention to the women, but they were oohing, aahing, and giggling over her, so I figured she had the situation under control.

"Is that Cary Grant sitting at the end of the captain's table?" I asked.

Scott turned in his chair to look. "I think so."

* * *

The Meyer Davis Orchestra played "Autumn Leaves" as we entered the ballroom with its crystal chandeliers glistening down from the ceiling like raindrops. Women in a bouquet of reds, yellows, greens, and blues floated across the floor on the arms of men in black tuxedos. We'd left Juliana in the dining room still talking to the entranced Captain Black at his table. Cary Grant had left.

"Do you think she'll sleep with him?" I whispered to Scott.

"Who? Cary Grant?"

"No. From what I hear, he's one of the few who *wouldn't* be interested. I meant the captain."

"No. Stop thinking like that. She's married. Dance with me." He scooped me up in his arms and foxtrotted me out to the center of the crowded dance floor.

"How are you, Scott?"

"Did I step on your toe?"

"No."

"Then why are you asking me that?"

"I worry about you."

"Please, don't. I'm fine."

"Was it wrong of me to take you away from Max?"

"Of course, it was." He smiled as he swung me around, stopping in mid-swing. "Did you hear that? That trill the pianist just played." He sighed and started dancing again.

A dark-haired man in a tuxedo came up behind Scott and tapped him on the shoulder. "May I?" he asked.

Scott said, "Sure." And backed away.

"But Scott, I should stay with you."

"Have fun." He stepped off the dance floor and my eyes followed him over to the bar. The man clasped me so tightly to his chest, I could hardly breathe. "Hello, I'm Dan Schuyler," he said.

"Nice to meet you. Could we dance over that way? I want to keep an eye on my friend. He doesn't know anyone here and . . . Oh, I'm being rude. My name is—"

"I know who are, Miss Huffman."

"You do?"

"Yes. That's why I cut in. You're close to Juliana."

A chill ran up the center of my spine. "I—don't think I know what you mean."

"Can we stop dancing a minute before I step on you? My wife says I have three left feet. I have a business proposition to make."

"A business proposition, Mr. Schuyler?" He walked me over to the row of red, barrel-backed chairs situated around small round tables that lined the perimeter of the ballroom. "Schuyler? Schuyler?" I said, "Why does that name sound familiar?"

"Well, you may have heard of me in connection with *The Miller's Daughter*. I co-produced that show with Martin Bilberbank."

"You were with Martin Bilberbank? I've heard good things about him, but I've never met him. I wouldn't remember you from that show, though, because it was before my time. I wasn't in the business then."

"No matter. I was merely in the background, co-producing."

"But I did hear some talk about that show. Old-timer Broadway scuttlebutt. It was a hit and then something happened, I believe, that almost closed it. I'm not sure what. I'm afraid I don't stay on top of Broadway gossip. I have enough to do keeping track of the supper clubs and cabarets."

"Well, it's best not to pay too much attention to rumors anyway. They can be so hurtful. Can't they, Miss Huffman?"

"Excuse me?"

"Like for instance, it's been rumored that I disappeared."

"Disappeared? My goodness. I never heard that one."

"Good." He spread his arms out wide. "Because here I am. I did go away for a time to gather my internal resources. I went to India to meditate. Shall we sit?"

"Yes, of course." He guided me into my chair. As I sat, I took in the measure of his thirtyish demeanor. He was slim in a well-made tuxedo, dark hair slicked back away from his brow. Nothing particularly distinctive.

"Meditation can put you in touch with your true self." He sat across from me. "So, you see I did not disappear, Miss Huffman, rather, I *appeared*. After much contemplation, I appeared to myself. What would you like to drink?"

"Nothing. If we're going to talk business."

"I always find business goes down easier with a martini."

"Then please have one, Mr. Schuyler. I personally find it best to have a clear head when discussing business matters."

He signaled the waiter and ordered his drink. "Miss Huffman, I have a script I'd like to speak to you about for Juliana."

"A script? But Juliana is a singer, not an actress."

"You're referring to that fiasco last season."

"Well..."

"That part wasn't right for her. I'm surprised you let her do it. The script I'm talking about is a musical. That's what she does. Sing. Like an angel. From hell."

"Well, I've never heard it put that way, but that description *does* sound apt."

"The script I have in mind allows room for that wonderful presence she brings to the stage without sinking her behind some dull character. She *is* the character. *You* know what I'm talking about."

"Yes, I do."

He reached into his inside pocket and pulled out a pack of cigarettes; he slid one away from the rest and extended the pack toward me.

"No thank you. I don't smoke."

"Ah, but these are Gauloises. French. Serious cigarettes, more so than our American brands. I make this trip three or four times a year and I always stock up. Can't I entice you to try?"

"I'm familiar with the brand. I have a friend who smoked these and Gitanes Brunes right after the war, but he found them both coarse, inferior to American brands."

"Oh?" He put the package back into his pocket without taking one out.

In the background, a girl singer sang "You Belong to Me" with the orchestra.

"Things are changing, Miss Huffman." He leaned close to me. "Can't you feel it in your bones? That's what I've been off thinking about. In India. Cabaret is changing. Music is changing."

"You had to go that far away to think *that*?"

"Distance brings perspective." He took the cigarette package out again and quickly lit one, returning the pack to his inside pocket. Damn, those inside pockets are handy. Why don't women have them? "Look what's happening. The cabarets are bringing in solo comics to do a whole evening."

"At both Max's Mt. Olympus and The Haven, we still headline singers."

"Yes, but how long can you continue doing that? People are coming less and less to hear singers. Even Swing Street is being infected with hoodlums and other unsavory elements. You must've seen that. That new rock 'n' roll music has a lot to do with making criminals out of the young."

"Mr. Schuyler, I don't think—"

"Audiences fearful for their lives are staying home. But, they still go to the theater where the grown-ups are."

"Perhaps, but the theater has been limping lately, too."

"True. But we've got some pretty good shows on the boards right now. *Carousel, Peter Pan, Damn Yankees. They're* making money."

"By busing in audiences from Ohio. New Yorkers are staying home to watch TV. I don't know if you can consider that a thriving theater."

"You wait. Theater will survive. And it will be musicals like the one I have in mind for Juliana, the big musical, that will bring back the crowds. Not those pesky social issue plays they're doing on off-Broadway that depress everyone. Broadway is about to explode once again with new talent. And you know—Juliana isn't getting any younger."

"Don't let her hear you say that."

"I mean no offence. She's maturing, which can work in her favor. Now is the perfect time for her to make the transition to something that doesn't tie her to only singing in nightclubs. If she had a hit musical, I bet it wouldn't be long before we were seeing her regularly on TV. Maybe she'd even get her own show."

"I like the way you think, Mr. Schuyler. But finding the money for a musical these days is no easy task. That's why fewer musicals are being produced. How do you purport to raise the money?"

"I assure you I can get the money, but you'll have to trust me on that one. May I bring a copy of the script to your stateroom tomorrow?"

"Certainly not."

"Or even better we could read it together on the deck after breakfast."

"Read it together? I think it would be difficult for me to concentrate if you were reading over my shoulder."

"I could read it to you."

"Mr. Schuyler, did you write this script? Because you're starting to sound like a writer and I don't do business with writers."

"Heavens, no," he laughed. "I don't write. My talent is like yours, Miss Huffman. I discover those with the savvy for writing, singing, whatever, and I exploit it."

"Well, 'exploit' isn't exactly the word I would have chosen, but your point is well taken. I would have used the word 'support.'"

"That's because you're a woman."

"Is that a problem for you?"

"Not at all. I very much like that you're a woman. As the French say, 'Vive la difference.'" He blew out a stream of smoke and winked at me.

"So—back to business, Mr. Schuyler."

He leaned toward me. "I know this script is perfect for your client."

"Richard Styles is Juliana's manager and he'd have to approve any—"

"Come on, Miss Huffman, I know your secret."

I felt the color draining from my face. "What secret? I have no—"

"Sure, you do. Mr. Styles is Juliana's manager in name only. *You* are the creative force behind her. I've been studying you for some time. I leave nothing to chance. I *know* you, Miss Huffman."

Sweat gathered around the waistband of my underpants. Was he playing a game with me or did he know something? I smiled. "I think I'll take that drink now."

"My pleasure." He signaled for the waiter. "What'll you have?"

"Uh, well, a side—no, a Manhattan."

"You heard the lady," he said to the waiter.

"Very well, sir." The waiter nodded and dashed off.

"So, you've been observing me." I tried to sound unconcerned. "Whatever on earth for?"

"To learn."

"What would I have to teach an apparently savvy man like yourself?"

"Oh, Miss Huffman, there is so much I have learned from you." He didn't take his eyes off me, so I didn't take mine off his.

"You are good at this business," he continued. "And you know it. Not only with what you've done with Juliana, but with Lili Donovan too. I may have something for her in another property I'm developing."

The waiter handed me my drink. I gripped the glass so hard I thought I might crush it, but I would not take my eyes off him.

"Your Buck Martin has a strong voice, but he was terrible in 'Hey There, I'm Here,' a ridiculous piece of fluff. Unworthy of Dame Margaret."

"And Buck Martin," I said. "Give him time and you'll see what he can do."

"Well, you do know how to choose your talent, so I'll believe you. I've also got my eye on Patsy LaRue, but she's got to change that name. It makes her sound like a stripper."

"So, you've been observing me because of my work with singers?"

"No, Miss Huffman. That's not the only reason."

"Oh?" I took a sip of my drink and switched my glass from one hand to the other, trying to appear at ease.

"You are a most fascinating woman. Are you married?" He leaned his elbow on the arm of my chair. Too close. *Don't react, Al. Keep calm.*

"Well, if you've been studying me as closely as you claim, you must already know the answer to that."

"You could have a husband tucked away in some dark closet, but I don't think so. A husband would get in your way. Wouldn't he?"

"And what does any of this have to do with the script?" I resisted turning my gaze from him.

"I'd like to invite you to afternoon tea tomorrow. Will you join me?"

"Mr. Schuyler, I am not married, but *you* are."

He leaned back in his own chair. "Divorced. Three years. I know, immoral. However, you know what they say about people in our business. We're all an *immoral* bunch. Aren't we, Miss Huffman?"

"I am an ardent spinster, Mr. Schuyler. Totally dedicated to my work." I couldn't believe I'd said that. There was a time that admitting to being a spinster would've crushed me under a heavy weight of shame. Now, I used it as my shield to protect me from the truth of what others might suspect.

The orchestra played, "Sway," the song Ethel, Lucille's friend, had sung while she took her clothes off for me at The Haven.

"Call me Dan, won't you?"

"No, Mr. Schuyler, I don't think so. We have business—"

"Dance with me." He hopped out of his chair and took my hand.

"What about the three left feet?"

"I lied."

"Why would you lie about something like that?"

He shrugged his shoulders. "I had to get you to sit with me and consider reading the script. Sorry. Business. Let's dance."

"Mr. Schuyler. I manage with the waltz and the foxtrot. Not terribly well, but I don't usually kill my partner. This is a rhumba."

"You were fine before."

"Fine?"

"No. Divine."

"I know I wasn't divine, but I was hoping for a little better than fine."

He pulled on my arm. "Come, you're stalling. I'll guide you through it."

"My friend!" I practically shouted, pulling back my hand. "Where is he?"

My eyes shot around the room. There was no sign of Scott. I'd forgotten to watch him.

"He looked like a big boy to me. I bet he can take care of himself. Let's go."

"No, you don't understand. I *do* need to find him."

"Then I'll help you."

"No, no, I have to go. But I do want to see that script. Where can we meet so you can give it to me?"

"Your stateroom?"

"No."

"How about that afternoon tea tomorrow? It's a real treat." He put on a poor English accent. "Veddy British."

I took his arm and guided him to the side. "There's one thing. You cannot tell Juliana we're talking about a script for her. If you do the whole thing will never happen. This has to be handled delicately."

"Not a word." He locked his lips with his fingers.

I dashed out of the room like Cinderella hurrying to catch her carriage before it turned into a pumpkin. I caught up with Scott on deck. He leaned on the railing, staring at the moon. As I walked toward him, the wind coming off the Atlantic almost knocked me over. Couples clung to each other and the railing as they made their romantic moonlight walk. One woman's hat flew off her head and her beau tried to grab it, but a gust of wind took it higher into the air and plopped it down onto the dark choppy water.

I took my hat off and held it under my arm as I stood next to Scott. The wind rearranged my hair into a wild mess. "Are you all right?" I asked him.

"Could you stop asking me that all the time? It makes me nervous. I start thinking you know something I don't."

"I don't ask you *all* the time."

"Yeah, you do, and then you look at me like that."

"Like what?"

"Like how you're looking at me now. All sad and worried. Like I'm a sick person that you have to be really careful around. I wish you'd treat me like you used to—normal. Max is worse than you. He's always got this stupid grin on his face and telling me to 'have some tea,' 'put up my feet,' 'don't work so hard.' He even cuts the depressing stories out of the newspaper before I read them. It's like trying to read Swiss cheese with advertisements. I won't be able to stand this kid-glove treatment for the whole trip. And no, I wasn't thinking of jumping in."

"You weren't?"

"No, I was thinking how beautiful it is. The ocean and the moon and the salt air. And I was thinking how beautiful you and Max were to me during that bad time. And how my grandma came all the way up from Lake Ambrosia. I caused everybody a lot of trouble, didn't I?"

"Yeah, you did."

"Thanks a lot."

"Well, you asked."

"You could have been a little more tactful, softened the blow some."

"You were a pain in the ass, Scott, and we went through all that because we love you. You said you want me to stop treating you like a sick person, so I'm telling you the unadorned truth."

The ship bounced up and down with the waves, and I pulled my wrap more tightly around me. We went up, down and up, and down and up and . . . "Uh, Scott, I think . . ."

"Don't look at the water. Look at the horizon."

"I'm not feeling so . . ."

He took my arm. "Come over here." He walked me into the glass-enclosed deck and sat me down on one of the chaise lounge deck chairs. He shook out a blanket that hung over the back of the chair and draped it over my legs. "Now look at me. Not the ocean." He sat on the chair next to me. "The

French call that green look on your face 'mal de mer.'"

"You speak French?"

"No, I met a French couple on deck a little while ago. They're on their way home. I used to go sailing with my father when I was small. He taught me all about avoiding seasickness."

"How are you, Scott? Really."

"Fine."

"You don't look so fine."

"Neither do you," he laughed.

"Yeah, but I have a reason. What's yours? Are you mad because I left you by yourself?"

"No. I like being by myself."

"How are things with you and Max?"

"Well, you know."

"No, I don't. You never tell me anything. You don't have to, but I thought we were friends. You never let me help you with anything."

"You do help me, Al. By being around and saying nice things to me."

"That obviously wasn't enough." I drew my wrap closer around my shoulders, trying to block out the cold.

"What do you mean?"

"You never told me that you were feeling so desperate that you wanted to—to die. Is that what you wanted? We were never sure if that was what you were trying to do or what."

Scott looked away. "Do we have to talk about this?"

"Yeah, I think we do. You're making everyone—me—feel so left out of your life. You went and did that, and you didn't say one word, not one word about how bad you were feeling. When the doctors told me what had happened, I was so mad I wanted kill you." I slapped my hand over my mouth, shocked at what I said. He laughed, and I joined him.

"I'm sorry, kid," he said.

"How can you call me kid? I'm older than you. And I'm your boss, so show some respect."

"Max calls you kid so. . . Look Al, you mean a lot to me, Al, and that was a lousy thing to do to you."

"You're not kidding, it was. What if you'd succeeded? Hah, that's success?

You have any idea how I would've felt?"

"I do now. It was thoughtless."

"And your God," I whispered, "may not care a whole lot for homosexuality, but you can be *damn* sure he hates suicide. There's no love in that."

"You're right. But you don't have to follow me around this ship all week. I'm not going to jump over the side."

"Why was it so bad you wanted to die?"

"This is going to sound strange, but I didn't want to die. I wanted to kill the pain. I went to this bar and ordered a drink because I was mad. Mad at me. Mad that I couldn't stop wanting Max in that way. I wanted the alcohol to kill the pain, so I kept drinking and drinking. This guy, a cowboy type, propositioned me, and the anger and pain in me was so deep and the alcohol wasn't killing it, so I went with him. We had sex. Please don't tell Max."

"I think he figured that out."

"When it was over, I told the cowboy about Max. I went on talking and talking and maybe crying, and I guess I broke the empty scotch bottle we'd been drinking from and I think I tried to stab myself. But I know this for sure, that when I picked up that piece of broken glass and stuck it into me it wasn't because I wanted to die. It was because I wanted to live. I'm okay now so you don't have to worry. Standing out here breathing in this air makes me think that maybe there may be another way to look at things. And maybe God *is* bigger than I've been giving him credit for. That's what my grandma says. So, go back to your stateroom and get warm. I'm fine."

"No, I think I'll stay here on this chaise lounge breathing in the salt air, hoping Juliana shows up soon. Tonight is going to be a special night for us."

CHAPTER THREE

I fell asleep on the chaise lounge on deck and didn't wake up until a pale blue haze rose in the sky. Zombie-like, I walked back to the stateroom and fell into bed. Juliana still wasn't there; she didn't arrive until the thin rays of sun peered through the portholes. She slept into the afternoon. I stood over her, watching her curled up into a ball on the couch covered with a blanket. A dull ache sat in my stomach. *Oh well, tonight will be our night.*

I stretched out on one of the chaise lounges on the open-air deck to catch up on my reading. I had begun reading a detective novel that had been popular a few years ago. I'd missed breakfast, but I dressed for lunch and went back to the cabin to change again for the deck. I packed a couple pairs of trousers, foolishly thinking I'd be able to relax on deck in them since a deck is sort of a beach-like place. But no, trousers were not permitted anywhere in our floating palace. Scott, in his sweater-vest and tie, took off after lunch to explore the ship; he thought he might find a shuffle board game he could join. A woman dressed in a pink, orange, and green short-sleeved day dress sprawled out on the chaise lounge next to mine, taking a huge relaxing and loud deep breath. "Oh, isn't this too delightful?" she said, stretching her arms wide. I thought she might be speaking to me, but I wasn't sure. "Oh. Look!" She sprung into a sitting position, pointing excitedly, the loose fat on her large arms flapping. She pulled herself so close to my ear I could smell the crabmeat salad from lunch on her breath. "Do you know who that woman is?" she whispered. "Straight ahead at the railing."

"I can only see her back so . . ."

"*I* saw her from the front at breakfast this morning. She's the Duchess of Windsor."

"No kidding?"

"The duke was with her this morning, so I suppose he's around here somewhere. I've heard they make this trip often. I'm going to go stand by the railing and see if I can start up a conversation. Ooh! The Duchess of Windsor." I watched her walk to the railing, curious to know how the duchess would react to this woman, but then Juliana showed up and I lost track of both of them.

Having come from the shipboard beauty parlor, Juliana had her hair tucked up into a scarf, which she covered with a wide-brimmed hat. The air was cold despite the bright sun. Deck stewards wrapped our feet in fluffy towels to keep us warm.

"So how was your evening with the commodore?" I asked.

"Pleasant. He took me up to the bridge to see how they make the ship go without crashing into anything. He told me I was the only passenger besides the Duke of Windsor he allowed up there. I'm in pretty good company, heh? But, you know, I enjoyed talking to his wife more. She was a WAC during the war and Captain Black took her home from England on this very ship. A fascinating woman."

"Juliana, you didn't . . . with his wife."

"Oh, stop."

"Well, you did come home pretty late."

"Are you keeping track of my movements?"

"No. I'd never do that. Only . . ."

"Oh. This is awful," Juliana whispered to herself.

"What is?"

An open copy of *Confidential Magazine* lay on her lap. In the center of the magazine spread out over two large pages there was a picture of Marlene Dietrich in a beret, slacks, and overcoat. The title read, "The Untold Story of Marlene Dietrich." On the opposite page, there was a picture of a woman in a tuxedo smoking a cigarette. "Now they're calling us 'Baritone Babes,'" she whispered. "What an ugly, humiliating name. They have pictures of Marlene's girlfriends in here."

"That's Hollywood," I said. "Nobody cares what we do in New York." I didn't believe what I was saying. I thought of the book that had been left in my office. The one I hadn't put there. The one that claimed, "female homosexuals" could be dangerous. The one where the author tells a story from an interview with Dr. Karl Menninger. Menninger was treating a "charming, tender girl" who was a lesbian. She'd been sent to prison because she'd beaten her husband to death with a hammer and left him in their apartment to die while she drove to a bridge party. Ah, yes, a charming girl. Despite that book and its thinly veiled threat by whoever left it on my desk, I had to pretend for Juliana's sake that none of it applied to us.

"I wonder why Paramount didn't stop them from printing this? she asked. "That's what all the studios do. Pay the bribe. Oh, that's right. She hasn't been working in film lately. She's only been playing nightclubs and supper clubs where there's no—protection." She turned toward me. "You wouldn't let them publish that I'm—"

"Of course not."

"Of course not," Juliana repeated, catching her breath. "Of course not." She pointed at a picture in the magazine. "This is Jo Carstairs."

Jo Carstairs looked very much like a man in her boy haircut and tuxedo.

"I met her in Paris before the war," Juliana explained. "She was seeing Marlene off and on."

"Marlene? You call Marlene Dietrich Marlene?"

"Well, we *did* entertain the troops together during the war. She's a good person. I bet that's why she keeps that husband she rarely sees hanging around. He makes her look 'normal.'"

I wanted to say, like Richard, but I didn't. "You never told me that when you entertained the troops it was with Marlene Dietrich."

"You never asked. Oh. Look at this page."

"We could've used that in your first PR campaign."

"They found out about the lesbian club she backs in Paris." She read from the magazine, "Carroll's—a favorite hangout for continental deviates."

I looked at the row of chaise lounges on either side of us. A few people in coats leaned on the railing looking out onto the sunlit water. I didn't see the back of the Duchess there anymore; no one stood close enough to hear. "Juliana, did you—did you sleep with her?"

"That's not a polite question to ask a person." She continued to stare down at the article on her lap.

"You did. Dammit, you did."

She turned to whisper, "Would *you* turn down Marlene Dietrich?"

"Uh—okay, no. How was she?"

"Al! That's private. You know I don't engage in that type of talk." She turned the page of the magazine. "But she *is* a generous woman." There was a wink in her voice.

"More generous than me?"

She smiled a smile I had no idea how to read and turned back to the magazine. "If—if anyone wrote this sort of thing about me," she said, "I . . . I couldn't take it, Al. When they said those things about me in the papers, about how bad I was in the play, I felt so ashamed. My mother. She would've been ashamed of me. I'll never go back on a Broadway stage again. Never. But this—this is even worse."

"With the right property . . . A musical. You'd be—"

"No. I can't take the chance that reporters will come nosing around in my private life."

"But no one bothers theater people about this. Look at all the gay chorus boys and girls."

"And I suppose that's why Gertrude Lawrence and Mary Martin are married to gay men. Because no one bothers theater people about this."

"Well, sure we can't talk out in the open about who we love, but . . ."

"Yes?"

"Okay. It's not so good in New York, either, but you'd be great in the right musical."

"I got booed, Al. That has *never* happened to me before. Ever."

"That was only a couple of rowdy—"

"And if this other came out too. I couldn't take it."

"I know." I wanted to hold her hand, to comfort her, to protect her from all the ignorant people who sought to destroy us. "It's okay. You don't have to." I slid the magazine off her lap. "Stop reading this junk. Why don't you close your eyes and get a few winks so you're in top dancing form tonight?"

She pushed the back of her chaise lounge down. "Yes. I'll lie here and rest," she sighed. "What are you reading?"

"*State Department Murders.*"

She lowered her hat over her eyes and yawned. "The homosexual did it with a little help from his friend, the lesbian. A wicked lot, those queers."

CHAPTER FOUR

Our days were filled with lifeboat drills, shuffleboard, deck tennis, shipboard movies, writing postcards in the writing room, and changing our clothes. We must've changed our clothes seven or eight times a day. Each meal and each new activity required different attire, but you couldn't wear what you wore the day before.

Sometimes I had lunch with an ambassador or diplomat's wife, sometimes Juliana joined us, sometimes *she* was having lunch with her own ambassador or diplomat's wife, which I encouraged. I was working on building my connections for Juliana, Max, and myself. I had breakfast one morning with a blonde starlet who'd been forgettable in some Hollywood film whose title I couldn't recall. She sat across the table from me in the dining room with her overeager, fifty-something agent who I suspected was her lover. Even though he didn't smoke, Scott was in the smoking room with the musicians, talking over the routines.

"Miss Huffman, I seen what you done for Juliana and Lili Donovan." She fluttered her eyelashes at me. "And I'm a Lili Donovan look-a-like, doncha t'ink?" She turned her face this way and that, fluffing her jaw-length hair in my direction.

"Don't do that, dear," her balding agent in a gray suit said, patting her on the shoulder. Ignoring him, she leaned her elbows on the table and shook her tits at me. She wore one of those V-neck sweaters that hugged her breasts. She obviously was wearing a bullet bra underneath, which made her breasts stick way out and taper into two sharp points. They were hard not to notice, especially since she kept swinging them in my direction.

"I would do anyt'in' to be a star like Lili," she oozed. "*Anyt'in'.*" Was she intentionally flirting with me? Straight women had a way of flirting with other women without knowing it, but this one . . . I pushed my chair a few inches away from the table. Could she know about me? I think that was the hardest part of being . . . different. The not knowing, the reading into everything everyone said or did and never knowing for sure if they were sending you messages that they knew, or worse, they would *use* what they knew against you.

"Take over my career, Miss Huffman," she said. Her bright red lips pouted and sucked at the air. "I know *you* can make a star outta me."

"Talk to me in New York," I said, knowing I shouldn't be giving her a reason to hope, but I had never learned how to get myself out of those awkward spots. I pushed myself away from the table, thanked the two for a pleasant breakfast, and headed outside, hoping not to run into them for the rest of the trip.

I had wrapped Mr. Schuyler's script in a mimeographed shipboard newspaper. I found a chaise lounge in the open-air deck and spent the morning and part of the afternoon reading it. Mr. Schuyler had been right. It *was* a good script. One that would show off Juliana at her best. Now, all I had to do was convince Juliana.

Every night we dressed up for another elegant dinner and later went dancing in the ballroom or sometimes on deck; other times we had cocktails in the cocktail lounge. I danced with the men and chatted over cocktails with the wives. I wish it could've been the reverse, but, oh well. Juliana danced for hours without resting. I loved sitting on the side watching the men buzz around her lining up for a dance. She was magnificent on the dance floor. Mambo, waltz, lindy, foxtrot, it didn't matter; she could do them all with ease and even make an awkward partner look graceful. Watching her move like that, so in control of all those men, made me burn for her. Being aware that they wanted her but could never have her, while I could . . . I could, couldn't I?

Juliana was in constant demand by senators and congressmen, well-known actors and artists, a diamond merchant, and even a bishop all wanting to buy her drinks and walk around the deck with her, probably dreaming of doing lots of other things with or to her. She seemed to have no time to be alone with me.

The second night, she collapsed into bed next to me in the early morning hours while I lay there awake, hoping she would put her arm around me and bring me close; she didn't.

On the third night, she slept on the couch in the sitting room explaining in the morning, "I didn't want to disturb you; I came in so late."

On the fourth night, the day before we were to dock in Le Havre, France, we were getting ready for dinner. I stood near the bed in my bra and girdle, mindlessly pulling up my stockings watching her. She sat on a chair before the mirror inspecting her hair. She'd come from the beauty parlor and it was piled up on her head. "Not bad," she said to herself, turning her face from side to side. She wore what looked like a man's shirt, no underclothes and bare feet. I wanted to come up behind her and . . . "What's that thing you're wearing?" I asked.

"Oh this?" she laughed. "It's the top to Richard's pajamas. Sometimes he wears the bottoms and I wear the top."

A cold chill ran through me. "Why?"

"No reason. We just do."

"Are you saving on the laundry bill or is . . . is this some kind of game you two play? A sex game?"

"Stop it, Al."

"What? I only asked a question."

"And you know I don't talk about that. Now, get dressed."

"Sure." I finished cinching my stockings. "It's just . . . Dammit, Jule, I've gotta feel you between my legs soon or I'm gonna go mad."

She took out her compact and lipstick and laid them on the table in front of her.

"Did you hear me?"

"I did."

"Well?"

"What do you want me to say?"

"Nothing." I stepped into my violet gown and pulled it up over me. "Have . . . have I done something . . . something to make you mad?"

"I'm not mad." She patted her cheeks with the powder puff.

"Then why . . . why haven't we . . . ? I thought if we were sharing a stateroom we'd naturally make love, but . . ."

"We don't make love. We have sex." She reached for the lipstick.

"No, we don't. We haven't had sex in months, almost a year. I thought it was because it was impossible to get together, but we've been 'together' this whole trip and still we haven't done whatever you want to call it. Why?"

"We've both been busy." She applied lipstick to her upper lip. "We've been meeting people. Isn't that the purpose of this trip *you* put together? Didn't you want me dancing with men, lunching with wives? Now, I'm supposed to do what else for you? I'm not your dancing bear."

"What? You wanted this too. Didn't you? Is that what this is? You feel like I pushed you into this? Something you didn't want?"

"No. No, this *is* a good idea." She blotted her lips. "I don't know why I said that."

"Then what is it, hon?" I put my hands on her shoulders. I felt her body stiffen under my fingers.

"I have to get ready." She slipped out of my grasp and got up. "Don't worry. There'll be plenty of time in Paris."

She unbuttoned the pajama top and let it fall to the floor. I watched her glide naked over to the closet and pull out her underthings.

"Are you trying to torture me on purpose?"

She looked at me, surprised, "Torture? No. I'm getting dressed. Would you finish up too?"

I slipped into my heels as she stepped into her white silk underpants and pulled them up. I watched as she reached around her back to hook her bra. She bent to pull up the garter belt and straightened to fix it around her waist. She put her foot up on the chair and slid a stocking over it, then slowly ran the stocking up the leg I hadn't touched in oh so long and secured them to the fasteners of the garter. Was there anything sexier than watching a woman dress? Yes! Watching her undress.

"Can't you tell me what's going on?"

"Going on?" She thumbed through her dresses, studying them. "I'm getting ready for dinner."

"Why won't you sleep with me?"

"Please don't push," she said. "You're beginning to sound like Richard. Do you like this dress on me?" She held the pale pink gown against her.

"Of course. You look good in everything. Tell me what's happened."

"Nothing's happened. We've both been busy."

"I'll zip you up." As I walked over to her, my body shivered with anger, frustration, fear, desire. My hand shook as I put it through the opening on the side of her dress and felt the warmth of her bare skin. I let my hand slip further around to the front and stopped below her breasts where the bra began. She didn't say anything. I slid my hand over her bra-covered breasts and onto the soft skin of her upper chest. She still didn't say anything. My fingers slid into the bra, seeking her nipple. She grabbed my hand— "No!"— and thrust it out of the dress with force. "We have to get ready."

My body shook with a wordless fear-rage. I stomped out of the room into the sitting room, heading toward the door.

"Al, get back here."

I threw the door open.

"Al! Listen to me. It's not you. It's me."

I turned back toward her. "Then tell me what the *hell* it is."

Her mouth moved, but no words came out. I waited. Finally, she said, "I have to finish getting ready."

"Yeah, you do that." I stomped out the door.

CHAPTER FIVE

In a blind panic of rage and terror, I dashed through the ship's passageways, vaguely aware of passengers in formal dress heading calmly toward the dining room. I knocked into people and pushed them out of my way as I charged into the cocktail lounge and, without hesitation, went right up to the bar. I'm sure I must have been stared at, a lone woman at a bar. I was too enraged to see clearly. The bartender eyed me from a distance, probably not certain what to do with me. In New York, it was against the law for a bartender to serve liquor to an unescorted woman, but we weren't in New York or even in the United States. We were in a kind of no-country.

"Maybe I can help," a man with white hair and a drink in his hand said. He wore a white dinner jacket. "*I'll* buy you a drink, honey." I heard a few women standing at his elbow giggle.

That snapped me back to myself and I slowly stepped away from the bar. "Uh, no thank you." But where would I go? I had to go somewhere. I had to do something. I was jumping out of my skin. Now, it felt like everyone was staring at me, laughing. I crept backward, confused by the glaring faces.

"What are you doing?" Scott asked.

"Oh. Scott, thank God." I threw myself into his arms. "Hide me."

"What's the matter?"

"I think those people at the bar think I'm a bad woman. I want a drink."

"I'll get you one." He put his arm around me. "What'll you have?"

"A side—no, a Manhattan."

"That's Max's drink. Don't you usually drink sidecars?"

"No more. Never again."

Scott walked me up to the bar and ordered my drink and a Coca Cola for himself. We took our glasses and found a small table in the back corner.

"Why would a nondrinker like yourself be in a bar?" I asked.

"Sometimes I come here with the guys from the band. I've met some nice people here. I think people who drink are friendlier than people who don't. But *you* don't look relaxed. What's the matter?"

"Nothing." I took a sip of my drink.

"Oh? That's why you stormed in here demanding a drink like some sort of floozy?"

I squeezed my eyes shut. "I looked that bad?"

"What's the matter?"

"Scott, you have enough of your own problems without me—"

"Come on, please. I *want* to hear your problems. I want to be let back into the human race."

I took another sip of my drink. "You may not like hearing this." I took another sip. "It's Juliana."

"Yes?"

"Well, it's not the sort of thing a Christian man like you likes hearing about. Max said you don't like knowing about *those* things . . . and you play piano for her."

"Max doesn't know everything about me. Tell me."

"Juliana won't sleep with me. You want to go to dinner now?"

"No." He took a deep breath. "I can listen to this."

I laughed. "Your ears are red."

"So? Tell me. I want us to be close again."

"And you're not going to tell me I shouldn't be sleeping with her anyway?"

"Of course not."

"Gee, that's a nice tux you're wearing." I touched his sleeve and felt the material. "This one's new."

"Max had it made for me. Now, quit changing the subject and tell me what happened with you and Juliana."

"That's just it. I don't know. We're sharing a stateroom. We've never had this much time to be alone together. We even have a private place with no worry that Richard will suddenly pop in. I thought we'd do it every night, but nothing. She always has some excuse."

"What does she say?"

"Nothing. She says there'll be time in Paris and that it's not me. It's her."

"So, you see?"

"What?"

"It's going to be okay. There's something about being on a ship that's making her nervous, but when you get to Paris she'll be on solid ground and—"

"That's ridiculous."

"I know. I wanted to help you, but . . . Could it be because there *is* so much time to be together?" Scott asked.

"You mean she only likes to be with me if we *don't* have time?"

He shrugged his shoulders. "Maybe."

"Oh, that would be terrific. Paris should be a real picnic."

"I'm no psychoanalyst. Maybe that's not it. It's just a thought that came to me."

I swallowed down the last of my drink. "I'm going to have another. But not a Manhattan. I want something else. Something I've never had before. I wonder what . . . ?"

"Me, too," Scott said.

"You? But you don't drink."

"I think I'm going to tonight and you know what else?"

"What?"

"I'm going to smoke a cigarette."

"No."

"Yes," he nodded, signaling for the waiter. "Bennie, could you bring me . . . What, Al? What brand should I get?"

"I don't know. How about Luckys? I like the way they square dance in the television commercial."

"Bring me a pack of Lucky Strikes," Scott told the waiter. "The square-dancing kind. And . . . what do you think we should order to drink?"

"What are those people having over there?" I asked our waiter, pointing to an older couple, the woman wrapped in furs and jewels.

"They're having martinis, ma'am," Bennie, our balding, middle-aged waiter answered.

Scott looked at me. "Well?"

"Let's."

"We'll take two martinis like they have," Scott told Bennie.

"Are we going to be bad tonight?" I whispered to Scott.

"Do you want to?"

"Yes. To hell with Juliana."

"Yes, to hell with her and to hell with Max and his Swiss cheese newspapers."

"Did you say 'hell' and not mean the place below our feet?"

"Yes, I did. This trip may corrupt me and maybe I'll let it. I'm sick of being good."

Bennie put our drinks in front of us and set the Lucky Strike pack next to Scott's hand.

We picked up our glasses and clinked them together. I was about to take a sip when Scott said, "Wait. Not yet. I want to make a toast." He raised his glass. "To being bad."

"Yes. To being bad."

We clinked our glasses together and took a sip. We both made a face at the same time. "Ooh," I said. "This may have been a mistake."

"I think it's one of those acquired tastes." Scott forced himself to take another sip. "Oh, this is rough, but I think we should press on. Try another sip."

I did. It took until the middle of the second glass before we'd acquired the taste. Or we were getting too woozy to notice it. We were also moving quickly toward a point of not caring what it tasted like. Scott sat back in his chair smoking his Lucky. "This thing is making my head spin," he said.

"That's what it always does to me too, so I don't do it."

"But the martini makes me not care that the room is spinning around."

"So, tell me," I said, my words beginning to slur. "Why to hell with Max? Is it only because of cutting up the newspaper?"

Scott leaned on the table. "No. There's more. Since my great overly dramatic event, Mr. Maxwell Harlington the Third has not fucked me."

"Scott! You said fuck," I whispered, then laughed.

"I did, didn't I? I don't think I've ever said that before. I've thought it a lot. I may even like the word. Fuck. Fuck. Fuck."

"Quiet. We'll get kicked out."

"That would make us *really* bad, wouldn't it?"

"I think so. But please don't."

"For you, my dear, I will restrain myself from yelling 'fuck, fuck.'"

"Thank you."

Scott raised his glass. "Another, my dear?"

"Another."

The place had grown less crowded since many had taken their drinks to the dining room for the second dinner seating.

"I think he sees other men," Scott said, as he sipped on his third martini.

"You really think that?"

"Yes, I do." Scott said. "He has needs, Al. Needs he will satisfy one way or another. You know I've heard he goes to Washington Square Park to meet strange men."

"How do you know they're strange?"

We exploded into hysterical laughter. Too loud, I think.

"But, Scott, listen. A lot of the gay boys do that. It's their meeting place. It doesn't mean anything."

"It does to me. But I can't get mad at him cause the last time we did it—right before my dramatic event—I screamed. Not in ecstasy. In terror. I had visions of burning in hell. I'm surprised he didn't kick me out of the house."

"Is that why you were with that cowboy?"

"I 'spose. Trying to learn to do it without screaming maybe. Stupid. I wanna do better by him, Al, but I think I may have ruined everything. Hey! What am I doing? We're 'sposed to be bad tonight, not sad. Let's go."

"Where?"

"I don't know. Let's get another drink and take it out on deck."

Once we had fresh drinks, Scott grabbed my hand and we swayed down the hall, bumping into the walls. We fell up the stairs heading for the Lido deck, laughing all the way. We leaned against the railing.

"Beautiful, isn't it?" Scott said as we stood looking out over the choppy ocean that bounced us around. The sun was setting, spreading yellow, orange, and red across a sky that was bigger than I ever knew it could be. A holy vision that I should be seeing with Juliana. For a second, I did see us—Juliana and me—standing a few feet from Scott and me—holding hands as we watched the sun slowly fall toward the ocean.

"Why can't we talk about who we love, Scott? Right out in the open. Why do we have to hide and feel ashamed?"

"I used to know. I used to think it was because we were sick, but now I'm not so certain."

"Well, I know I have never once had one communist thought."

Scott laughed, "Me either."

"And right now, I want to yell out that I'm in love with Juliana. I want the whole world to know."

"Go ahead. Do it. Tell the sun and the ocean and anybody else who happens to pass by."

"I will." I filled up my lungs with salty air and was about to shout, "I'm in love with Juliana!" But I stopped. "You know what would be even better? Let's go down to the ballroom and tell everyone there."

We ran, holding hands, slipping and sliding into the ballroom. Everyone was doing the boogie-woogie to the 'Chattanooga Shoe Shine Boy.' "He's playing that like an old lady," Scott said.

"Huh?" My gaze focused on Juliana, wiggling her damn hips and throwing in a little bit of tap. A half circle of men had formed around her, clapping the beat, their wives standing behind them not looking happy. I told her to watch out for that. Oh, who cares if the wives gang up on her? She deserved it.

"He's dragging it out, no pep," Scott said. "Come on. It's an emergency." He grabbed my arm. "Don't mind Juliana. We've gotta save that song."

"But I gotta make my announcement," I said.

He pulled me to a set of back steps and both of us tripped our way up into the balcony where the orchestra played. "Scott, what are we doing?"

"Saving that song before that guy kills it. Hey, pal." He leaned on the grand piano, close to the piano player. "Remember yesterday you said I could tickle your ivories? Well, here I am."

"Not now. I'm working."

"Move over." Scott sat on the bench and pushed the guy over with his butt. He played the song to a fast boogie-woogie beat. "Hey!" the guy complained, trying to keep up. Scott was playing so fast the guy gave up and watched him. "Man, this boy can wail," he announced to his fellow musicians.

The other musicians perked up to Scott's playing and joined him. The people down on the floor noticed the difference and were looking up at the orchestra, some dancing to the new faster rhythm. I stood next to Scott snapping my fingers to the beat, and suddenly I was dancing up there, twirling around, not caring what anyone thought. The real piano player grabbed me into his arms and we boogie-woogied. I broke loose from him and wiggled around by myself, my hands in the air, thinking I really should tell everyone who I loved. Yell it, even.

I turned to the orchestra. "Do you guys know 'Sandman?'" Well, of course they knew 'Sandman,' I laughed to myself. What orchestra didn't know 'Sandman'? The girl singer came over to me. "Dear, maybe you don't want to do this. You've had quite a lot..."

People stared up at me from the dance floor. Scott played and the men in the orchestra sang the "bump, bumps." I snapped my fingers and sang the words into the microphone. Well, the ones I could remember. When we got to the part where it said, "Mr. Sandman, make him the cutest . . . and let him have lots of wavy hair like Liberace." I stopped, voicing aloud something I'd always wondered about. "Why would this girl want Liberace?" A blurry image of Juliana staring up at me from the dance floor, not happy, and I. . .

CHAPTER SIX

I woke up in bed the next morning—no, I think it might have been afternoon. I heard Juliana's voice in the other room, saying, "Thanks, Oscar, and here's a little something for you."

The bed tilted downward under her weight as she sat next to me. I squinted up at her, but when the light hit my eyes I shut them again. My head throbbed, and my stomach wasn't doing too well either. "Here, drink some of this," she said.

I opened one eye. "What is it?"

"Tomato juice. It's good for hangovers."

I pushed myself up on one elbow, every part of me stiff and aching. She held the glass to my lips. I sipped and fell back onto the pillow.

"I'll leave it over here for you," she said, placing it on the end table.

"Are you mad at me?" I asked.

"A little."

She walked over to the closet, her burnt-orange chiffon robe floating around her body.

"How's Scott?"

"I would guess about the same as you. I'm going over there in a little bit to bring *him* some tomato juice."

"That's nice of you."

She gathered her clothes into her arms and headed toward the doorway.

"Where are you going?"

"I'm going to get dressed in the sitting room so I don't disturb you."

"You won't disturb me."

"Torture you, then."

I fell back onto the bed. Images of myself dancing and singing on the balcony came back to me and I cringed. I think I fell over the railing of the balcony and landed . . . somewhere. I dragged myself from under the covers and threw my legs over the side. I was in my nightgown. She must have changed me. That was a pleasant thought.

I pressed my hands to my forehead, wishing the pain away. Juliana walked back into the room in slacks and a form-fitting, navy-blue, wool sweater, her nightclothes folded in her arms. She bent to slide open a drawer at the bottom of her trunk and placed the clothes inside.

"Juliana, I have to talk to you about something. Not about you and me. It's only about you. I have a meeting today." I looked at my watch laying on the end table. "In an hour. Oh, God." I pressed my hands into the sides of my head as if I were holding it on. "Mr. Schuyler. Dan Schuyler. I think you met him, maybe you danced with him."

"Yes."

"He gave me a . . . Don't say no till you hear me out. He gave me a script. A musical that he's producing on Broadway in the spring. It's perfect for you."

"Can I say 'no' now?"

"We have to expand your career. Cabaret is shrinking. This play, this musical, will show a huge audience what you can do. It could open up Hollywood to you, expand your radio and television careers beyond the gourmet cooking shows and the occasional talk show. I'm asking you to trust me here. Let me tell him yes, you'll do it."

"I can't."

"Can't trust me?"

"Can't do it. I'm sorry I'm letting you down."

"You're not. But I think you're letting you down."

I limped over to where she stood and put my arms around her. She quickly slipped out of my grasp. "You should get more sleep," she said, pushing the drawer in.

"Juliana, are we splitting up?"

She slid a few bangle bracelets onto her wrist. "Splitting up? How can we split up when we've never been together?"

"We haven't?"

She sighed, not turning to me. "Dammit, Al, we're not Shirl and Mercy and you know it. I never pretended to you that we were. I'm married."

"You've always been married, but still we've been close, loving. So why now?"

"This." She held her arms out wide. "This. All this."

"What?"

"Richard's supposed to be here. We are not Shirl and Mercy." She took a breath. "I have to bring this tomato juice to Scott. There are aspirins in my purse for your headache."

She took the glass of tomato juice from the tray that lay on the vanity and walked out.

* * *

Despite the throbbing in my head—Juliana's aspirins weren't working—I got dressed in a business suit to meet Mr. Schuyler in the cocktail lounge.

I passed by the chapel but backed up when I saw Juliana seated in a middle pew with a veil over her bowed head, her rosary threaded through her fingers. I stood near the door watching her for a few moments, my body filling with pain and rage. I wished she'd explain her faith to me and why it made it so easy for her to deny I had any part in her life. I headed for the lounge.

"Miss Huffman," Mr. Schuyler called from a corner table, standing. One couple sat at the bar laughing, a few others were scattered about, chatting at tables. A pianist played softly in the background.

"Good afternoon, Mr. Schuyler."

He helped me into my chair and returned to his seat. "Your drink is a sidecar, I believe?"

"No. No, I never drink that," I said nervously, wondering how he knew since I'd taken the precaution of not having one single sidecar on the ship. He must have been studying me closely in New York to know my preferred drink. More closely than I would expect from someone who merely wanted to "learn" from me. I took off my gloves and placed them in my purse. "I don't think I'll have any alcohol this afternoon. A ginger ale would be nice."

"Yes. Good for the stomach. I imagine after last night your stomach *is* a little raw." He signaled for the waiter.

"I'm so sorry about that. It's not something I'm accustomed to doing."

"I know. I found you entertaining, though. You have a sweet voice."

"But we're here to talk business."

"I'm eager to hear your response to the script, Miss Huffman. The writers are waiting with bated breath to hear that Miss Juliana will sing their songs."

"Then I'm indeed sad to have to disappoint them."

"She said no?"

"I'm afraid so. It's a beautiful script and I know you'll find someone else who'll—"

"There *is* no one else, Miss Huffman. Go back and make her."

I laughed. "Oh, Mr. Schuyler, no one 'makes' Juliana do anything she doesn't want to do."

The waiter placed our drinks in front of us.

"*You* can. She simply must do this. There is an investor who insists—"

"What investor?"

"I can't tell you, but you have to convince her. My career depends on it."

"There is no bigger fan of Juliana than myself, Mr. Schuyler, but even *I* know that there must be someone else who can—"

"There isn't. You have to change her mind."

"I'm sorry. There's nothing I can do."

"It was written for her."

"Why would you commission a script before you knew if she would be interested?"

"I didn't commission it. The gentleman who paid the writers did. Our major investor is in love with her. He will accept no one else. I told him I could get her for him. There must be something you and I can—"

"Perhaps you shouldn't have said that before you asked Juliana. Now, if you'll excuse me, Mr. Schuyler."

I started to rise from my seat when he said "No!" and placed a firm hand around my wrist.

"Mr. Schuyler, please, let go of me."

"I'm sorry," he said, still holding on. "Sit down, Miss Huffman. I'm not finished with you."

"Excuse me? Do I need to call for help?"

He leaned close to me and whispered, "I *know*."

"You know what?"

"You know what I know."

"You're sounding needlessly mysterious, Mr. Schuyler. Thank you for the ginger ale." I tried to pull my wrist from his firm grasp but couldn't.

"I know what you two are."

"What *are* you talking about?" My heart banged against my chest. I stood straighter, attempting to appear composed.

"Sit and I'll tell you what I know."

I sat down and he released my wrist.

"I told you I've studied you. I don't need to say out loud what I know about you two, do I?"

"What is this about, Mr. Schuyler?"

"I had hoped never to have to say this to you, but it's simple. I have an opportunity to revive my career, my reputation, if I put up this musical with Juliana. I have a secret investor who will only support this project with her in it. If she doesn't sign these papers . . ." He reached into his inside pocket and took out a fat envelope and pushed it across the table toward me. "I will publicly declare what I know about you two, and I have a witness who'll back me up."

"A witness? A witness to what?"

"Well, perhaps we should call this person a colleague. Could we go so far as to term this person a friend? It's hard to say. Inevitable, I suppose, in your line of work—a maker of careers—to alienate someone without knowing it. I mean, they wouldn't tell you and risk losing your goodwill. Would they? A terrible thought, though, to think there could be someone in your circle who has betrayed you. A colleague, a friend, someone who has put me wise to the ugly truth of you two. It would make such a scandal, don't you think? And think of the headlines. The newspapers would love it."

"You're talking blackmail, Mr. Schuyler."

"Well, I suppose you could go to the authorities and report me, but if you do, nothing will keep your secret out of the papers, Miss Huffman. And you know what that will mean to both of your careers. Not to mention the worldwide humiliation Juliana would be subjected to. He leaned toward me. "If you're thinking Juliana can ride this out, wait till it blows over, recall what the public did to Ingrid Bergman when she tried to come back into our country."

"But *she* was pregnant with that Italian director's baby, while she had an American husband at home. Juliana has *never* done anything remotely similar."

"No. *She's* done something much worse." He chuckled. "Remember that Senator Johnson from Texas yelling from the Senate floor that Bergman was an 'influence for evil,' 'a terrible role model for women.' I wonder what he'd say about Juliana?"

"Please. You can't do this." I knew I sounded as weak as I felt and that was not good with a guy like this.

He sat back in his chair once more. "Look, I hate putting you under this strain. I do. I like you. I wish this could've remained simply a friendly business arrangement, but I see it can't be that way. My numbers are on those papers. Call me in Paris when they're signed. Don't take too long." He stood. "Enjoy your ginger ale, Miss Huffman. I shall settle the bill with the waiter. I am no cad."

Dazed, I left the cocktail lounge, walking through passageways and around corners without direction. I couldn't bear to think. *What am I going to do?* I leaned on the railing looking out across the endless expanse of sea and sky. *They* were calm. A wisp of cloud feathered by. The sun's rays cut through them like sharp spears. Ingrid Berman's face from *Casablanca* popped into my mind. Such a beautiful film and she was spectacular in it. The critics and the public had been in love with her, but five years ago... In a day, she went from darling to slut. Hedda and Louella went after her like hungry wolves, the public boycotted her films. She'd never come back to the U.S. again, not unless she wanted a mob to tar and feather her. All of that was for heterosexual sins. What would they do to a—homosexual, a beloved cabaret singer who hid who she truly was by flirting with men? A married woman. It'd be bad for me, but for Juliana... She'd have nowhere in the world to go. Not even Italy. I imagine Richard would divorce her. My stomach ached.

I pushed myself away from the railing to walk—to walk away the pain, to walk away the fear. I blindly bumped right into Juliana. "Oh. Excuse me," I said as if she were a stranger.

"Are you all right?" she asked.

"Sure," I said, trying to move past her.

"Can we walk?"

"Sure."

She'd changed into a short-sleeved blue-and-white striped dress made of crisp cotton; it was cinched around her waist with a blue belt.

We walked in silence, the air warm, not sure how to reach across the chasm between us. Plus, I couldn't stop worrying. —Who was this colleague, or "friend" who betrayed us. He specifically said it was *my* friend or colleague, not Juliana's. *I* had brought us to this edge. My heart pounded like a demented kettledrum banging against my rib cage. I quickly flipped through my mental wheeldex of friends: Shirl? Never. Mercy? Why would she? Max? Ridiculous. He'd have as much to lose as me and nothing to gain. Scott? No. Marty? He's my buddy. I backtracked to Scott. Could his fear of being gay have allowed Dan Schuyler to blackmail him? A pang of sadness. No. Maybe. Who else? Virginia? Absurd. She can barely carry on a conversation. Richard? He came under *Juliana's* "friends," plus I was sure he didn't know; if he did, we wouldn't be here. How did Dan know who my friends were? All right, yes, he observed me, but a person like that . . . Could he tell the difference between a friend, a colleague, an acquaintance, or even an . . . enemy? Did I have those? What could I have possibly done to this someone that would make him . . . her? . . . want to destroy us? How would I ever tell Juliana that she had to do the very thing she was most afraid of doing, because if she didn't the worst thing she could imagine happening *would* happen? *I* had brought Juliana to the brink of some cliff and I was going to be the one to push her off. How could I tell her? Of course, Max would have no choice but to fire me. I'd lose all my clients. Who'd want to be represented by a mentally disturbed, potentially criminal, unnatural woman? A thing. I'd lose my gay clients too, like Marty. It would be too dangerous for him to be represented by me. I'd never work again, at least not in show business or government or civil service; Is there anything left? I'd be poor again. Maybe scraping by in low level jobs like my father. I'd hate that. I did have savings and stocks, so I could hang on for a while. But my work in cabaret. I must have that. It was my life. Still—I'd survive it. Somehow. But Juliana . . .? She was used to being adored. If it came out that she was . . . The worst for me would be that this would most likely be the end of us, and *that* I didn't know how I would live through.

"You know," Juliana spoke into our silence. "You were pretty good last night."

"Oh, please," I hid my eyes behind my hand. "Every time I think of it I cringe."

"You have a nice voice."

"For singing to babies and in the shower. That's what Max told me a long time ago."

"Is that why you stopped singing? Because of Max? He can be cruel. I remember when you and I first met, singing was one of the things you wanted to do."

"It hurt when he said it, but I think he ultimately saved me a lot of heartache and wasted time steering my life in the wrong direction. And then, of course, there was you."

"Me?"

"The first time I heard you sing, it was like the gods were playing their harps inside my body."

"That sounds more like sexual excitement than singing."

"It was both. They're both tangled up together pretty tightly when it comes to you. And when I heard you sing up close without a band or orchestra. That first time in your apartment. Well, I didn't know it then, but I guess that was *my* gift. To know brilliance when I heard it, singing that touches the divine."

"Except when I sing ballads."

"No. You've gotten way past that. You can sing anything now."

"Thanks to you."

"I didn't do anything but bring out what was already there. That's what I do. And when I heard you sing, I knew *my* voice would never come close to yours."

"Well, I had a lot of training and advantages you didn't. That doesn't mean you can't sing. You can, and you should. Let's go in here."

She dipped down and slipped past a railing. I held back. Could Dan's witness be on the ship? Scott? Could someone be watching us now? Dan? "Uh, Juliana, maybe we shouldn't. It's close to teatime."

"I want to show you something." She headed down a set of wooden steps.

I looked around before I went under the railing. All I saw was the sky and a few passengers standing on an upper deck talking. I followed Juliana down onto the lowest deck where they kept the cars that were being transported to Europe. It was packed with different kinds of expensive motor vehicles. We walked around them. "Look at this Rolls Royce," Juliana said. "Richard wants one of these, but I keep telling him they're too expensive. And too showy."

She bent to peer through the window. "Look, it has a red interior."

"And over there," she pointed. "Another Rolls." She ran over to it. "White and black interior."

Juliana leaned her back against the shiny black car. "When I was around three and Mother and I were coming back from the States to Paris, I played on a deck very much like this, running around and crawling under the cars."

"Only three and crawling *under* cars all by yourself? That sounds dangerous."

"No. Sometimes, Mother had 'company' if you know what I mean, and I couldn't stay in the cabin when she was—you know, uh, 'entertaining' a guest."

"I've always wondered about your mother 'you know-ing' with different men. Didn't that make your father mad?"

"Quite a bit," she laughed. "It led eventually to them separating permanently." A sadness fell over her; she seemed suddenly alone. "I never should have left her there by herself," she said, but not really to me.

"What?" I asked.

She smiled, washing the sadness away. "I was living with Shirl and she practically had to tie me down to keep me from getting into some real trouble. I would do anything in those days. I was wild. I wanted jazz, dancing, sex. I slept with two, three different girls a week. White girls, Negro girls, Caribbean girls, Spanish girls. I even smoked marijuana for a while."

"You smoked reefer and didn't get addicted?"

"No. I got high. You go to a lot of parties with musicians. Haven't *you* ever indulged?"

"No," I said, defensively. "I wouldn't do that."

"You are so good."

"I am not."

"I didn't mean that as an insult. You're naturally good."

"I'm not."

"Okay, okay, you're not. It was quite pleasant. The marijuana. How did you manage not to at least try it? You must've had plenty of opportunities."

"Sure. But I saw this movie about it way back when I was little. My church showed it. It scared me to death. After a while, I figured out that the movie was exaggerated. None of the musicians I knew got crazy like in the movie, but I can't get past the fear."

"It made me eat a lot, so I decided to stick to bootleg hootch. I didn't want to get fat. I'm no stranger to hangovers. Only when *I* woke up with them, I was sixteen, not thirty-two."

"See? I *do* know how to be bad."

"Yes, you do." She had a big grin on her face. "Shall we go in? How about the one with the red upholstery?" She hurried over to that Rolls and pulled on the backdoor handle.

"We can't. Someone owns this."

"So? We're not going to drive it. We're only going to sit in it. "

"Like Bette Davis and Paul Henreid in *Now Voyager*?"

"Exactly."

"I don't know, Juliana." I looked around the deck. Could someone be hiding somewhere, under a car, in a car, watching us?

"Have you ever felt the interior of a Rolls Royce?" she asked.

"No, but . . ."

She crawled into the back seat. "Come on in. Close the door."

My eyes scanned the area again. I didn't see anyone, so I tentatively crawled in beside her, leaving the door open. "Jeepers," I exclaimed. "This leather *is* soft."

"Uh, huh." She leaned over me to close the door.

"No!" I squeaked. "It's, uh, I mean, warm in here, don't you think?"

She stretched her arm across the back seat, feeling the softness of the leather. "A little piece of heaven."

"You wish he was here instead of me?" I couldn't look at her as she answered, so I looked out the back window.

"I never said that."

"You said Richard was *supposed* to be here."

"He was. That was the plan before his mother became ill. I know how to handle Richard when we're together in a husband-wife situation. I don't know what to do with you. That's all I meant."

"Do with me? Like a poodle?"

She laughed. "I don't think of you as my poodle. It's uh, two women, uh. . . the world's set up for a man and a woman so I don't know how. . . Oh, I can't do this. Look, Al, I don't have the words to explain. *You're* the one who's good with words. But since we're on the topic of Richard . . ."

"Do we have to talk about *him*?"

"No. Except—there is something I probably should tell you because of your involvement with my career. Richard's been, uh, talking about having a baby."

"Then let *him* have it and leave you out of it. You're too old."

"Thanks a lot."

"You know what I mean. It's not safe to have a baby at your age. You're thirty-eight. You could be forty before you get pregnant. That's dangerous."

"Forty. I haven't heard it said out loud before. I keep trying not to think about it."

"Then don't. You don't have to. We're still building your career. It's going to get much bigger. Now is an important and sensitive time." Dan Schuyler's face whooshed through my mind. My stomach turned over. "No. You cannot have a baby."

"Should I tell Richard you absolutely forbid it?"

"Yes! Jule, you've never talked about wanting one. Is this something *you* want?"

"Well, it's something women are supposed to want. All the magazines say you're not a real woman until you have a baby. My gynecologist said I should hurry. If I get much older it wouldn't be advisable for me to get pregnant, but if I don't have a child, she said I would it regret it for the rest of my life. Haven't you ever wondered. . . ?"

"No! Jule. You are a *real* woman. No baby could make you any more real than you are right now. You don't need a baby. You need to sing." I turned to stare out the window again. "Thinking of him on top of you—sweating, huffing and puffing, making ugly gurgling sounds. He's hairy, isn't he? I bet he is. All hairy like a gorilla, bouncing up and down on you and slobbering all over you and putting his thing inside you and—"

"My goodness," she laughed. "You make it sound like such a miserable ordeal."

"Well?"

She put a hand on the side of my face and, bending toward me, she kissed me, and oh, wow, did she kiss me. "Take your clothes off," she whispered.

"Are you out of your mind? Someone could come."

"They won't."

"Jule, we're not kids anymore. We can't do things like we used to. We have a whole stateroom upstairs where we can—"

"Not there. I can't. I want to see you naked against these red cushions." She kissed me again and started to unbutton my blouse.

"Jule, no, this is not the place." I held her hands in mine; I imagined Dan Schuyler opening the car door behind her. I'd been waiting for almost a year and four desperate days on this ship to be this way with her. Damn that Schuyler. If I pushed her away now, would she hate me forever? She loved having sex in places you weren't supposed to.

"I know what you like, Country Girl," she said, running her fingers up one of my legs. I was melting at her touch. There was no Dan Schuyler, no betrayer, no Broadway musical. "I bet Bette Davis and Paul Henreid didn't do this in the back seat of *their* car," she said as she unsnapped one of my nylons and pushed it away from my garter belt. Her tongue dabbed at mine and I was falling, falling . . .

There was a bang. I jumped away from her. "My God! What was that? We're not alone down here." My heart pounded. And not with passion.

Juliana looked out the window. "A police dog."

"A police dog!"

"In a crate. A German Shepherd. Not loose. My goodness, calm down. You'd think someone was after you. Poor guy, stuck in that crate. And he's none too pleased about it. Can't say I blame him. They keep the dogs their owners are taking to Europe down here. Relax. Why so jumpy? You need this."

She slid her hand under my skirt and unsnapped the second nylon.

"Uh, Juliana, we shouldn't . . ."

"I know." Her fingers crawled up my leg again. I was growing more powerless by the minute. She slid to the floor and pulled my underpants down to my knees.

"Uh, Jule . . ."

"I know. We shouldn't, but I gather I've put you through a lot this trip. This'll be my gift." She slid my underpants down to my ankles.

"Oh, Jule," I moaned, "you are making it so hard for me to be sensible."

"Good." She slipped off my shoes, then pulled my stockings and underpants all the way off. She tickled the insides of my legs. My good sense had almost evaporated. "Uh, uh, Jule, suppose someone walks by the car."

"Smile," she said as she put her head under my skirt.

CHAPTER SEVEN

Alone on the deck, my body wrapped tightly in a shipboard blanket, I lay on a chaise lounge. We were moving quickly toward Le Havre, and yet it felt as though we weren't moving at all. The whole world had gone to sleep. There was only me and the ship and the largest sky I'd ever seen. No stars. We were drifting in the upper half of a huge eggshell with a visible line marking where the sky met the ocean. It wasn't hard to imagine why the early explorers feared falling off the edge of the earth.

I stood, dropping the blanket. I was so small within that expanse of sky. A dot in the ocean. Barely seeable. And yet—I knew. In that moment, I knew what I had never known before and may never know again. I mattered . . .

* * *

It was dark and cold as we stood on the deck of the ship watching the tugs pull us into the dock at Le Havre, France. I could smell the thick fishy smell of the water and hear the slosh of the ocean against the side. We stood huddling near the railing, our coats wrapped tightly around us. It must have been the damp cold that was keeping us awake at half past three in the morning.

Despite the cold and dark, the deck was alive with activity. Stewards ran back and forth with luggage, and women held onto their hats, fighting against the wind. People scurried every which way looking for family members, friends, and misplaced luggage. Waiters ran about with trays of coffee, drinks from the bar, bowls of Post Toasties in milk, and blankets to keep the cold at bay.

Scott leaned heavily on the railing, looking down at the water as the ship came close to the dock and ropes were thrown to the waiting workers. He wore a tan cashmere jacket that I was sure Max's tailor had made. I stood near the back wall beside an empty chaise lounge, watching him. Had there been any sign? Anything that would point to him as my betrayer? How do you look within another person's heart to see what's truly there? I had to give it up. Scott and I would be working together in Paris. I couldn't work with him in a cloud of suspicion, and he'd done nothing to make me suspect him. I had to give it up or I wouldn't last this trip. He was my friend. I needed to hang on to that. Unless he did something that made me think . . . He wouldn't. We were going on this foreign adventure together.

He lit a Lucky. "Scott," I said, running over to him. "Don't tell me you're still smoking."

"Oh, yeah. One or two or nine a day."

"What?"

"I didn't expect to like it so much. I should stop, shouldn't I?"

"I don't know. I thought your religion . . ."

"Yeah, well, this trip has given me time to possibly rethink some things."

"No kidding? Like what?"

A few stevedores jumped onto the ship and worked together to secure it. The waves rolled gently under our feet.

"Hey, Scott," the sax player said, coming over to us. "I don't like the way they're handling the instruments down there. I'm worried."

"Let's go," Scott said as he led the way down the steps to the lowest deck.

He's so conscientious, I thought. If he'd done what Dan said, he would literally shrivel up and die of guilt.

I turned and saw Dan Schuyler talking to Juliana. My heart sank into my stomach, and for a moment, I didn't move. Was he telling her? Blackmailing her right on the ship? Implicating me?

He offered her a cigarette and she accepted. She only smoked when something upset her. He lit her cigarette and then his own. I took a deep breath and marched over to them.

"Hello, Dan," I said with the strongest, most commanding voice I could muster. It was the first time I'd called him Dan.

"Hello, Alice. Or should I call you Al?"

"Alice will be fine, Dan." I tried to stand taller and make my voice deeper.

"Well, Miss Juliana," Dan said, "it's been a pleasure sailing the ocean with you. I know the time will come when I shall have the honor of working with you and your great talent. You belong on Broadway, and I am just the man to bring you to that majestic height."

"I appreciate your kindness, Mr. Schuyler—Dan, if I may."

"You may."

"Alice told me that you have a script you'd like me to consider."

"Yes!" He beamed.

"But I am a nightclub singer. That's where my career began and that's where it'll end. I love the closeness of the audience, the personal contact."

"Well, maybe Miss Huffman can convince you. What do you say, Miss Huffman? Are you going to convince Miss Juliana that Broadway needs her?"

"Juliana does what *she* thinks is best for her career."

"Oh, does she now?" He grinned at me like we were co-conspirators.

"Well, I must join my party. I'll undoubtedly see you both in Paris. Won't I, Miss Huffman—Alice? With good news." He nodded at us both and left.

"What is he talking about? What good news? I'm *not* going to do his play."

"I know. He likes hearing himself talk."

"You're sure there isn't something I should know?"

"No. Nothing. It's nothing."

She took a puff of her cigarette and blew out the smoke as we floated under the inky dome of sky that spread over us. Passengers exited down the gangplank. Juliana joined them with me following behind her. As she stepped onto solid ground, she lit another cigarette that she bummed from one of her fans. She was oblivious of the large muscled stevedores in torn T-shirts that were rushing past us onto the ship to get the trunks. They yelled to each other in a hoarse French that I surmised was laced with French cuss words. The night was still thick with dark, and the air was wet and smelled of salt. Lights from a nearby bridge sparkled in the distance.

I had no time to wonder at my new surroundings or marvel at the strange sounds of another language dripping easily from the tongues around me. There was work to do. "Scott, Scott," I called, running toward him as he put his suitcase down and lit a cigarette. His eyes scanned the crowds, looking for me.

"We're over here." I pushed through the people hurrying to greet loved ones. "You get yourself, the guys, and the instruments through customs. The train's supposed to be on the other side. When you get to Paris, take everything over to the Lido before you check in at the hotel. Juliana and I will meet you at the hotel this evening for dinner."

He nodded and headed toward the musicians, who were lighting up cigarettes.

Juliana stood near the docks, her silk shawl draped loosely over her head. She stared out at the ocean as she lit another cigarette. There was something bothering her. It worried me. It worried me that what was bothering her was me. Me being here with her in France. "We're not Shirl and Mercy," echoed through my brain. What had she meant? I walked over to her. The sky seemed a little lighter and the moon a little fainter. A yellow beam from an approaching tugboat floated through the early morning fog. The Seine lapped rhythmically at the dock. "Are you all right?" I asked.

"Home," she sighed and blew out a stream of smoke.

CHAPTER EIGHT

I took a sip from my brandy. "Isn't it a little early to be drinking?" Juliana asked, stepping into my room. She wore her peach and white chiffon bathrobe. "It's only nine in the morning and you've been up all night. You don't want to end up singing, 'Sand Man,' down in the hotel lobby. Do you mind that I walked in without knocking?"

"Of course not." There was a small pain at the bottom of my stomach that she even needed to ask.

"I wanted to thank you, Al."

"For?"

"For this. Arranging the separate accommodations."

"Oh, that." I took my drink to the picture window, pushing aside the curtains. Beyond the window was a shallow balcony and beyond that—Paris.

"Well, we do have this convenient door between us," she went on.

"That's because it's a suite."

Paris was out there and I should be overjoyed, but all I felt was weighed down and burdened. The oppressive heat in our unair-conditioned room wasn't helping. Juliana and I were in separate rooms with a "convenient door" between us, and Dan Schuyler lurked beyond these walls, ready to tear down everything Juliana and I had worked for.

"This is a lovely hotel you put us in." She went on trying to make light conversation. "I guess my room is larger than yours, especially for Paris. Rooms are usually so small here."

"You're the star."

"But both are decorated nicely."

"No, they're not. A lot of beat-up wood." I sipped my drink and continued to stare down onto the street. Richard, not wanting to spend too much money on our Parisian experiment, had reserved a moderately expensive hotel. Juliana's canopy bed was the most striking thing in the suite with its many-layered, lush-green curtains draping the bed in delicate folds.

"The rugs are shabby and the elevator shakes," I went on.

"Perhaps. I've been going over the schedule you arranged for me. It's quite extensive."

"Let me see." I put my drink down on the desk and sat on a nearby chair. "This schedule's impossible. You can't do this."

I'd set up a grueling schedule for Juliana to keep her so busy Richard would have no time to . . . to do whatever he might want to do with her. But now Richard wasn't here; I was. It was me who was stuck with this schedule. Damn.

"You get right to bed," I told her. "Now. You've got a gigantic day tomorrow. I'll work on getting you out of some of this."

"You must have thought all of that was important when you made the arrangements. I'm not complaining. I know you're only doing what's best for my career."

Am I? I looked down at the list in my hand. She was booked at the Lido for two weeks. That's all I could get, but I was hoping for an extension. In between rehearsing at the Lido, I had arranged for her to be interviewed on a few French radio stations and I'd set up some live television appearances. In case they didn't extend her at the Lido, I had her booked at a club in Provence and another in Marseille. No breaks in between. She was scheduled to open the new show at the Lido in only three days. That would barely be enough time to load in the sets, rehearse the costume changes, and get comfortable on a stage she wasn't used to. Billy Preston, the director who'd been working on this new show with her in New York, wouldn't be flying into Paris until tomorrow night. How could I have done this to her?

"Let's go out tonight," Juliana said, sitting on my bed. "It's your first night in Paris. We can't spend it in the hotel sleeping."

"We're here for your career. You need to be in top form. That means lots of rest."

"Okay, okay, I'll rest, but let's go out tonight."

"You've got to eat." I picked up the house phone. "Bring up a glass of . . . Huh? What? English?"

"Let me try," Juliana said, taking the phone. She made some lovely sounds into the phone and my heart swelled. She held the phone against her breast. "He *does* speak English, but only to certain people. You just became one of those people. Don't abuse the privilege. His name is Monsieur Girard Fournier. Address him as Monsieur Fournier and always begin with 'bonjour' before requesting *anything*. When you're ready to hang up, always say 'merci monsieur.' He's on during the day." She handed the phone to me.

"Uh, hi there. Bring up a glass of—"

"Monsieur, monsieur!" Juliana whispered loudly.

"Monsieur!" I shouted. The monsieur shouted back at me, "Bonjour!"

"Oh, yes! Sure. Bonjour! Bonjour!"

Juliana hid her eyes behind her hand, shaking her head.

"Bring up a glass of orange juice and one scrambled egg white for Miss Juliana. Thanks. I mean, merci, Monsieur Four—Girard."

Juliana moaned, "Fournier. Never call him by his given name. You don't know him. The French don't understand our informality."

I hung up the phone and both Juliana and I took a relieved breath.

"I can't eat before I sleep," Juliana said. "I'll get fat. You eat. I'll drink the orange juice."

"You have a long way to go before you get fat. You have to eat a little something or you'll be a rag."

"Scrambled egg white? That sounds terrible."

"It probably is, but I read it's good protein. That's what Rocky Graciano eats when he's training for a fight."

"I'll eat it if you let me take you out tonight."

"Jule, you need to rest."

"I will. I promise. But tonight, we go out."

"Okay. If you eat now and sleep all day, I'll go out with you for an hour tonight."

"Make it two."

"Okay, two. But that's it."

"We'll see. I'm going to sponge down in the bathroom now."

"Sponge down? Why don't you take a long hot bath? Relax your muscles so you can sleep."

"That sounds lovely, but French hotel bathrooms don't have bath tubs."

"What?" I ran into the bathroom and found two ceramic basins molded out of one piece sitting on top of a ceramic base. A hot and cold brass faucet pointed to the center of each basin.

"Two! We've got two basins," Juliana exclaimed from behind me. "This *is* a good hotel."

"It is? What about the shower?"

"No shower," Juliana said, leaning against the bathroom doorway filing her nails.

"There has to be, at least, a toilet. Where's the toilet?"

"Down the hall. With the communal tub. Oh, and there are also the public ones outside."

"Outside? I'm a private kind of person, especially about those things."

"When in Rome . . ."

"Yeah, sure, and I suppose that other thing over there is the . . ."

"Yes. The bidet. I'm going to wash up now." She slipped her nail file into the pocket of her bathrobe. "You want to help?"

"Yes, but no. We've got to stay serious. This is your career. You will go in there and get washed alone. And then you'll sleep."

There was a knock at the door. "Service de chamber," the masculine voice on the other side said.

"Bring it to me in the bathroom." She winked, letting her robe slip off her shoulders and down her deliciously naked body.

"Juliana . . ." I whined.

CHAPTER NINE

The driver stopped the cab in front of Chez Moune and I drew out a fistful of francs from my pocket. Juliana counted out the right amount and handed it to him. He looked quizzically at her, then at me. He turned back to her and said something with an ugly smirk on his face.

"Monsieur, vous nous déposez ici." Juliana said sharply. Then to me, "Come on, hurry."

I slid out of the car. "What'd he say?"

"It was nothing."

"It got you upset."

"He thought this was a mistake, that we didn't want to get out here. Forget it."

I followed her down three flights of stone steps. The air was thick with humidity, and I wished I could throw off the coat I wore. On the way down, she told me that we were in Montparnasse, a section of Paris that used to be sort of like Greenwich Village. Before the war, it had been a home to a great many artists and writers who came from all over the world. The war and the occupation had made it too hard for them to stay, and once they left, they never came back.

Chez Moune, a woman's club, was first opened back in the thirties, and Juliana used to go to it when she was a kid before she went to live in the US. It was hard to imagine they had a women's club way back then, but Juliana told me that those kinds of clubs had always existed, even in the US, only they were secret to most of the world. Juliana said she would never go to any of the gay bars in New York City because they were bars, not clubs, and they were for low-class people. Shirl and Mercy sometimes went to those kinds of bars and they'd ask me to come, but I never wanted to take a chance on getting arrested and Max having to fire me. Juliana said in France the police didn't bother much about the women's clubs, but they did raid the men's since it was against the law in Paris for two men to dance together. That seemed strange since the French had legalized homosexuality way back in 1791.

I wore the suit and tie that Shirl, or maybe it was Mercy, had snuck into my trunk. Juliana warned me that, although our kind of people weren't illegal in France, regular people didn't like us much more than the people in the U.S. did; they considered us a "social plague." That meant I had to be careful to keep my coat closed till we got inside the club.

Juliana was wearing an orange and green chiffon dress held up with spaghetti straps. She'd thrown an airy chiffon shawl around her shoulders.

When we got to the bottom of the steps, Juliana pushed through the heavy wooden door and we were in a darkened room with plush couches and tables, a dance floor, and a bar. The thick heat followed us into the room, and there was a faint smell of bodies. An orchestra played a foxtrot I didn't recognize, and all the musicians were girls. I'd never seen anything like it. Girls in suits and ties like me danced with girls in dresses like Juliana. There were some girls in suits who danced with other girls in suits. The waiters, all girls too, wore tuxedos like they did at the 181 Club in the US. The difference was there were no queens in this place, just butches and femmes. And no one was performing for the straights because there were no straights. We had a place to be ourselves without fear that some guys in uniform would burst through the door ready to arrest us. Years of tension I didn't even know was wound up in me seeped out, and I felt like I could breathe, maybe for the first time.

Juliana told me there were some women's bars like Le Monocle where a single woman could sit at the bar and try to attract another single woman, but at Chez Moune that was frowned upon. At Chez Moune, you had to come as a couple and leave as the same couple.

"You can take your coat off now," Juliana said. "You'll be safe here."

"*Safe*." I breathed the word in, and out. I decided not to think about Dan Schuyler.

She walked me over to the hatcheck girl, who was a cute young thing in a little bitty outfit. I gave the girl Jule's shawl and my coat.

A blonde woman in a suit who looked to be in her forties hurried over to

Juliana. "Ah, Julien." She took Juliana's one hand in her two and put a kiss on each of Juliana's cheeks. Juliana did the same to her. The two spoke in a wild, excited French. Listening to Juliana speak French sent thrills up my legs. There was something so sexy and feminine about those sounds, at least the way they came out of Juliana. The woman seemed happy to see her.

"Bon soir, Madame Moune. Comment-allez vous?" Juliana said.

Smiling, Madame Moune said something back to Juliana.

Juliana turned to me. "Je voudrai vous présenter Madam Alice Huffman."

"Welcome to Chez Moune," the woman said in a heavily accented English, then she kissed me on both of my cheeks. "Australian?" She looked to Juliana.

"No. American."

"Oh." Madam Moune took a few steps back. "Well, you are a friend of Julien so drink, dance, relax yourself."

She spoke again in French to Juliana, and they seemed to have a little banter back and forth along with a few laughs before Madam Moune returned to sit with her friends on a long couch in the corner.

"What was that about?" I asked.

"She wanted me to sing."

"Tell her to buy a ticket to the opening."

"I didn't put it quite so crudely, but I knew how you would feel about it. Shall we have a drink first or a dance?"

"Dance? You mean—you and me? We can . . . Right out in public?"

"Right out in public. And dancing here is about as public as you and I will ever get. So? Shall we?" She opened her arms and I took one of her hands in mine. I put my arm around her bare shoulders. Despite the heat, her skin was cool against my fingers. She pulled me close, holding me tight; I felt her breasts beating against mine as she led me slowly around the dance floor. I hadn't danced with her since that first time in her apartment when she kissed me. A new life pulsed through me. A girl stood in front of the orchestra, leaning into a microphone singing in English, "Time After Time," and I got lost in Juliana's eyes. There was no one left in the world, only Juliana and me. The music and our bodies swirled through a timeless space filled with just us. If Dan Schuyler's face hadn't kept popping into the back of my head, it would've been perfect.

I laid my head on Juliana's shoulder and her hair tickled my face. She hummed the song so that only I could hear. Her hair smelled of lemons. She kissed me right on the lips in front of everyone. It was a short kiss, but a good one. I was so filled with love; how could I let Schuyler tear it all away from us? I held her tighter. Nothing would ever separate us.

There was a tap on my shoulder, wrenching me from my Juliana-Al world. I turned to look.

"Hi." Andy grinned. "May I cut in and dance with the prettiest girl in the room?" Andy's dark, slicked-back hair glistened under the dim lights. I remembered how the girls at Club 181 practically drooled when this he-she mounted the stage and sang like Frank Sinatra. Even the straight girls swooned over her. I wanted to stomp on him—her—right there. Instead, I was about to concede, the way men do, when Juliana said, "Andy. Al and I have never danced together. Do you mind, terribly?"

"Uh, no," Andy said, backing away. "She's all yours, Al. You lucky dog, you." She turned to Juliana and winked. "I'll talk to you later, doll face."

After Andy left us, I held Juliana so close she couldn't breathe. "Easy, Al. Give me a little room."

"Oh. Sorry. Thank you for doing that. Did you used to go with her or something?"

"Or something. Your dancing has improved."

We danced all night. And drank and talked to Juliana's friends. Some of them spoke English, but most didn't, or *said* they didn't. Juliana tried her best to keep up with translating for me, but there was a lot I didn't get. Still, it was a marvelous sensation to be in a place where Juliana and I were a couple, and everyone accepted us like that. No one treated us as if we were mentally ill or two criminals on holiday. They were like us, and nobody was hiding. How lovely not to be hiding. It all felt so natural. The jams were always calling us unnatural. What did that mean? Here, with these women, dancing with Juliana, everything felt natural. I thought about how often I'd watched straight couples huddle around tables at the Copa or The Mt. Olympus or The Haven. They'd have their arms around each other; sometimes they'd kiss. I'd be so envious, but this night at Chez Moune, Juliana and I were like them. Except *they* didn't have a Dan Schuyler lurking somewhere waiting to tear it all apart. *Stop thinking about him.*

Around midnight, showgirls came onto the stage to sing and dance. It was hard for me to sit back and enjoy the show; in my mind, I kept casting this one or that one for the floorshow at The Haven.

A couple of the girls came up to Juliana and asked her to sing, and my manager-self jumped in. "She has to rest her voice. She's got a big show coming up in few of days at the Lido. We'd love to see you there."

"Sorry," Juliana would shrug. "Al's in charge."

Through much of the night, Andy sat at another table, balancing one of the showgirls on her knee while drinking one mug of beer after another. She-He watched Juliana closely. Sometimes Andy's and my eyes would lock for a moment. Then I'd go back to listening to all the French flying around me. At one point during the night, I looked over at Andy's table and she was gone.

Juliana and I didn't get home till almost dawn. "Bed. You have to get straight to bed," I whispered as we got off the elevator and stepped into a black hallway, with not even a window to let in a bit of moonlight. "Jule, I can't see a thing. How are we going to get to our room?"

"There," she yawned, pointing at a button that glowed through the dark. "That button. Press it."

I did, and the hall was awash in bright light, but as we stumbled toward our door, a little tipsy with drink and lack of sleep, it went out. "Jule! Are you still there?" I called out.

"Right here," her voice came. "The light doesn't stay on long. It's the way the French save money."

"You stay there," I told her as I crawled along the wall, feeling my way back to the button. I pressed it and ran like hell, grabbing Juliana as I went by. The light blinked off before I could fit my key into the keyhole. "Damn! I can't find it."

Juliana laughed as I struggled. "Shh. Everyone's sleeping."

My key finally went in, and I pushed open the door on Juliana's side of the suite. I flipped on the light and we fell into her room, laughing. She collapsed onto her bed, instantly falling asleep. I pulled off her dress and underthings.

"Come on, Juliana, you've got to help a little. I'm trying to get this nightgown on you. And gosh, it's sweltering in here. They must have a fan somewhere. I'll ask tomorrow." I had gotten the nightgown over her head and it bunched up around her neck. I struggled to get her arms through the sleeves. Her eyes opened, and she broke into laughter.

"Juliana, stop laughing." I said, laughing too. "You'll never get through tomorrow, I mean, *today's* rehearsal, which is soon. Put your arms through the sleeves."

She put her arms through the sleeves, and I pulled the gown down around her.

"Did you have a good time tonight, Al?" she asked, her eyes closed.

"Lift up," I said.

She lifted, and I slid the nightgown under her rear. I sat on the bed next to her. "It was a magical night, Juliana."

"Are you happy?" she asked, her eyes two sleepy slits.

"Very." Dan Schuyler's face popped in to dilute my joy.

"I want you to be happy," she said.

I slid my two hands under her nightgown, pushing it up a little, and lay the side of my face against her pussy because I needed to be there. A tear rolled out of my eye.

"Al, is something wrong?" she asked, putting her hand on my head.

"Just happy." I squeezed my eyes around my tears as she ran her fingers through my hair.

CHAPTER TEN

"Eleven o'clock?" I shot up in bed and threw my watch back on the end table. "Oh, no. Juliana!" I jumped out of bed and ran through the door that separated us.

Her bed was empty, the sheets thrown back. There was a note pinned to her pillow.

> *Al, I'm off to rehearsal. I'm meeting Scott and the boys there. I wish I could show you around the city, but that doesn't look possible. At least not today. Take yourself out. Relax in a café. Have a French breakfast. Go see the Eiffel Tower, take a day trip to Versailles, or go for a ride on the new Cityrama Tour Bus. You'll love it. I saw a picture of it. I can hear you saying it looks like something out of a Buck Rogers comic strip. Don't spend the whole day working. You're in Paris!*

Well, the idea of spending a leisurely day sightseeing sounded wonderful, but totally out of the question. I had research to do. And I had to find a fan. Today! The top of my nightgown was soaked. With Juliana gone, it seemed like a good time to put a call through to Shirl to see if she knew anything about Dan Schuyler. First, I opened a window trying to get some air. Cars and buses honked and screeched. Clouds of exhaust drifted in, making me cough. I closed it again.

"Monsieur Fournier? No? English? You don't? You're not pretending, are you? I don't understand. No je n'cest . . . forget it. English por favor. No, that's Spanish. I—need—an—English—Eng—lish," I overpronounced. "Op—er—a—tor. Never mind. Okay. Okay. Yeah, c'est bean."

I hung up and immediately dialed the desk again. "Hello, Girard—No! I mean, Monsieur! No, don't go. Bonjour, Bonjour!! Thank you, thank you! I need to place a call to the United States. Could you help me? New York City. The number is SPring 3-5743. Call me when you get through. Do you know about how long that'll be? That long? Thanks, I mean, merci, monsieur. I'll be here."

I dashed into the bathroom. I had time. Girard said it could take an hour. I leaned over one of the basins washing myself in the freshly filled water basin with a rough cloth and a bar of soap. The phone rang. I had a mouthful of toothpaste. This is not an hour! Pushing my toothbrush to the side of my mouth, dripping toothpaste, I wrapped myself in a couple of thick white bath towels and ran to pick it up.

"Yes. Yes. I'll be right down."

I threw off the towels, ran back into the bathroom to rinse and spit. I dashed back into the bedroom and pulled my clothes from the closet and out of the drawers. Keeping Shirl waiting down there was costing me a fortune. I jumped into my underwear, blue day dress, stockings, flats and sped out the door and down the carpeted steps. I was afraid the clunky elevator would take too long.

Breathless, I grabbed the receiver of the international phone lying on the desk. "Shirl?"

"Al? Is that really you?" she asked.

"Yeah! Shirl, I had—"

"All the way from Paris," Shirl mused. "Our little Country Girl, calling all the way from Paris. So grown up."

"There's something I wanted to—"

"Where's Juliana? I want to talk to her too."

"She's at rehearsal."

"Too bad. You're settled into your hotel? Mercy, come. It's Al."

"Shirl, I wanted to ask you—"

"Is your hotel 'tray chick'?"

"Nice, but the reason I called you was—"

"Mercy!" she yelled. "Hurry! Al, say hello to Mercy. She's never talked to anyone in Paris."

"Not now. You see—"

"Here Mercy. Say something."

"Hi, Al," Mercy shouted. "This is so exciting. You're calling all the way from Paris?"

"That's right." I held the phone away from my ear, afraid her shouting was going to burst something. Be patient, I told myself, but it was getting hard.

"Are you having a good time?" Mercy shouted again. "How was the ship?"

"Nice, but you don't need to shout. I can hear you fine. I need to talk to Shirl. It's business."

"Oh, business." She continued to shout. "Here's Shirl back. Say hi to Juliana for me. And you have yourself a grand time."

"Shirl, have you ever—?"

"Bring me some hotel soap with the hotel's name on it," Shirl said.

"They don't give you soap in French hotels. You have to buy your own."

"Well, that's not convenient. Then bring me towels. Hotel towels are always the best."

"That's stealing."

"Oh, pish posh."

"Shirl please, this is costing a fortune. Have you ever heard of Dan Schuyler?"

"Hmm. I did know a Schuyler once, but not Dan. Tony. Tony Schuyler was his name. He was the lead producer on a few of my early ventures into Broadway investing, but that was years ago. Why?"

"Did he have a son?"

"Yes. Gave Tony a lot of trouble. A bad seed, the way I heard it. I never met him, but I seem to remember something about problems with the law. Oh, wait! I remember now. My memory's slower than it used to be. Tony's son worked with Martin Bilberbank on one of his shows."

"Co-producer?"

"Hardly. More like a gofer. He was a kid. As I remember it, Martin was trying to help Tony straighten the kid out, so he gave him a job. This is going back ten, maybe fifteen years. The kid got into some kind of trouble. Something having to do with box office money. A good bit of it was missing. Nearly closed the show. Martin said Tony paid back the money out of his own funds to keep the story out of the papers and the kid out of jail. After that mess, Tony was broke; only had enough for a modest retirement. Sad. He was a good producer. The kid disappeared, and Tony spent what little he had left trying to find him."

"Did he ever find him?"

"No. Broadway folks used to say he died trying. Why are you asking about such old news?"

"I think I found Tony's son."

CHAPTER ELEVEN

"Are you all right?" Scott asked.

"Huh? Oh. Yeah. Sure. Fine." I'd forgotten Scott was sitting across from me at the Paix de la Cafe. We sat at a small round table packed together with others sitting at their own small round tables under a green awning; patrons yelled in French at harried waiters—I mean garcons—who squished in and out of tables carrying trays of baguettes, cheese, and coffee. For a moment, I imagined seeing Emile Zola and Guy de Maupassant sitting across from us. I was here. For real. Paris. In this famous café. I wished there were more time to *feel* Paris, instead of having to prepare for Juliana's opening and worrying about what to do about Schuyler.

"Drink your café au lait," Scott said. "It's getting cold,"

"I'll never get used to drinking coffee out of a bowl. I feel like a horse at a trough."

Scott smiled and lifted his bowl between his two hands. He whinnied like a horse and drank.

"And it tastes funny." I squished up my face as Scott drank.

"That's because of the boiled milk."

"Boiled?"

"Oh, yeah, I met this middle-aged American couple who've lived here for years. They said to be careful of the milk because the French don't pasteurize or refrigerate it?"

"Don't refrigerate it?" I pushed the bowl away from me. "And don't pasteurize it? That's against the law."

"In the U.S. We're in France."

"Oh, yeah, I forgot."

"But it's okay. This American couple said as long as it's boiled, it's safe, and quality places like this always boil their milk. I'm getting to like it. I can hardly believe I'm sitting in a café in Paris. Can't wait to send Grandma a post card."

"It *is* fantastic," I agreed, taking a moment to breathe in the French air before I went back to worrying.

But the worrying did come back. I kept tossing around in my head how I might get more information on Dan Schuyler's background. Given what Shirl told me about this guy's youth, I was sure there had to be something I could use to put us in one of those Mexican stand-offs. But how would I research it in Paris? I'd have to get Max involved.

Scott opened his copy of *Le Figaro*. "Wish I could read this thing."

I'd been talking through a translator to the French press for the last few days, following up on what I had started in the States. I made sure things like photos from the Copa were in their papers, as well as stories of her being raised in France, and of her coming to France's aid during the war. Every French paper would be at her opening, along with other foreign language papers. The only press that wouldn't be there was US.

I'd gone to the *Times* Paris office and gotten nowhere. I'd made calls to the New York papers to get them to run something about her opening at the Lido, but they wouldn't budge. Richard was bothering them from his mother's bedside in Omaha, but still, nothing. Juliana was old news. If we didn't make a big showing at the Lido, Juliana's career could be over. Richard went every night to church to light a candle for her. I supposed that's about all he could do from Omaha. And who knows—maybe it would make more of a difference than what I was doing.

Scott asked, "Is thirty degrees Celsius hot? It sounds cold, but it's been plenty hot the past few days."

"I'll pick you up a *Times* at the American Express office," I told him. "Do you need any francs? I'm going to cash in some traveler's checks when I'm there."

"Yeah," he said, pulling his wallet from his back pants pocket. He handed me a couple of traveler's checks. "If you don't mind."

"Not at all."

The arguments that had begun in the states with Billy Preston, Juliana's director, continued, but now the fights were with me, not Juliana. I absolutely forbid him to fight with her. Juliana must not have any additional stress. My first big fight with Billy was in New York before we even left. I was furious he insisted on flying instead of coming with us on the ship. The cost of flying was double the cost of sailing on the *SS United States*. But *he* said he had some "life-changing meetings" with Broadway people and he couldn't waste five days on a ship when TWA could get him to Paris in only fourteen hours. We should be overjoyed to spend more money on him; after all, *he* was the star. I wanted to kill him.

When Billy started rehearsals at the Lido, he immediately crossed out most of the new songs we'd agreed upon in New York. He wanted most of the French ones off the bill and he started crossing out the ones in English that were new and had been especially written for her. He wanted to stick her with a lineup of old ones, "standards," he said, hers and others. "That isn't what Juliana does," I told him. "She doesn't sing other singers' hits."

"Everyone sings everyone else's songs," Billy shot back. "Especially if they're trying to claw themselves back up to the top."

"Juliana is not everyone. Juliana is Juliana. She sings mostly her own material, with only a few 'old standards' from other singers." I looked down at the list of songs I'd clipped to my clipboard. "What's this? 'Aba Daba Honeymoon'? That's that song about the talking chimpanzee. No! Definitely not."

"It's a good song. Debbie Reynolds had a hit with it."

"It's silly. Juliana and Debbie Reynolds have *nothing* in common."

"I know. Debbie has a career."

I took in a deep breath. "Juliana will not sing that song."

"But I love Debbie Reynolds. Everybody does. What's wrong with *you?*"

"Then do 'I Like the Likes of You,' but let Juliana do it *her* way. It'll be a good flirting song if we play with the beat. And work in a fun, sexy dance routine for her and have the boys dance around her."

"Hmm, that's not bad."

"I know."

"You're pretty smart for a girl."

"Am I supposed to say thank you for that?"

"Well, it *was* a compliment."

"Was it?" I went back to looking over the list.

"No, Billy, she will not sing 'La Vie En Rose.'"

"Why? It's French. *She* wants to sing in French. *You* want her to sing in French. *That's* in French, but it's familiar. People like familiar."

"It sure is familiar. Piaf made a hit with it in '47. You will not put Juliana in the position of competing with the French people's beloved Little Sparrow."

"It'll work. They'll connect Juliana with Piaf and—"

"Forget it, Billy. I won't compromise on this one. Juliana will not sing that song or any Piaf song."

"I gave you a French song. Don't forget that." He grabbed his hat and stomped out. He came back again in a few hours while I was scrambling around trying to find another director while keeping the news from Juliana. He finished directing the show and never mentioned that song again.

Billy and I continued to fight over almost every song through to opening night. I got most of the French songs put back. He won on a number of those old standards he was so fond of, but not all. All the while, I kept reminding him that he had to keep smiling for Juliana. She could not know there was any controversy between us. It was exhausting.

"Scott, you've been such a doll through this whole thing. Listening to me growl and moan," I said, pushing my bowl of coffee further away from me. "My nerves have been pretty frazzled, and you've been so calm. How are you doing today? This is *your* big opening too."

He took a bite from his croissant. "I like this flaky roll. What is it called again?"

"A croissant."

"Did you know you can get them with chocolate on the inside, too?"

"Yes, and you're not saying how you are."

"I'm going to get one of those chocolate ones next time." He lit a cigarette.

"Are you avoiding my question on purpose?"

"No."

"Well? How are you, dammit?"

"Don't curse."

"Don't smoke. What's the matter?"

"I'm scared to death. I've never played for an audience as large as the one that's going to be at the Lido tonight and this kind of music . . . What if I ruin it for her?"

"You won't. I have faith in you, and so does Mattie. You be sure to wire her today and tell her this is your big day. Save the postcard for later. It'll take too long to get to her." He still looked anxious. "Look, Scott, opening night jitters are normal. Do the topless dancers bother you? Is that what it is?"

He grinned, "They don't bother me as much as they bother *you*."

"They don't bother me. I'm as sophisticated as, uh, uh . . . Does it show that much?"

"Yes. But I know you. I don't think anyone else notices you squirming."

"The worst is watching Juliana having casual conversations with them during a break as if it were nothing. Like yesterday, this girl stood yammering away in French with Juliana, smoking a cigarette without a stitch on top. I can't imagine what they could've been saying while the girl is standing there like that. How does Juliana do it? When the girls come up to me to ask something, I don't know where to put my eyes."

"How about back in their sockets," Scott laughed.

"Yesterday I asked Juliana how she did it and you know what she said? She said, 'You are so American.' What does that mean?"

Scott shrugged his shoulders.

"Of course, I'm an American. What else would I be? Sometimes I don't understand Juliana at all. And I suppose you haven't noticed any of those cute boy dancers in the tight pants."

"I try not to. I have a lonely gentleman at home who needs taking care of and I feel bad if I. . . I don't want to lose him, Al."

"You won't."

"I worry sometimes. I put him through a lot."

"Are you recovered from your fear of the hell fires?"

"I'm working on it."

"Oh, gosh, the time." I threw my napkin on the table and jumped up. "We've got to get over there. Jiminy, I've got so much to do before tonight."

"Jiminy?"

"I didn't curse, but you're still smoking."

He threw his cigarette on the ground with a scowl and shook some bills at the waiter.

CHAPTER TWELVE

Despite the problems between Billy and me and Scott's nerves, Juliana was a smash. I thought I'd go mad waiting for her to make her entrance. She was scheduled to be in both acts, but first we had to wait for the ice skaters and the comic, George Matson and the Oriental Dancers. Finally, Les Bluebell Girls created a beautiful entourage of bright colors and bare breasts around her as she entered through an opening in the ceiling. The boy dancers pushed a spiral staircase to meet her, and Juliana, singing her hit song, "Johnny, I'll Never Forget," floated down the steps toward the stage, her white and blue gown flowing around her body, her long blue gloves lightly touching the banister. I heard the audience emit a collective "oh" as she appeared, and who could blame them? She *was* glowing and self-possessed, so in charge of us all. Sexual sparks sizzled through the audience and no one was ordering more wine; all eyes and hearts and probably genitals too were on her.

In the second act, Les Bluebell Girls—dressed elegantly in black gowns, breasts bare, white mink stoles wrapped around their shoulders—danced onto the stage in high heels; they were surrounded by tuxedoed gentlemen. Water fountains illuminated in pink and yellow jumped up from the center of the stage. They sang a bouncy French tune as they danced around the fountain and through it.

Out of the fountain came women dressed in prison uniforms. Edouard Fleming, the man who had danced practically naked right after Juliana's number in the first act, came onto the stage, dressed in tights with a bare chest. He dragged one of the women out of the fountain by the hair and threw her onto the floor, stepping on her. The woman pushed him off, got up, and with a dramatic dance movement, threw *him* down, but before she could step on him he had knocked her to the floor again. After a few more dancing fight bouts, the man subdued the woman under his foot.

The lights came down on that act. When they came back up, Juliana was standing center stage in a black leotard with dark stockings, high heels, a tuxedo shirt, and black tie; a top hat, cocked to one side, sat on her head and her hair was pinned up into a feminine boyish look. Rhinestones dotted the lapel of her tuxedo jacket. Accompanied by an accordion, she sang of the sexy sights of "Pigalle." The Bluebell Girls slowly danced onto the stage with seductive looks. They were all naked legs, arms, and breasts. Playing prostitutes, they ran their hands over Juliana's shoulders as if she were a man. She undid her tie and whisked it from her neck, as she opened her shirt buttons to just above her breasts; the audience cheered, hoping for more. There would be no more. Instead, she winked to keep them on edge.

The audience loved her; she was one of them. More than half the songs were in French. She spoke to them in French, she flirted with the men in French, she nodded at the women in French. She knew all they had suffered and now she'd come home to them. Anyway, that's what the newspaper ads I'd run had said. At the end of the show, the applause went on and on like it would never end. She did eight encores before they finally let her leave the stage. This audience was far more expressive than the ones in New York. It was almost scary. We had to sneak her out the back door onto a cobblestone side street where the driver met us with the car so she wouldn't be mobbed.

The opening night party at Le Crillon, the elegant five-star hotel on Place de la Concorde, beat anything Juliana had ever had before, even at Sardis. She was the Queen of the Ball. She wore a simple black dress that hugged her waist. The V-neck gave a subtle indication of the full breasts that lay beneath. Around her neck was a simple strand of pearls that matched the earrings that dangled, one pearl on either side. Her dress was the least ostentatious of all the women clustering about her, and yet she naturally stood apart from them all. Her classic beauty was perfectly suited for simple. For me, Juliana chose the white chiffon with a daisy pattern from all the dresses Max had selected for me to pack. She thought I looked best in flowers.

As she entered, the orchestra played a medley of her songs, while stiff-legged young men marched among us with serving trays filled with glasses of champagne.

The people I met had titles like Duke and Duchess Whachamacallit and

Lord and Lady Whoknewwhat. This I gathered was the British side of Juliana's family who had made their way across the Channel to hear their darling sing at the world-renowned Lido. Juliana, herself, introduced me to her beloved Great Aunt, Lady Florence Viola Dankell-Smythie. They both said I could call her Aunt Sally. I wasn't sure where they got Sally from the long list of her names, but it sure helped. This charming grande dame in her mid-eighties—who expected the world to do a little bowing in her direction but wasn't overly obnoxious about it—had a deliciously snooty British accent. She wore her thick white hair piled on top of her head, gold-rimmed spectacles that kept sliding down her nose, and she obviously adored Juliana. That instantly won her over with me. She was Juliana's father's mother's sister or somebody like that. Coming from a tiny family with only a very few relations like I did made keeping track of all those apostrophes difficult. I did pick up that Juliana's visits as a child to Aunt Sally's summer home on Juliana's father's estate was a special time for her.

There were French uncles, aunts, and cousins too, some who weren't exactly blood and others who may have been. They swarmed around Juliana excitedly babbling in French. I imagined bemoaning the hot weather as all conversations in English, French, and probably Swahili seemed to begin by talking about the dog days of summer. I didn't mind not understanding, because Juliana sparkled with joy and that was enough for me.

I looked over the heads of the throng to see a large man—not fat, just big, with squared off shoulders—standing at the top of the steps waiting to enter the room. He held his top hat in his white-gloved hands. His stance was as imposing as his size. He wore an exquisite tuxedo, the front of which was covered with a gold medallion held on by gold chains draped across his chest. Most of the dukes and viscounts appeared to have thought it best to leave their insignia—symbols of their specialness—home, but not this man. As annoyingly ostentatious as he appeared to be, he commanded everyone's attention, even mine, as he took firm, deliberate steps down the staircase to walk among us mere mortals.

Juliana had been deflecting the advances of the young, pimply-faced, and slightly awkward Earl of Whatever. He looked like someone who, if it hadn't been for the accident of his birth, would have been the kid the other kids would've stuffed into a locker. She slowly turned to face the approaching man with the large medal on his chest. The man nodded at her and managed a half smile. "Father," I heard Juliana say.

You're kidding.

"Yes," he said. "Juliana, I was quite impressed." There was no emotion in his voice, and his body remained frozen in an impossibly straight posture. "Your mother would have been proud." He spoke mechanically, as if saying something Aunt Sally had told him he should say.

"You were there, Father? You saw the whole thing?"

"I did."

"Do you think Mother would've liked it?"

"I do," he said to the ceiling, still not giving any hint of what he might be feeling. Or *if* he were feeling.

"Because it's so important that she be proud," Juliana went on. "Do you think she knows? I want her to know, Father. I want her to—"

"That is quite enough. You are becoming overwrought."

"Yes, of course, you're right." Juliana said, reigning in her natural passion. "You'll stay for the supper?"

"No, I'm sorry, I can't."

"Drinks. You'll have a drink, Father. Please say you'll have a drink with me. "Garçon! Garçon!" In a panic, she signaled to one of the men walking by. She took a glass of champagne from the tray. "Here, Father, it's the best." She held it out for him.

"Champagne," he scowled. "You know I don't drink champagne."

"I can get you something else. What would you like, Father?"

"I'm fine with this." He took a sip and screwed up his lips into a corkscrew as if it were the worst thing he had ever tasted. That look of displeasure reminded me of my mother, minus the medals on his chest, of course.

"Waiter! Waiter!" Juliana called, desperately. "Bring my father, Lord Ruthersby. . . What, Father? Whatever you want."

"I told you I am fine with this." He spoke firmly, as if chastening a child. "I did not expect to have to repeat myself."

"No. I'm sorry, Father." She was beginning to sound like a penitent in the court of Henry VIII before he said, "Off with her head."

"Hey, Juliana, aren't you going to introduce me?" I marched right up to this Lord Ruthersby with the gold all over his too-puffed-up chest, my hand extended. *I* was an American. I didn't have to fall for this bull caca.

"Oh, Al." She sounded relieved to see me. "Father, this is my friend, Alice Huffman. Alice, this is my father, Lord Ruthersby."

"Howdy, partner," I said, taking the American motif perhaps a little too far. I'd felt awkward all night, sometimes doing a clumsy curtsy or bow because I didn't know what the hell to do around these people. Aunt Sally whispered to me, "Oh, dear, please do relax. No one expects very much from Americans." But I think turning into a cowboy was probably a little *too* relaxed.

"It's a pleasure to meet you, Miss Huffman," he said to the ceiling in his formal British accent, taking three of my fingers into his huge hand and awkwardly shaking them around.

"Help me take Father around to meet my other guests." I was honored that Juliana wanted my help, but I had no idea what exactly she wanted my help with. I didn't know these people.

As we walked about the room, Lord Ruthersby said, continuing to talk to the ceiling, "Yes, an entertaining show."

"Then you *do* think Mother would've liked it? Do you think she knows? I like to think that she knows and maybe approves. Daddy, do you think she—"

"Daughter! Control yourself."

"Yes, Father, I'm sorry."

I was starting to hate this guy.

"Yes, the program was quite entertaining, but dear, don't you think that some of it was—"

"Was what? You didn't like it?" Juliana asked, anxiously.

"Perhaps, a little risqué. I'm not criticizing, but . . ."

"Perhaps," she agreed.

"You know your mother always hoped you'd sing opera."

Juliana stood frozen, her head bowed like a needy child.

"Lord Ruthersby," I said, "I hate to steal your extremely talented daughter away from you, but there are some foreign dignitaries who have only arrived, and they are demanding to see her."

"Al?" Juliana looked at me, questioning.

"I understand," Lord Ruthersby said, sounding relieved. "You must attend to your business as I must attend to mine." He turned to Juliana. "I said I couldn't stay long."

"When will I see you again?"

She wants to see him again?

"Well, we shall see," Lord Ruthersby said. "It was a pleasure, Miss Huffman." He did an about face and marched from the room.

"Okay?" I asked.

"Why did you do that? Chase him away. I hardly ever see him."

"He was hurting you. I can't stand it when someone, even your father, hurts you."

"He doesn't mean it."

"Maybe not, but the results are the same. You have a show to do tomorrow and I won't have anyone undermining your confidence."

From the corner of my eye, I glimpsed Dan Schuyler by the bar.

"I guess I should say thank you," she said.

"No. Just enjoy your night. Oh, Scott! Scott, we're over here."

Scott made his way over to us and Juliana gave him a hug. "You were stupendous tonight."

"Who cares about me?" Scott said. "You were a walking dream."

A few of the guests came over and whisked Juliana away from us while I watched Schuyler; I was careful not to let him see that I was watching him, but I was sure he was watching me. Who let *him* in? This party was by invitation only. I turned to Scott and laughed loud and high.

"I'm glad *you* think it's funny," Scott said. "I don't."

"Oh, I'm sorry. I thought of something funny. What were you saying?"

"I still haven't gotten a letter from Max."

"You spoke to him on Wednesday. I'm sure . . ." Schuyler was still at the bar, but I could see that now he was speaking to Lady Philomena Quakenbush.

"You're sure of what?" Scott asked.

"Huh? Oh, Max. He'll write soon."

"Maybe not," Scott whispered. "And then it all would've been for nothing."

"What?" I asked.

A bell chimed, and we walked toward the dining room for the late-night supper, which was really the early morning supper. Schuyler had Lady Quakenbush, a stout woman in her thirties, on his arm a few steps away from me.

At the head of the line was Billy Preston, dressed to attract autograph seekers in his one-of-a-kind, navy-blue tux with satin lapels. Everyone wanted to know the "famous" American director who they had read about in *France Soir*. I was sure it never occurred to Billy that those articles were the result of *my* hard work. He had a few Duchesses and Viscountesses hanging from his arms, and I had no doubt that before the night was over, he'd have a couple in his bed, too.

"Well, well, Miss Huffman. How nice to see you again." A chill went up my back as I turned to see Schuyler smiling at me.

"Why are you here?"

"I imagine for the same reason you are. To celebrate Juliana's great triumph. There'll be nothing to stop her when she gets home to the states. Will there? Hello." He looked at Scott and put out his hand. "We met on the ship."

"Yes. I remember," Scott said. "You beat me at shuffle board."

"No hard feelings, I hope."

"Of course not. It's good to see you again."

"And you, too. Allow me to introduce you to Lady Philomena Quakenbush. She's investing in the new musical I'm bringing to Broadway in the spring."

"I've never invested in a show before," she giggled. A woman with an upper-crust English accent shouldn't giggle; it sounded all wrong. "It's risky," Lady Quakenbush went on. "But since I met Denny, I've learned to throw caution to the wind and live, live, live." She threw her arms about and smiled up at her 'Denny.' "He's convinced me that investing in this show will be stimulating. And," she lowered her voice to a whisper, "he won't tell me who the star is to be. It's a secret. Isn't that thrilling? He says when he announces the name, it is sure to cause a great stir on the great white way." She giggled again. She really needed to stop doing that. "Maybe *you* should consider investing in it, Miss Huffman."

"Yes, Miss Huffman," Schuyler said. "Maybe you should. Give me a call. Soon. It could be dangerous to wait too long."

"Oh, isn't he simply adorably mysterious?" Lady Quakenbush enthused.

"Ta-ta," Schuyler said, giving Lady Quakenbush a shove. "I must get my hungry investor to the trough."

"Uh, Al?" Scott leaned toward me, whispering. "Did he just call Lady Quakenbush a pig?"

"I think so."

Scott and I took our places at the elaborately adorned table with gold settings and all manner of sparkling things, but I barely noticed them. All my joy at Juliana's opening had been squashed by Dan Schuyler.

* * *

As soon as the car left us off at the hotel, I said a quick good night to Juliana and Scott—we were all bleary-eyed anyway—and hurried to my room. I threw the early newspapers we'd read at the party onto my bed. The reviews were glowing. Juliana was headed back to the top. At least in Paris. I tossed my satin wrap across a chair. I peered out my door into the hallway to be sure no one I knew was out there, then I ran like hell down the stairs to the desk.

Monsieur Blanc sat behind the desk in his blue uniform, wearing his usual stern expression; he was proud that he spoke no English. I cleared my throat and with my heart pounding, I approached him. I slid out a folded piece of paper from my purse that Juliana had prepared for me and read, "Bonsoir or —is it bonjour—oh, well, one of them—M. White c'est une belle soirée aujourd'hui, n'est-ce pas?"

He grunted without looking up. He didn't even take a moment to agree with me that it was a lovely evening. *If* it was evening and not morning. I didn't have time for this. I was exhausted. "'Téléphone?'" I said abruptly, forgetting Juliana's lessons in French politeness.

M. Blanc nodded at the phone sitting at the edge of the desk. I guess that was my signal to make the call myself. I picked up the heavy receiver, and the French operator rattled off something in my ear. "English?" I pleaded.

She rattled off another string of words and I hoped in there somewhere was 'I'll get you an English Operator.'

After a few moments of silence, an English operator did come on and told me she would place the call to New York. M. Blanc kept grumbling behind his desk while I paced in the lobby waiting for my call to go through. Finally, the phone rang, and I grabbed it.

"Max! Max!" I said as soon as the English operator connected us.

"Who is this?" Max yawned into the phone.

"It's Al."

"Do you have any idea what time it is?"

"Yes, it's ten thirty there and you should be up. You have two clubs to run. Max, have you ever heard of Dan Schuyler?"

"Who is this?

"Al."

"Who?" he yawned.

"Al, dammit."

"Don't curse. It's not ladylike. Al! It's really you? How'd she do?"

"Fantastic, but that's not why I called you."

"I knew Paris would come through. How are the reviews?"

"The morning reviews are gifts from the gods. We're still waiting for the evening. Please Max—Dan Schuyler?"

"Who?"

"Schuyler. Have you ever heard of him?"

"I've heard of a Tony Schuyler. Never met him, though."

"No. Dan. Do you know anything about a *Dan* Schuyler?"

"Doesn't ring any bells."

"You have connections all over the place, the cops, the mob."

"What kind of guy do you think I am?"

"I *know* what kind. Ask around for me. Try to find out anything you can about him and let me know pronto."

"What's this about?"

"I can't talk about it now."

"Are you all right, kid? You in some sort of trouble?"

"Uh, no, no, I'm fine." Part of me wanted to tell him, wanted him to be outraged at Schuyler, wanted his comfort and advice, but the other part of me felt responsible. Like I had done something to cause this. Like I'd been less than discreet at some time that I couldn't remember or had been too honest with some friend who wasn't a friend. Or a colleague or . . . I didn't want Max to hate me like he would if Schuyler followed through with his plan.

"And how's my Scott?"

"He's fine, but you need to write to him. He's beginning to think you don't care about him."

"We kind of had a thing on Wednesday."

"What thing?"

"A thing. It'll pass."

"On an international phone? That's crazy. Fix it. You can't have a thing with him while he's here. He has to concentrate on his work. We need him. Juliana needs him."

"I think about him every day."

"Yeah, well, he doesn't know that unless you *tell* him. In a letter. Better yet, send him a cablegram. It's faster."

"You want me to say romantic things to him in a cablegram while the cablegram guy takes down every word? And when it gets to Paris the next cablegram guy—"

"No. Bad idea. A letter then. But send it today."

"All right, all right. I *am* running two businesses practically by myself while my manager and accountant are off vacationing in Paris."

"Vacationing? Are you certifiable?"

"I thought that'd get you. It's hard, isn't it?"

"Damn hard."

"Good. You'll come back better than when you left. Then I'll get something out of this too."

"I've got to go. It's four thirty here. That's a.m., and I'm about to collapse. And this call is costing me a damn fortune."

"Give my boy a kiss for me."

"Cable me back if you find out *anything*. Anything about Schuyler. And please, *please* find something."

I fell onto my bed without pulling down the bedspread. As I drifted off—faces, names—Bertha. . . Lucille. . .maybe. . . Who betrayed. . .?

CHAPTER THIRTEEN

"The car will pick you up at the hotel at ten this morning and take you over to the salon, nails first," I said. I wiped the sweat from my eyes with a handkerchief, so I could see my list.

Des Magots was my favorite cafe and I went there most mornings. I went alone so I could eavesdrop. I loved listening to the fascinating people who gathered to argue politics and philosophy. The air was hot with their passion. I struggled to understand the words that flew around me. No one seemed to notice me sweating over my used French phrase book that I got from one of the booksellers on the quay near the hotel. I soon realized phrases like "Puis-je atterrir?" (Am I clear to land?) or "Quel est l'etat de piste?" (How is the surface of the runway?) were not going to help me a great deal. The book was left over from the war. I'd have to find something more contemporary. Every once in a while, though, I detected a few English words. Juliana told me that they were yelling about that philosophy, existentialism, that I'd heard bandied about at the Jumble Shop on Eighth Street in the US.

"My hair," Juliana said. "Did you get me an appointment with Rene?"

"He'll be waiting for you." I was pleased I could please her.

"I think I'm going to get it cut short in that new Parisian style."

"Don't you dare."

"This shoulder-length style is out of date and I'm bored with it."

"Your hair is perfect the way it is. We can make different looks from it: piled on your head, down, whatever. You're a success in that hair. We can't risk changing it. After you're finished with Rene—wash and set—that's it, Jule . . ."

She leaned across the table and whispered, "You're so sexy when you're bossy."

"... the car will take you over to ... to what do they call it? You know, the TV studio for the interview." I lifted my bowl of coffee with one hand. "Do you really think that?"

She winked and a surge of hormones shot up through the center of my body.

"Then you come home and rest," I continued. "It's practically a day off and there won't be many of them."

"You'll still meet me at three for lunch, won't you?" Juliana asked. "I want to take you shopping along the Rue de Faubourg St. Honore, so you can see where the real French shop. Here, take this. It's a plan, or map in English. It's quite helpful for showing you how to get around the city by subway, bus, whichever you prefer."

"Can we make it two, so you can get an extra hour of sleep?"

"Nothing will be open at two, remember?"

I sighed. "Oh, yes, that siesta thing. How do the French get anything done if they stop working every day from twelve to two-thirty?"

"It's not a siesta," she laughed. "That's Spain. It's just a midday rest. Good for the mind and body. You're too much of an American. Work, work, work."

"I'll meet you at three, but I want you in bed by six."

"Yes, boss."

"I'm serious, Jule. You need lots of rest to keep up with this schedule." I looked down at my notepad. "Tomorrow at nine you have a dance lesson. Right after that is your private exercise class. I've arranged for the new vocal coach to work with you at the hotel. He said the piano in the basement will be fine. The guy comes highly recommended by Monsieur Guerin, at the Lido, so he should be good. Still, I'm doing all of this through a translator, so if anything turns out not to be to your liking, tell me right away. Here. I've written your appointments on this."

She took the list. "You certainly are thorough."

"That's what I do."

"But there's one thing ..."

"Yes?" I asked, panicked that I could have forgotten anything she needed.

"My opera coach. No one's listed here."

"But you don't sing opera in the show."

"I sing opera for my life. I must have it. I'll call my teacher in New York; he can recommend someone."

"You still study opera in New York?"

"Of course."

"How come I don't know this? Oh well, give me your teacher's number. I'll contact him for a referral."

A shadow crossed our table. "Julien, como c'est va?" Margarite spoke in a slow lilting voice, obviously flirting with Juliana.

"Margarite. English, please. For Al."

"Yes. English for the American child."

Margarite sat herself down at our table, her back turned toward me as if I weren't there. Did she follow Juliana wherever she went? She pulled at each finger of her beige gloves, slowly removing them. "Oh, Julien, I must look a fright," she said, puffing her lips out at Juliana, knowing she looked absolutely gorgeous. She wore an obviously costly multi-colored silk dress and a maroon hat with bird feathers all around the brim. "I didn't get a wink of sleep last night," she continued. "All I could think of, well . . .I was dreaming. Of you. And I—I couldn't help touching myself you know where."

"Margarite," Juliana admonished, "a café is hardly the proper place to speak of such a thing."

"Oh, pu, pu, where is the proper place, ma cherie . . .?" She ran an index finger up Juliana's bare arm, ". . . when you burn, you know where?"

"You know, that could be bugs," I offered. "French drug stores take turns staying open all night so . . ."

"I do not have bugs," Margarite said, indignant.

Juliana held her napkin to her lips and swallowed down her laughter. "I'll speak to you later, Margarite. Al and I have—have business. Excuse us."

Margarite stood with an indignant "humpf" directed at me and swished out of the café just as Juliana broke into peals of laughter. I loved making her laugh.

"You have a devil in you, Al, and I love it."

"Why do you let that silly woman come around you?"

"Margarite isn't a bad sort once you know her. And I've known her a long time. Since we were both nine. Well, at least, *I* was nine. She was eleven, but even then, she was lying about her age. We studied music and dance at the same school. But *she* graduated from the Conservertoire instead of dropping out like I did. That's quite something." She had that faraway look of regret she sometimes got. "She heard I was appearing at the Lido, so she quite naturally wanted to be at the opening."

"She was at the opening? I didn't see her."

"She didn't come to the reception. Too many people. She hates crowds. They make her nervous. I spoke to her the next day."

"Did she like the show?"

"Yes, as a matter of fact, she did. Oh, Al, don't look like that. I know she puts on airs, but there's more to her under the surface; you have to take the time to see. Life hasn't been easy for her."

"Hah! She struts around like a dancing peacock in her fine feathers, making me look like a pigeon."

"A pigeon?" she laughed. "You don't look like a pigeon. It's an act, Al. Margarite is acting. I just can't tell you her private business. I hope you can understand that. It wouldn't be right. But. . . she *has* suffered and I feel some responsibility."

"But why?"

"That's all I can say. So—tell me about the rest of my day."

CHAPTER FOURTEEN

After the cab dropped me off in front of the hill, I started the climb upward toward the old church Juliana had told me about. It was once used as an opera house because the acoustics were so good. She had sung there as a girl. She said the acoustics were better in that old building than in any other she had ever sung in since. Later, it was converted into a church for the local residents. Now it was rarely used; it lay in disrepair on the top of a long zigzag line of craggy stone steps in the shadow of Sacre Coeur. Few people knew about it, especially not tourists.

All morning I had run from office to office, first stopping at American Express to pick up the mail and send an update wire to Richard, then running to the post office to mail Scott's and my letters to Max and Juliana's letter to Richard and my post cards to Shirl and Mercy. I set up key appointments for Juliana while opening up possible doors for Lili Donovan and Patsy LaRue. The French weren't so put off by Patsy's name. To them she sounded French, not like a stripper. Of course, they weren't so put off by strippers, either. I thought I might call Patsy to come over and introduce her around. Marty was too distinctly American to fit into a Paris nightclub; Parisians were cautious around anything "too American." They pretty much considered all of us a bunch of clumsy gangsters who had no appreciation for the finer things of life, even those things that came from our own country like the works of Steinbeck and Faulkner. I was following Broadway closely from my faraway perch, certain I'd find something for Marty soon.

It was a hard climb up those steps with a rickety handrail that was difficult to grip without getting splinters. By the time I reached the top, my legs ached, and my clothes were wet with sweat. I limped to the single step in front of the door and sat to take off my shoe. I shook out the pebbles that had collected there and tried to fan myself with my hand. It wasn't terribly effective.

With the door slightly ajar, I could hear the dramatic sounds of two women's voices blending as they sang an aria. My shoe still in my hand, I leaned back against the outer wall, listening to the sounds and drinking in the afternoon breeze that drifted over me. I could see the whole town of Montmartre, including Sacre Coeur, spreading out before me. I felt I could have spent all afternoon there, not moving, only breathing and feeling gently alive.

As I listened more closely to the singing, I heard the sound of a piano accompanying the voices. I put my shoe back on, stood, and went into the foyer of the building. The music swelled around me and in me, and I breathed deeper to take more in. I tiptoed toward a torn red-velvet curtain that separated me from the singers. I pushed it out of my way and saw that I was at the top level of a rather large raked auditorium. Far below me on a wide but shallow stage was Juliana in her Jacques Fath wide-brimmed navy-blue hat, her long dark hair tucked into the hat, because of the heat. Margarite, wearing a small hat that hugged the back of her head, stood next to her. They sang together. To the right of them was a heavy man with a goatee. He wore a well-made gray suit and played the piano; a large wooden crucifix hung crookedly on the back wall behind them.

I took a seat in the top row so that Juliana wouldn't see me right off. I hardly ever got to hear her sing opera, so now was my chance, even if it was with Margarite. As they sang, I kept wishing Margarite would sing off key, but she didn't. Her voice blended and intermingled perfectly with Juliana's. Maybe this was what Juliana meant by looking under Margarite's surface. When they'd finished, the man at the piano stood clapping. "Bravas! Bravas! Bravisimas." He spoke with an Italian accent.

"Oh, Margarite! Such fun!" Juliana said.

I could hear everything perfectly from where I sat. Juliana had been right about the acoustics in this building. And as long as I stayed quiet and squished down in my seat, I was the proverbial fly on the wall.

"It's been so long since we've sung together, dear Juliana," Margarite said in her too-fancy French accent, threading her fingers through Juliana's. "Time does keep flying away, does it not? Oh, did I tell you I have a new husband?"

"No, Margarite," Juliana laughed. "Not another one? What number does this one make? Six?"

"I think he might be number seven, but who's counting? He's only a man. And you know how men are."

The Italian man cleared his throat and said, "No, I do not know how men are. Please do tell, Margarite."

"Armando," Margarite giggled, throwing her arms around his neck. "I did not mean you. You are a special man."

"I should think so," Armando said.

"And so is my new husband." She took Juliana's and Armando's hands in hers, drawing them close. "He's an Italian like you, Armando. And so handsome. Also like you. And he's royalty. A duke from the House of Savoy."

"A duke? Of which province? What is his name?" Armando asked. "A duke? But, alas, these days the Savoys have no—"

"Let's have another song," Juliana hurriedly interrupted, as if trying to save Margarite from some truth that Armando might discover.

"Juliana, a solo," Margarite suggested.

"But we said Armando would be next," Juliana said.

"Oh, but Juliana, I bow to your greater gift," Armando said, bowing. "Please, dear, you must sing."

"Yes, do, Julien," Margarite said. "I will keep my mouth closed up tight all the time." She planted a quick kiss on the back of Juliana's hand. "As a matter of fact, *I* shall sit in the audience."

She scurried down the proscenium steps and sat in one of the theater seats in the front row. "Now you may begin," she called to Juliana and Armando.

Juliana looked over at Armando, who'd seated himself behind the piano. "Ebben? Ne Andro Lontano," she said, taking off her hat and throwing it to Margarite.

Her hair! Short. I told her not to . . . I almost jumped out of my seat and ran down there. I'll kill her!

"An excellent choice," Armando said, playing a few notes.

And yet, the style looked good on her. Maybe even more alluring. The way Ava Gardner's been looking these days. Still . . . she's supposed to listen to me. That's the deal.

Juliana took a stance, opening her mouth, and the most otherworldly sounds came out of her. I forgot about her hair. The sounds poured forth softly at first, like wisps of clouds, then stronger, deeper, heavy with pain; they swirled around the auditorium and pierced my body. I swore that those sounds shook the crucifix behind her. Or perhaps the Christ was showing his pleasure at being bathed in Juliana's holy vibrations. This was a sacred place. Her voice made it so. As the song drew toward its end, I saw droplets of tears roll down her cheeks as well as mine.

For a long moment, there was only silence, and no one moved. I thought soon I would show myself, once I could breathe again, and walk down the steps to her. Oh, how I wanted to throw my arms around her, kiss her, worship her, make love to her. As I slowly pushed myself from my seat, Margarite dashed back up the steps, crying out, "Darling, oh, darling, c'est magnifique."

Armando left his piano bench to come forward and bowed, "I kiss your feet, dear Julien. We must serve you. You are the grand dame of all musique."

Margarite grabbed Juliana's arms and the two women fell into an embrace. I sat back down to wait for a better time to present myself. Margarite placed her lips upon Juliana's lips and Juliana did nothing to stop her. Instead, she put her arms around Margarite's back and pressed their bodies together; breast to breast, stomach to stomach, their satin dresses melting into each other as she returned the kiss. Anger welled up in me as their tongues danced in each other's mouths. I slipped out the back before the kiss had ended.

*　*　*

It was as if I'd been skinned of my outer layer and nothing was left but raw organs and blood about to splatter upon the pavement. Hours or minutes went by. What difference did it make? I walked by artists sitting at easels; a woman in high heels and a party dress—or was that a cartoon for my mind—carrying a long loaf of unwrapped bread. Like a drunkard, I stumbled over rough cobblestone streets. I walked along the Seine past the used bookseller stalls. A fat woman sold ice cream from a cart and a song sheet vendor sold sheet music while his wife played the violin. I didn't stop. I was in Paris with sights so strange to my eyes I should have wanted to stop and see everything, but I didn't. There may have been a bus or two along the way. I couldn't be certain. Blind, I headed in no direction; I only moved without plan or thought. My body wanted to flail, lash out, hit someone. Finally, I ended up back at the hotel. I went in because there was no other place to go, but I didn't want to be there either. I had no place I wanted to be; I wanted to be no place.

I heard myself slam my door. That momentarily roused me from my stupor. I stared at the closed door, then down at my hands, saying, "I did that. Who was it that slammed that door? That was me. I think it was me. I think I slammed that door. I think I did that."

Beyond my open curtains, the day was turning gray. How gray the day, I thought. That rhymes. I laughed to myself. What should I do now? Sleep. Sleep would be good. Heavenly unconsciousness. I yanked the bedspread off the bed and squeezed under the tightly tucked blankets, still in my day dress, nylons, and shoes. I would sleep and when I awoke, none of it would be real. But hadn't I known all along?

"Al!" A voice very much like Juliana's broke into the room. "Where have you been?"

I turned, groggy, toward the voice. I didn't know if I'd been sleeping or not, but the afternoon's daylight was gone and beyond my curtains there was only black. I saw a shadowy outline of her standing in the doorway of our two rooms.

"What?" I said.

Juliana switched on the lamp beside my bed and I squinted at her, hardly able to make her out. "What?" she asked. "Is that all you have say to me? Where have you been? I've been going out of my mind with worry."

"Why?"

"Why? Have you been drinking? We were supposed to meet at the church in Monmartre, go to lunch and shopping. When you didn't show up, I didn't know what to think. Were you lost? Were you kidnapped?"

"Sorry I upset your lunch plans." I pulled the cover over my head.

"No. You will not do this." She yanked down the cover. "You're not even dressed for bed. Get up. Tell me what happened. Scott is out looking all over Paris for you right now, and it's pouring out."

"He is?" I threw my legs over the side. "Gee, I didn't mean to worry *him*."

"But *me* you did?"

"I see I didn't worry you too much. You're in your nightclothes. But gosh, I hate that cold cream all over your face."

"It's not cold cream. It's egg white and sweet cream. An old Parisian beauty treatment."

"And that rag around your head. You look awful." I picked up the phone. "Hello, room service? Bring me up a bottle of gin and some ice. Well, get me someone who *does* speak English!" I yelled into the phone.

Juliana took the phone out of my hand. "Bon soir, monsieur—je suis deisolée pour toute confusion. Mon amie ne parle pas Français. Je voudrais commander un verre de lait, et s'il vous plait annuler la commande pour le gin. Merci beaucoup."

As she hung up the phone, I yelled, "Hey! I understood some of that. You cancelled my gin. And I won't drink milk in this place. You're trying to kill me, aren't you?"

"What?"

"They don't pasteurize it or refrigerate it or anything. Their milk will kill me, and you know it. And you can't go around cancelling what *I* want." I picked up the phone.

"Yes, I can. Because it appears that at this hour, only the French speaking help are available." She took the phone from me and hung it up. "Now, what's the matter?"

"Take that gunk off your face, whatever it is. I can't talk to you when you look like that. It makes me want to laugh, and I don't feel like laughing."

Juliana heaved a sigh and went into her room. I flipped off my shoes and stood at the doorway while she sat at her vanity, taking out little jars, white cloth squares, and powder puffs. "I only went to bed because *you* told me to. I didn't sleep at all, you know. I've been pacing this room . . ."

"When did Scott leave?"

"A couple hours ago. I hope he didn't wander off into the slums."

"Paris has slums?"

"Every big city has slums. Since the war, ours happen to be in the suburbs, but not far from the center of Paris." She took off the scarf she had wrapped around her head and shook out her hair.

"I told you not to cut your hair. You're supposed to listen to me. That's our deal."

"Our 'deal' only extends to my career. Not my whole life. And certainly *not* to my hair."

"Your hair *is* your career and you're lucky it looks good or I'd be walking out of here right now. Gosh, I hope Scott's okay. I'd hate anything to happen to him because of me."

"Yes, well, maybe you'll be a little less cavalier about standing people up in the future." She took a cloth and began wiping the white stuff off her face.

"Cavalier? Do you think that's what I was?" I leaned on her vanity. "Well, I *did* show up at the church."

"You did?" She stopped wiping and looked at me. "Why didn't you let me know?"

"You seemed to be too busy."

"I was with my friends, and we were singing, but—" She stopped suddenly, remembering. "Oh."

"Yeah. Oh."

She removed the last of the cream and tossed the soiled cloth in the trash bin beside her. "That was nothing." She patted some clear liquid on her face. "Margarite is emotional. The French *are*, you know."

"Now, you're lying to me. I don't think you've ever lied to me. You've done lots of other crappy stuff to me, but—"

"I have?"

"But you've never lied to me, so why now? You're sleeping with her, aren't you? You've been sleeping with her for a long time. All the time that you and I have known each other. I've been a jerk, haven't I?"

She dabbed a powder puff over her forehead. "You're being melodramatic."

"It makes everything so much clearer. Especially the separate rooms. You'd rather be with her."

"Don't be ridiculous. I couldn't stand being with Margarite for more than a few hours."

"Only enough time to frig her."

"Don't be crass. It doesn't suit you."

"But it suits Margarite, doesn't it? You like her whispering curse words in your ear?"

"Margarite is incapable of *whispering* anything. She has the voice of a fog horn on an extremely cloudy day."

"Is that meant to be funny?"

"No. I don't think any of this is funny." She furiously dabbed powder on her nose. "You're the one who told me I needed to rest. How can I rest when you're wandering around the streets of Paris in the dark, mispronouncing the few French words you know? Parisians hate that. And they hate Americans, so I'm pacing in my room thinking they're going to find you in some ditch bloody and who knows what else?"

I pushed myself away from her vanity and headed toward my room.

"Like you care."

"I do." She was standing when I turned back around to face her.

"You do what?"

"Nothing." She busied herself with putting away the bottles and cloths that were spread across her vanity.

I crept back toward her. "You said you care."

"Of course, I do," she said stiffly. "Now let's stop talking about it." She tried to tighten the top of one of the jars, but her grip slipped, and the top flew off. "Dammit."

I picked it up from the floor and handed it to her. "Why does it make you so nervous when we get close to calling the thing between us love?" She kept recapping her jars and wiping white gunk from the vanity glass. I leaned onto the glass, my face looking up into hers. "I love you," I said. She flinched. "I love you, Jule. I love you. I love you."

"Well, you don't have to keep repeating it." She moved away from the vanity toward the sofa in the center of the room.

"Yes, I do." I leaned back against the wall, feeling some return of power. "I get to say it as much as I want. And you have to listen to it without giving me that nonsense speech about how two women can't love each other in the same way that a husband and wife, blah, blah, blah. It seems to me I delivered pretty damn good on my end of the deal. You wanted me to help Richard make you a success. Well, look around. You're the toast of Paris. And today I got a wire from Jules Podell." She turned to face me. "Yes, he and I will be negotiating a good contract for you long distance. You're on your way back up in New York, too." I pushed out of my mind the intruding Dan Schuyler and his blackmail. "And in exchange, I get to say I love you as much as I want and you have to listen to it. That's not such bad deal, huh? I love you. I love you. I love you. I can even do it in French. Je t'aime. Je t'aime. Je t'aime."

"All right. All right," she said as if I were throwing knives at her.

"Everyone in France is in love with *l'amour*, except you."

"The French don't approve of our kind of—of... any more than

Americans do."

"That's the reason you keep this long-term arrangement with Margarite, isn't it? Because with Margarite there is no love."

"Stop trying to 'figure me out'; there's nothing to figure out. I'm not complicated like you. I'm just me. I don't understand why you're even bothered by Margarite. She doesn't have anything to do with you."

"She sure the hell does."

"It's just that with Margarite . . ." She walked back toward the vanity. "You know, I never speak about private things that happen between other people and me, but, uh, maybe I'll bend a little so you'll see that this isn't something you need to be concerned with." She sat back down at her vanity, placing her jars into the drawers. "I can do things, sexual things with Margarite that—"

"That you can't do with me? Why? Anything you want to do I'll—"

"Don't do that. Don't twist yourself into something you're not. I don't want that."

"What makes you think I'm such a 'scaredy cat' that I couldn't do anything she does, only better?"

"Because you use expressions like 'scaredy cat.' Which is charming," she hastened to add.

"I'm charming? Like a kitten?"

"No, like a country girl. I enjoy your homespun, down-home ways. You're gentle. That's a lovely quality. I don't want you to change. There's nothing about you I'd change. We've had some beautiful times together, haven't we?"

"Of course, but I never thought I was sharing you with the world."

"Margarite is not the world."

"Richard?"

"Oh."

"Yeah. Oh. Tell me how Margarite is different from me? Beyond the obvious."

"I've already said more than I should. Do you *really* want me to break my rule, a rule I value greatly, knowing if I do I'll feel terrible afterwards? Do you want that?"

"Yes." I crossed my arms over my chest.

She sighed. "All right. I don't feel at all good about this, but if it will help you. With Margarite I can . . . Well, she likes things a little rough. There's nothing more you need to know."

"You think I'm not sophisticated. You think I can't know about these kinds of things. You're treating me like a child."

"In business you are extremely sophisticated, but in sex . . ."

"You talk like you think you're the only woman I've ever been with."

"Well?"

I gave her a wink and a nod and sauntered over toward her bed like a swashbuckling Errol Flynn.

"*Have* you been with someone else?"

I sat on the end of her bed, leaning my head against one of the canopy posts. "Maybe."

"Who?"

"I don't kiss and tell."

"Who?" she repeated more firmly.

There was a knock at the door. "Service de chambre," the voice on the other side said. Juliana hurried to open the door, signed the check, and retrieved my warm milk. "I guess you don't want this."

"Oh, but I do." I snatched it from her and sucked on the glass like it was an elixir from the gods without drinking it. "This is going to make me sleepy, you know." I yawned with vigor. "I better go to my room."

"You're not going anywhere until you tell me who." She blocked the doorway.

"Oh? You're hurt."

"I am not. Only surprised. It doesn't matter who . . . Who was it? Was it someone I know?"

"You might."

"You're making it up. You've never been with anyone else, any other *woman*. You're making up a story to impress me."

"Are you impressed?"

"No."

"And I'm not making it up."

"Tell me. I told *you*."

"No, you didn't. I figured it out."

"You're making it up in retaliation." She walked away from the doorway and sat at the vanity. She looked in the mirror, poking and fluffing her hair. "You're jealous so you've concocted this story about some make believe, mysterious—"

"Virginia Sales."

"You're kidding. But she's straight."

"Not with me she's not." I was really reaching if I thought that one time on the ladies' room floor with Virginia could compare to what I imagined Juliana was doing with Margarite, but it was all I had.

"I didn't think Virginia even had the necessary equipment down there to get the job done."

"Don't be mean 'cause you're hurt."

"I'm not hurt."

"Yes, you are." I bounced around the room. "You are. You are. Juliana's hurt. Juliana's hurt."

"Now you *are* acting like a child."

I leaned on the vanity. "What do you do *specifically* with Margarite that you haven't done with me? Maybe I did it with Virginia."

"You didn't."

"How do you know?"

"All right. All right." She slapped the vanity glass with her two hands, marched over to her walk-in closet, and disappeared for a few moments.

She returned with one hand held high, and hanging from it was a leather belt, a rubber penis dangling from the center of it. "Well?" she said, her voice and eyes challenging me.

She was trying to intimidate me, and I couldn't let her know it was working. "I know what that is," I said. "It's a, a . . ." My throat clogged, and I couldn't get the word out.

"A dildo, yes. And you and Virginia used one of these?"

"Sure," I puffed out my chest as far as it would go. "Sure we did. Lots of times. All the time. Shirl and Mercy gave one to you *and* me. What happened to that?"

"I have it."

"Well? Give it to me. I'll show you I know how to use it."

"Al, you don't have to prove anything."

"Oh yeah, I do." I barged into her closet. "Where is it?" I pushed her clothes out of the way looking for it. "Come on, Jule, they gave it to both of us. You have no right—"

"All right. Don't wrinkle my clothes. It's here." She stood on tiptoe and pulled down a box from the top shelf and handed it to me.

I opened the box and grabbed out the phony penis. It felt strange, kind of a mushy rubbery feel, not at all like Henry, my ex-fiancé. "I'll show you I know how to use this thing. I'll be right back. I marched out of her room into mine, holding the pretend penis in my hand like a spear.

"Uh, Al." She stood at my door. "Unless you're planning on gluing that on you'll need this." She held up the leather belt with the rubber penis still hanging from it.

I watched as she wiggled it out of its holder. "You have to use the harness. Come here. I'll help you."

"I know how to do it."

"I know," she said. "I'd like to help you."

Slowly, in the middle of her bedroom, Juliana began to undress me.

"Uh, Juliana, I'm mad at you."

"I know," she said, lifting my dress off over my head.

"If you undress me, I'll get excited."

"I know," she said, throwing off my slip and kneeling to unsnap my nylons.

"But if I get excited . . ." My excitement mounted as she slid down my garter belt . . . "I won't be able to stay mad at you."

"I know." She removed my bra and put her mouth around one of my nipples while her fingers stroked the other one.

"Oh gosh, oh gosh, Jule, you're, you're manipulating me. Again."

"I know." She slid my underpants down to my ankles.

She fitted our dildo into the center metal hole of the harness and pulled two of the straps up my legs. Then she wrapped the leather belt around me and cinched it. When she stepped back to take a look, the thing slid down to my feet. She covered her mouth, trying not to laugh, but the laugh exploded out of her anyway. She laughed so hard her legs got weak and she fell back on the bed.

"It's not *that* funny."

"Oh, yes, it is."

"I guess I'm a lot skinnier than Margarite."

"You are." She pulled the harness back up around me and cinched it into the last hole. "But *I'm* usually the one who wears it."

"You? I don't think I'd like seeing *you* in a penis."

She smiled and stepped back again. "Let's see how you look."

I put my hand over the protruding thing, trying to hide it. "Jule, I feel silly."

She covered her mouth, so she wouldn't laugh out loud again. "That's how you look. But it's not the look. It's what you do that matters."

"Uh, Jule . . . I—I don't really *know* what to do with it."

"I know. I'll teach you. It's the same idea as when you put a couple of fingers in me or I do that to you, only this is more so."

I put my arms around her and held her close. "What am I going to do with you, Jule? You're killing me."

She let her bathrobe fall to the floor and lifted her nightgown over her head. We stood together naked with the dildo pointing at her pussy. "Well, tonight I think you're going to make love to me. After that? Who knows?" She kissed me deeply. The rain beat against the windows as I melted into her.

A knock at the door. "Juliana!" Scott yelled. "I can't find Al anywhere. We gotta call the police."

CHAPTER FIFTEEN

I woke up the next morning in Juliana's bed. Juliana's head lay on my pillow, she was that close. I loved looking over and seeing her there, even if her black hair didn't quite fan out over my white pillow case anymore. I loved watching the barely perceptible rising and lowering of her breasts to the rhythm of her gentle breathing.

It'd been kind of awkward when Scott was knocking at our door with Jule and me both being in our naked condition and with me wearing the dildo. We ran and grabbed robes and let him in, but the whole time Scott was there saying how glad he was I was okay and drying his hair with Juliana's towel, I kept worrying the dang dildo would poke out of my robe and scare him half to death. I don't think we were as receptive to him as we should've been.

I carefully slipped from the bed, not wanting to wake her, and dashed into the bathroom. I wanted to get clean before I went back to her. Especially my teeth. As I leaned over one of the basins, reaching for the tooth powder, I watched the dildo jiggle up and down. I stared at myself in the mirror from all angles. I was getting to like how it looked on me. I brushed my teeth, soaped up, and rinsed in the two basins, but I didn't ungirdle the thing. I liked having sex with this thing. One time when I was on top. That was fun for me, but not so much for her. Juliana turned me over onto my back and she got on top of me and pushed herself down onto it. Was that how she and Margarite did it? That way worked out best for her. And when I moved my hips to meet her movements while she touched her clit and I played with her nipples, she damn near exploded. I thought they might send the hotel detectives in to arrest us. Wearing that thing made me feel strong and in charge. I liked being that for Juliana.

I watched myself in the mirror as I dried my body with one of the big fluffy hotel towels. I wrapped the towel around my waist and made fists of my hands. I curled my arms and flexed my muscles. Only there weren't any muscles. My arms were skinny sticks. As I studied my arms, the towel slowly unfurled from my waist and slid into a heap around my feet. There was the dildo, bobbing up and down on my boyish frame. I remembered overhearing conversations from musicians talking about their penis being big or hard or whatever. They always seemed to be talking about their penises if you listened close enough. Even if it sounded like they were talking about buildings or business or musical instruments, they were really about their penises, only in code. Wouldn't they have loved this one? Always big. Always hard. You could take it off when you didn't need it and keep it in a drawer.

I ran into my room, threw open one of my dresser drawers, and grabbed a T-shirt I wore when I had my men's suit on. I pulled it over my head and flexed my muscles in the mirror over my dresser. I thought, I looked stronger with the T-shirt on, so I left it on with no underpants to surprise Juliana with my great prowess.

I tiptoed back toward her bed, but I quickly saw that it was empty. My heart sunk. I'd wanted to spend at least a few hours with her in bed before I had to go back to being serious and thinking about things like Dan Schuyler.

"Good morning," Juliana said, exiting the bathroom in her frilliest bathrobe covered with pink and white lace. "Well, look at you."

I flexed my non-existent muscles and she smiled, pulling me toward her. "You're a quick study."

"Did I please you?"

"You know you did."

"That's all I want to do, Jule. Please you. I thought maybe we could spend some time in bed before we have to—"

"Come here," Juliana said, putting her arm around me and guiding me back toward the bed. She sat down on the edge and I sat next to her, worrying about what she was going to say. Something serious. I didn't want to be serious. Not yet. I didn't want to think about serious things. I didn't want to think about the serious things I knew I *had* to think about. And soon.

"There are some things you wanted to know that I didn't tell you."

"You mean about you and Margarite?"

"Sort of."

My stomach did a somersault. "Can you tell me in bed?"

"I suppose." She stood and threw off her bathrobe. She wore a silky nightgown that hugged her body.

She climbed into the bed, but I touched her arm. "Could you take your nightgown off too? If you're going to tell me something bad, I think it'd be easier to take if you don't have clothes on."

She laughed, shaking her head as she threw off her nightgown; she climbed into bed and I got in beside her. "I'm afraid," I told her.

"Of what?"

"Of what you're going to tell me about you and Margarite. I tried so hard to please you last night, but she's better and . . ."

She put a finger to my lips. "Shh. Could you stop thinking in those categories for a few minutes?"

"Categories?"

"Good. Bad. Better. Best. I've been invited to a party to catch up with some old friends. Friends who go a long way back. Before the war."

"And Margarite is going to be there, right?"

"I don't know. I don't keep track of Margarite's social calendar. Do *you* want to come?"

Ecstasy bubbled up in my stomach. "I'd love to go. When is it?"

"Tuesday when I'm not working."

"That's good. Tomorrow I'm at the Moulin Rouge to check out their new show, but I haven't scheduled any business yet for Tuesday, so I'm free too."

"You might not like this type of party and Al, please, don't turn yourself inside out trying to make yourself like it. It doesn't matter to me if this isn't something you want to do."

"Well, I'd be with you and meeting your friends. How could I not like it?"

"It's a sex party."

"Oh."

"Remember I said I do certain things with Margarite that I don't do with you?"

"Yeah."

"Look, you know, I never talk about other people's private business. I'm only doing this because you felt like I was lying to you and—"

"You've been to these parties before? With Margarite? In New York?"

"These kinds of 'things,' 'activities,' have been around for a long time, but not officially. They only started opening clubs for these 'games' in the States within the last ten years. After the war. Clubs like these have been in France a lot longer and some of the GI's brought the ideas back to the US. Most of them are for straights and some extremely secret ones are for homosexual men. But a few people have parties in their homes that accommodate gay girls."

"And you've gone to these parties? Participated? In France *and* New York?"

"Occasionally. Not a lot."

"I can't believe this. How could you?"

"I knew you'd react like this. That's why I haven't told you. You're shocked and upset." She grabbed her robe and got out of the bed.

"No. I'm fine. Tell me. What kinds of party games are usually planned at these gatherings?" I plastered a big phony smile on my face as if she couldn't see through it.

"You don't need to know about this. Let's go to the zoo this afternoon."

"The zoo? Like I'm ten?"

"I didn't mean it that way. I meant . . . The Louvre. We could—"

"Please, Jule, tell me about this party. I won't be shocked. For Pete's sake, I run a club in New York City. I hear and see lots of disgusting things all the time. I just don't participate. I go home instead. I was thinking about your career. If it ever got out that you—"

"You were not thinking of my 'career.' You were shocked and you had that look on your face."

"What look?"

"The one you get when you're disappointed in me. That look of horror, the one that says, 'Oh, Julie, how could you?' It makes me feel awful. You're so good and I can't be."

"I'm not good. You just don't know in what ways I'm not good. But I'm not. Tell me what you do with Margarite."

"And you won't give me that face?"

"Not if you take off your robe and come back to bed with me." She let the robe fall and we both crawled under the covers. "So, tell me," I said, facing her, my head supported by the flat of my hand and my elbow. "I won't make any faces."

"Do you know about things like voyeurism and exhibitionism?"

"Of course. Voyeurs are those creepy guys who go around peeking in women's windows trying to see them undress. You know, Peeping Toms. And exhibitionists are those sick ones who go up to nice girls in parks and subways and show them their privates."

"Well, those are *some* examples. But there are others. You see, there are some people who are discrete and decent who would never want to hurt or impose themselves on anyone, people who have the kinds of urges that 'nice' people don't think are so nice. At a party like this, they can play games and indulge their fantasies and . . . urges without upsetting the 'nice' people."

"Well, what do they do?"

"An exhibitionist might, say, for instance, if she were a woman, she might undress while others watch her."

"A woman would do that? In front of polite company? You mean Margarite—" I slapped a hand to my mouth, took a deep breath, wiped my look of horror off with my hand, and smiled pleasantly. "Oh, how interesting. And tell me, would a woman who was an exhibitionist be likely to take off her clothes while in the parlor with other guests who are on the sofa enjoying their cheese and baguettes?"

"She might."

"How illuminating." I said, struggling to hold my facial expression in neutral. "And that would have no ill effect on the other guests' appetites?"

"Well, it depends on what you mean by appetite. If the other guests are voyeurs, they would enjoy it quite a bit."

"I see." The scene of that girl, Ethel, who auditioned for me the time Lucille played the piano, flipped through my mind. She stripped down to nothing right in the club and I hadn't minded watching her. Well, if I were going to be honest with myself, I kind of liked it. If I hadn't been afraid of getting caught or killed—that was a pretty big knife she was dancing with—I probably would've let her continue her dance. Did that make me a voyeur? "Is that all?" I asked. "That doesn't seem so bad."

"Some people like to be tied up or have a blindfold placed over their eyes when having sex. There are others who enjoy having their clothes torn off by their partner or perhaps a stranger; others prefer being bent over a chair or a lap and having their bare behind spanked or lightly whipped. And there are those—"

"In front of everyone?"

"You see? You're doing it again. You can't help yourself. It's your upbringing. It's all right." She started out of bed.

I grabbed her arm. "Don't be mad."

"I'm not mad at you, Al. I wish I knew how to get you to understand that. I'm not asking you to change a thing. I'm simply asking you for my right to be who *I* am." She took in a breath. "Right now, I am a little frustrated because you keep asking me to tell you something you don't want to know. Let's go have breakfast. I know a pleasant little bistro near here where—"

"All right, all right, maybe I am a little shocked. That doesn't mean I don't feel a little excited too by what you're telling me."

"Do you?"

I took a deep breath. "Yeah. A lot. I think we should go to that party."

CHAPTER SIXTEEN

"Magnificent," Juliana mused, taking a sip of her Blanc de Blanc. We were looking out at Notre Dame from a window six floors up in La Tour d'Argent, the oldest restaurant in Paris, founded way back in the sixteenth century. It was also one of the most expensive restaurants in Paris. I couldn't help thinking of such things. The place was dripping in elegance with waiters running around in black ties and tails and the tables set with fine china and Christofle silverware. Our drinks were served in Waterford Crystal stemware and all the tables had different hand-blown glass ducks from Murano, Italy. Our particular duck had outstretched wings colored in a translucent violet. It was truly exquisite, a small piece of art from an unknown artist sitting right on our table.

Juliana looked lovely in her Jacques Fath sleek black dress with the scoop neckline; it hugged every curve of her body. She set the ensemble off with matching opera gloves and a wide-brimmed hat. She caught every male eye, and some female, as she sat there simply sipping her drink and musing at the view. Me? I don't know how "lovely" I looked. I just put on the dress Juliana said would be right for this place. A silky one with blue and red flowers—I was too distracted to pay attention to which designer—and red, open-toed heels. Oh, but such a view of the city we had, sitting above it all. The sun was still bright.

"Jule, do you ever wonder if you deserve all this?"

"All what?"

"All this. The view. The elegance of this place. The prices."

"Well, if you're worrying about the cost, tonight's on me."

"Thanks, but I didn't mean that. Sitting here makes me think of all the people who can't sit in our seats and take in this view or eat the food we're going to eat. Some may be lucky to get any food. Do you ever think about that?"

"No. I guess I take it all for granted. I've always had it, so I always expect it."

I think that was the biggest difference between Jule and me. She expected it always to be there and *I* knew how easily it could slip away. Was it slipping away now? Today? Could Schuyler make all this wealth and beauty disintegrate in one brief moment? "My father worked in a gas station," I said to Jule, "from early morning to the end of the day."

"I know. You've told me."

"He hardly ever had a day off. Came home exhausted and poured himself into bed. During the Depression, he took any odd job he could get and every time they let him go, he felt ashamed. Mom tried to work, but . . . well, I told you she was sick, something with her mind."

"Is everything all right, Al?"

"You know during the depression, if employers found out a woman was married, they wouldn't hire her. They'd yell at her for trying to take a job away from a man. When a woman lied and said she wasn't married when she was, employers looked down on her for *not* doing what women were supposed to do. My mother wasn't strong enough to take any of that."

"Has something happened?" Juliana asked "Are you worried about your parents? Is that why you're talking about this now?"

I kept staring out at Notre Dame, getting lost in its gargoyled walls. "You know, people don't talk about the women who roamed the country during the Depression in search of work, eating out of garbage cans, sometimes getting raped. They write songs about the men and how they suffered during those times and they did. I'm not denying that, but where are the songs for the women who were hopping those same freight trains? Nobody even knows about them."

"Lady hobos is an interesting topic, but why are you talking about them *now*? We're sitting in this lovely old restaurant, with a splendid view."

"Yes, but for how long?"

"Excuse me?"

"Everything is fleeting, but you're right. It all is so terribly beautiful. So beautiful it hurts my heart." I took a few sips of my chardonnay and sighed as I stared down at the Seine flowing past Notre Dame.

"Juliana, Juliana," a trim man in an excellent three-piece suit called, hurriedly approaching our table.

"Claude," Juliana called back, rising to greet him. The two hugged and planted kisses on each other's cheeks. They excitedly rattled off French words that I didn't have a hope of deciphering. Juliana turned to me and, speaking too distinctly in English, I gathered for Claude, said, "Alice Huffman, let me present Monsieur Claude Terrill, the owner of this restaurant." We shook hands, and Juliana and Claude went back to rattling off a string of sounds that made no sense to me.

"I haven't seen him in ages, Juliana told me as she sat down again. "Ever since the war. His father was still living when I was last here. Claude's a brave man. When he was a boy, twenty I think, the Nazis stomped through this magnificent edifice thinking they could have culture simply by taking it, but never endeavoring to incorporate it into their inner beings, the fabric of their souls. One of Goering's men stormed in here demanding to see the wine cellar. The Nazis took away 80,000 bottles and I imagine, thought themselves very smart. They didn't know Claude had single-handedly built a brick wall where he had hidden a remaining 20,000 bottles. That became the basis of the huge collection they have now. In Paris, a good wine collection is much like a good art collection, and often as valuable. He fought in Le Cleric's Free French Division, you know. A brave man."

"You know a lot of people here."

"It's my home."

"Is it more your home than the US?"

She stared out the window, considering the question. "No," she said simply and picked up her glass, finishing the last of her Blanc de Blanc. "Drink up. Claude is having the sommelier bring over a bottle of their best champagne."

"That'll cost a fortune."

Juliana shook her head. "It's a gift. You sound like Shirl. I wonder what's keeping Scott?"

"He went over to the American Express office to pick up the mail. He's hoping for a letter from Max. It's been longer than usual and he's worried."

"International mail can be tricky. I'm sure everything's okay."

"That's what *I* told him. And Max is running both clubs, so he may be writing fewer letters. I hope he gets here soon. The waiters won't let us eat without him. I mean, they won't even give us a dang menu until the "man" gets here, and *he's* the only one who gets the menu with the prices on it. Doesn't it make you mad that *our* menus won't have prices on them? Especially since *you're* paying."

"No. We're women. They're treating us special. Why should I mind that? I'm sure Scott will be here soon. Why don't you let yourself relax? Be a tad less American for a few hours. Tonight is to be our night of pleasure."

I took in a deep breath. "Yes. An excellent idea. I wish I had a cigar."

"What?"

"It seems to relax Shirl."

"If I *ever* catch you—"

I laughed, "I'm joking. I don't even like cigarettes." I sat way back in my chair, trying to look relaxed, trying to pretend that I wasn't a little worried about the sex party we'd be going to later that night.

"I'm concerned you'll be bored tonight," Juliana said.

"Bored?" How could I possibly be bored at a sex party. Terrified maybe, but bored?

"Well, most of the people who'll be there either don't or *won't* speak English. Everyone will be speaking either Italian or French except perhaps—"

"You speak Italian too?"

"My Italian isn't as good as my French, but I manage. Close your mouth. You'll catch a fly."

"Flies at these prices! Gosh, Jule, Italian too. That's almost obscene."

"I needed it to sing Italian opera, and my mother and I often took our holidays in Milan when I was a child so . . ."

"Being an American is important too, you know," I said a little too forcefully. "And so is speaking English."

"I *am* an American and I *do* speak English."

"I just wanted to remind you." I drank down the last of my wine. I'd miss white wine when we went home. It wasn't so easy to get in the States.

"Madam." The garçon stood near Juliana with a telephone in his hands. "You have a call."

"Merci, monsieur," Juliana said, taking the phone from him. I knew it couldn't be Richard. The garçon had brought the house phone. If not Richard, then who? Richard usually called around this time. We generally left our destination at the hotel desk, so he could track us down. Juliana spoke French into the phone. Her voice and face became increasingly more animated as the call progressed. I wasn't sure if it was anger or something else. When she hung up, her eyes had a blank sheen that I couldn't read.

"Who was *that*?"

The garçon returned and removed the phone.

"My brother."

"Your *what*? You never told me you had one of those." I vaguely recalled years ago when Juliana had gone off to join the troops at the front, Shirl had said something about there being a brother in France.

"Yes." Juliana's forehead wrinkled in thought and she seemed far away.

"Is he all right? What's the matter? Is he going to be at the party tonight?"

"Uh, no—no."

What a stupid question. Who has their brother come to a sex party? I wished I were back in my room, so I could kick myself.

Scott approached our table, pulling out a chair. "Sorry I'm late."

"Excuse me a moment?" Juliana said. "He wants to meet me downstairs in the Musée. I told him I'd have a quick drink with him."

"Where's she going?" Scott asked, lighting a cigarette.

"To talk to her brother."

"She has a brother?"

"I guess so. Did you get your letter?"

"No. Nothing. It's been over two weeks, Al. Do you think he's sick or . . . found someone else?"

"No. I think the mail is slow. Give him a call tonight."

"It's awkward trying to talk to him by the desk. I have to be so careful about what I say. And if I call and can't find him at the club or at home, I'm going to have awful thoughts."

The garçon returned to our table. "Another call for Mademoiselle Juliana. From the United States."

"Richard Styles?" I asked. "I'll take it."

"Oui," the garçon nodded. "Follow me."

"Excuse me, Scott. I won't be long."

I followed the waiter to the desk where the international phone was kept. He handed me the receiver. "Richard, hi. No. Juliana stepped away for a bit. Yes, the Ladies. How are you? And your mother? Oh, that's good. You've been talking to Jules Podell? Good. Yes, we're almost finished knocking out a few kinks from here, but doing it by mail and cablegram makes it slow. No messengers to run changes back and forth. Once we have it, I'll have Jules send a messenger to you with a copy. It'll take a couple more weeks so don't get impatient. Let Ben read it too. Both of you should sign it. It's going to be a good contract. No, not good; it'll be great. Don't muck it up."

"What? He contacted *you*? Don't sign anything with *him* and do not, you hear me, do *not* speak to Juliana about this. She has to concentrate on what she's doing here. Yes, I'll take care of it. Promise me, no *swear*, swear Richard on one of those statues you pray to that you will not mention this to Juliana. It's not that I don't trust you. It's just— Yes, the play is good, a musical; it's perfect for her. That's why I don't want you to mention it. If she digs her heels in against it, we'll never get her to do it. Yes, Richard, this time you and I *are* on the same side."

I hung up the phone, my heart pounding. I couldn't believe Schuyler would stoop so low as to contact her husband. How could I not believe it? Expect the unexpected. That's what Max taught me. I was no babe at this. Schuyler *knew* Richard would tell me. That's why he did it. To tighten the screws.

"What was *that* about?" Scott asked when I sat back down at the table. "You have no blood left in your face."

"Nothing."

"That call was *not* nothing."

"I can't talk about it now. Please don't push me on it."

"You don't trust me?"

"Of course, I trust you. It's just . . . Scott, for now, trust *me*."

"All right. I suppose."

"Now that *you're* here they'll give us menus. Could you see about that, please? I'd like to eat."

Juliana rejoined us just as the waiters were taking our orders. Throughout dinner, all I thought about was Richard coming to Paris to meet Dan Schuyler. I think I convinced him not to, but still I worried. The thought ruined the taste of the special champagne Claude Terrell had arranged for us, and it ruined the taste of the duck that La Tour d'Argent was known for that they prepared right at your table and cost more than my father made in a month. I put a goofy smile on my face as I imagined Schuyler sitting down in a café with Richard having one of those "man-to-man" talks that men had, telling Richard the truth about Juliana and me. I saw the headline in *Variety*. "Juliana, Nightclub Headliner: Her Secret Life as a Pervert," and the article in *Confidential Magazine*: "The truth behind Juliana's singing success—Alice Huffman, her very own baritone babe." I cringed while I saw our careers crumbling into dust and our strange relationship turning into an embittered war between us, first hot, then cold. A jumble of feelings rose up in me, all the while I sat there smiling and nodding in polite conversation.

Between each bite, Scott twitched his eyebrows at me. He knew how to read me. He could see that I was tormented, and I knew when he and I were alone he was going to pump me, but I couldn't tell him *this*. I couldn't tell him before I told Juliana, and I couldn't tell Juliana because the terror of it would render her unable to function and all that we had accomplished in Paris would crumble into ashes. I had to avoid Scott as much as possible.

* * *

Four hours later, we *finally* finished our dinner and all the extras that went with it. We watched the sun slowly set as it spread out pastel pinks and yellows across a fading blue sky. The restaurant was now romantically lit with candles on the tables and perched in holders on the walls. From where we sat finishing up our dessert, we could see the Paris street lamps popping on one-by-one, with Notre Dame still the biggest and proudest presence. We went back to our hotel, so I could change.

As I changed into a pair of pants and a shirt, I fumbled through my desk drawer digging out the envelope Schuyler had given me on the ship. I kept eyeing the door behind me, hoping Juliana didn't pop in. She was in there freshening up her makeup and fluffing her hair. I pulled the papers out. On top were Schuyler's two Paris phone numbers. On the wall, hanging from a hook, the telephone for local calls. I'd never used it before. Who did I know in Paris to call? But now I had to. I sat at the desk, taking out some paper and my new French phrase book. I wrote out a sentence that might help to get me to the right person. I stood and went to the wall where the telephone hung on a wiggly hook. I picked up the receiver, praying that an English-speaking operator was working the desk down in the lobby. "Hello, monsieur? Bonjour, no Bonsoir! English? Girard! I mean Monsieur Fourier. You're working late tonight. Thank God, thank God! Thank God!" I breathed out, relieved. I was about to give Girard the number when Juliana poked her head in. I hid the phone in my unzipped pants.

"They're bringing the car around in a few minutes," she said. "You ready?"

"Sure. Almost done. Thought I'd put on a pair of suspenders."

"Cute." Juliana winked, going back into her room and closing the door.

My heart thudded against my chest. "Girard. I mean monsieur. Sorry. Bonsoir. Gosh, there's so much to say before you can even get started. Are you still there? Good. Could you please get me, INV-02-93?" I waited, listening to the sound of static. Finally, an old woman's voice said, "Allo."

I read the sentence I'd written down on a pad into the phone, painfully trying to pronounce it correctly through a racket of static screaming at me. "Vou—drais—par—ler a Monsieur Schuyler, s'l vous plait."

She said, "Comment?"

Comment? You mean I have to say it all over again. I shortened it to "Schuyler?" with hope.

"Oh! Monsieur Schuyler. Oui, oui."

"Yes! I mean oui. Speak, uh, parle him?"

"Monsieur Schuyler n'est pas la . . . 'E's outside les houses. She rentre demain." I think she was trying to speak English. Thoughtful, but…

"What?"

"Demain, demain. Monsieur Schuyler demain."

"Friday? He'll be there Friday?"

"Non. Demain."

"What, uh, quelle est, est l'adresse?"

It took a little while to decipher the address she was giving me, but I finally got it and wrote it down. I thumbed through my French-English dictionary looking for "demain" before I forgot it. My finger stopped on the word and slid across to "tomorrow." Okay, Mr. Schyuler, I'll see *you* tomorrow, I said to myself. I tried the second number, but there was no answer.

The car we rented, a Citroen DS blue and white two-door convertible, was waiting for us in front of the hotel. It had a long sleek body and according to the French, it was something from the future with a lot of special just-invented new features that I didn't understand. All I knew when I asked Juliana to translate a magazine article about it was that it was one expensive car.

Despite the warmth of the evening, I wrapped myself in a long cloth coat to cover up my suit and tie. As Juliana, Scott, and I entered the foyer of the lobby heading for the front door, Juliana's fans surrounded us, waving their autograph books in her face. Juliana graciously signed them all and spoke their language, and I could see the oohs and ahs in their eyes. I was proud; it was because of me that these people pressed close wanting to touch her. Then I saw Schuyler's face in my mind and got an image of these same people throwing tomatoes at her. Or perhaps rocks.

On the outer steps beyond the doorway, the young valet who had driven the car over to the front of the building greeted us. His face was slightly pimpled and he'd tried to cover it up with some pink gunk. He hurried to hold open the driver's side door for Scott, then ran around the car to open the passenger side for Juliana. The doorman bowed as Juliana bounced down the steps with Scott and me following behind. The doorman and Juliana exchanged a few words in French and he kissed her gloved hand. As she was about to get into the front passenger seat, the valet put his hand over his heart and spoke softly. I, of course, couldn't understand the words, but one look at his beaming face, pink gunk and all, gave away what he felt for her. I remembered myself plastered against her dressing room wall, afraid to speak or even breath. I was about the same age as this boy. She slid into the passenger's side, while Scott sat behind the wheel. The boy hurried to open the back door for me. He was pleasant enough, but he sure didn't look at me the way he looked at her. I felt terrific about that. Until, of course, Schuyler's face popped into view.

Scott drove the car around the corner, stopped in a secluded parking lot, and got out. Juliana slid behind the wheel and I got into the front seat. Scott was our ruse. He knew we wanted to spend some time alone together. Of course, he didn't know *where* we wanted to spend that time. Still, two women leaving a hotel together at night in a rented car could be seen as strange, and we couldn't have Juliana's fans suspecting the truth.

Scott planned an evening of walking along the Seine and stopping at various cafes to write a page here and there to Max about what he was experiencing.

I'd never seen Juliana drive before. I didn't even know she knew how. She said it had been years, but she hadn't wanted to take a cab or hire a driver for this particular sojourn. She wanted to be assured of complete secrecy.

We drove along the Champs-Elysees, guided by its bright lights on both sides. It was crowded with cars cutting in and out, horns blaring. Juliana seemed to be managing it, but I found myself digging my fingers into the seat cushion. "How do you feel about going to this party tonight?" Juliana asked as she jerked the car out of one lane into the next, passing the Renault in front of us.

"Uh, me? Well, it'll be fun. Won't it?"

"I think that's why we're going but remember you don't have to do anything you don't want to do."

"Sure, sure." My heartbeat sped up. "This doesn't bother me. In my line of work, I've seen all sorts of bizarre things." I stared out the window, watching the trees and lights whiz by in one big blur. I had seen so much since Huntington. Bart having sex with a customer in the alley outside the club, Virginia being forced to orally copulate that creep, Moose, Jimmy the Crusher chopping off the creep's hand. There was no reason this party should rattle me at all. My work had made me tough. So why was I rattled? My breath was coming too fast; I made a conscious effort to slow it down. My mother whispered... I couldn't quite... Something... something... sex. "I want to do whatever you and Margarite do," I said with force.

She didn't say anything, and we drove a long while in silence. She made a turn off the Champs-Elysees, down a dark side street, and suddenly, right in front of us was another car speeding toward us, its headlights streaming into the windshield and our eyes, blinding us. I gripped the dashboard, ready for the crash.

We came to a rocking screeching halt, dust flying all around the windows. But we were in one piece. A Frenchman jumped out of his car and stormed over to us. Juliana lowered the window and let the man scream at her for a while. When he seemed to run out of steam, she said something apologetic to him. The man walked back to his car grumbling.

"What was *that* about?" I demanded as Juliana backed up the car.

"I forgot that after the war they made quite a few of these side streets into one-way roads to control traffic."

"You forgot? You forgot?" I shouted at her. "Juliana, you can't forget a thing like that. We could've been killed."

"But we weren't, were we? Do you even have a bump?"

"No." I wished I could say yes.

"Well, then? I've got this car under control and you have nothing to worry about. I'll be more attentive to the signs."

"Please do."

She turned the car onto a street with a sign pointing in the direction she wanted to go. I had a passing fantasy that I was seriously injured in the car accident that didn't happen. So seriously injured that Juliana would feel bad for me and not get mad when she found out about Schuyler. She'd forgive me and even say she loved me.

Juliana wrapped her hand around mine as it lay on the seat. "Don't worry. These are my streets. I know them."

She let go of my hand when we started to bounce over cobblestone side streets and around sharp curves. We drove into an area that was near Montmartre on the Right Bank. In the faraway distance, I could see Sacre Coeur all ablaze with light on its hilltop.

"Did you go to church at Sacred Core when you lived here?"

"Sacre Coeur," she corrected. "Sometimes. But I often preferred the simpler, less showy churches. There's a little chapel not far from Notre Dame that I liked to go to. It has the most beautiful stained-glass windows."

"You think a church with stained glass windows is simpler and less showy? The church I grew up in had only one real decoration and that was the wooden cross behind the altar. We were lucky if we could keep the paint job looking fresh. One time, one of the teenagers in the Sunday school got mad and punched a hole in the wall by the stairs going up to the sanctuary. It took two years for them to get it fixed, because that's how long it took for them to raise the money."

"I'm sorry," Juliana said with real sincerity. "I'm sorry your childhood was so hard."

Tears came into my eyes, so I couldn't say anything back. My tears didn't have anything to do with a two-year hole in my crummy church or my crummy childhood. They had to do with Schuyler, but I couldn't tell her, so I felt like I was building a wall between us at a time when she was opening.

She stopped the car. "Is this it?" I asked.

"No. I need to look around a bit to see which way I have to go."

"You don't know?"

"Everything looks different. I haven't been here in more than ten years."

I rolled down the window as she turned off the ignition. A man and a woman sat on the curb in torn clothes. They stared at me with not very pleasant expressions.

Juliana opened her door.

"Uh, Jule, I don't think you should get out here. It doesn't look safe."

"Nonsense," she said, getting out. "This is my home. Maybe we can find someone to direct me back to the main road. All those one-ways have me confused."

I made sure my coat was buttoned all the way from top to bottom before climbing out. It was dark, not at all like the bright city lights of Paris that the guidebooks always spoke about. As far as I could see, there were makeshift shacks and people occupying apartment buildings with no stairs, walls that were half there, no doors. Laundry hung over balcony railings. I saw one woman on a balcony peeking out of a torn curtain. Near one of the shacks was a homemade wooden sign with French words written in what looked like charcoal: "Defense de passer." I reached into my pocket and slid out my phrase book, but it was too dark to read so I put it back.

As I walked next to Juliana, I could hear the broken cobblestone crunch under my feet. Only the moon and a few streetlights with their glass globes smashed in lit our way. Scrawled across one building were the words "Yanky Go Home" and "Americains and dogs no enter." On an opposite wall, painted in a shaky hand, was the word "Communiste." A baby carriage with three wheels lay deserted in the gutter. Lining the broken sidewalks and hollowed out buildings were a few men hidden in shadows smoking and watching. No one ran to greet us. No one was impressed with who Juliana was. I doubt they knew. They only stared. And they spoke to each other in hushed tones, watching every step we took.

"Juliana, I think we're trespassing on something we don't understand. We should go."

"Yes, well, let me try asking this gentleman."

This "gentleman" was slouched against the side of a wall wearing a pair of loose fitting coveralls heavily smeared with dirt and mud. His shirt, hair, face, the fingers he smoked with, were all painted in grime."

"Monsieur," Juliana said stepping toward him. "Bonsoir. Excusez-moi, ne vous . . ."

The man straightened up to his full height and grinning, let his eyes run up and down her body slowly as she stood there in her slinky, form-fitting black dress, only a light shawl covering her shoulders. He stuck his cigarette in the corner of his mouth and focused his entire gaze on her breasts. She pulled her shawl down over her chest, but didn't move.

"We gotta go, Jule."

"Yes, yes, I think you're right."

But before we could turn back to the car, a drunken man sprang into the open and pulled at the skirt of Juliana's dress, laughing. She jerked herself away.

"Let's go." I wanted to grab her, but if they saw how I was dressed, there was no telling what they'd do.

"Yes, let's go." Juliana was about to run.

"Don't run," I told her. "That makes you look scared."

"I am."

"Keep smiling," I whispered to her. I turned back toward them and waved. "Au revoir. Au revoir."

Some of them waved back. I could hear the drunken man's steps crunching against the pieces of cobblestone behind us. "When we get to the car, get in as fast as you can."

"Al, I don't think I've ever been this scared before in my life."

"Don't worry. I'm going to take care of you. Keep walking easy, like you're strolling along the Seine. Au revoir," I called again and got a chorus of "au revoirs" back in return. I took a quick look behind me to see where that drunk guy was. He fell down, got up again, and swayed toward us, getting closer. I guided Jule over to the driver's side door without touching her. As I had my hand on the door handle ready to pull it open, the drunken guy grabbed Juliana's shoulder. She screamed. I pushed him back and flung open the door, but the guy came at her again; he put his arms around her, trying to kiss her. I got behind him, pulling on his shoulders, but I couldn't budge him. Suddenly this big bruiser guy came out of nowhere and moved me out of the way like I was made of feathers. He pulled the drunken guy off Juliana and pinned both his arms down to his side with one of his massive arms. He walked backwards away from us with the drunk's feet bobbing up and down over the crumbly road. "Au revoir," he called, waving at us with his free hand.

Jule jumped into the car and leaned over the seat to throw open my door for me. I yelled out one last "au revoir" to our savior and hopped in. Jule wasted no time in backing us up to the main road. We didn't speak until we'd gone a good distance away, but I held my French phrase book near the window, letting the light from the street help me decipher the words I'd seen on the homemade sign: 'Defense de passer.' It meant "Keep out." They sure weren't kidding.

Juliana pulled the car over to the side, breathing heavily. We were safe. The lights of Paris once again sparkled around us. "You okay?" I asked her. I wanted so much to take her in my arms.

"In a minute. I need a minute." She leaned her forehead on the steering wheel. "Would you get my rosary out of my purse? It's on top."

"Sure." I opened the purse and took out a small gold case shaped like an octagon. "This?"

I held the box up and she took it. I'd never seen her with these before. The only rosary I'd ever seen her with was blue with no case; these were a translucent red.

I waited, watched her as she held them, threading them through her fingers, her eyes closed and I guess praying.

After some moments, she kissed a few of the beads, letting her lips linger as if trying to suck peace from them. She placed the rosary back into its case and held it out for me. "Thank you."

"These are new."

"My brother brought them to me tonight. They were my mother's. You can read the inscription if you want."

I turned it over to the bottom. It simply said, 'To Grace, with my fondest love, John.' "Grace. That was your mother?"

"Yes."

"And John is your . . . ?"

"No. John is not my father. But he may have been my mother's murderer. Al, I don't know how I would've gotten through that tonight without you."

I slid my hand across the seat and interlaced my fingers with hers.

I thought, hoped actually, that after all that she'd say she didn't want to go to the party; I thought perhaps we'd go home and make love.

She turned the ignition on. "And so off we go. My friends will be wondering what on earth has happened to us. And won't we have a story to tell?"

CHAPTER SEVENTEEN

"Well, here we are," Juliana said, stopping the car at a curb in front of a group of buildings tightly packed together. This neighborhood looked nothing like the one we'd just come from. There were no runaway three-wheeled baby carriages in this neighborhood or people in ragged clothes sitting on stoops. The bricks were dusty, but the curtains that hung in the windows weren't torn.

"Down a few doors is my friend Armando's home. Shall we go?" She took a few steps down the sidewalk, her heels clicking against the cement. I pulled her arm back to stop her. "You mean men are going to be at this party?"

"Perhaps one or two, but they'll be gay. They won't bother you."

"Oh." We walked a little further on until we came to a building with three small steps in front and a door that looked freshly painted. This building wasn't covered in laundry.

"Al, you understand," Juliana said as we stood before the steps, "these people might not be as friendly toward you as we both might like. They might seem abrupt or standoffish. They're cautious around Americans. Keep in mind they have their reasons and those reasons have nothing to do with you. Luckily, you won't have the slightest idea of what most of them are saying."

As she was about to knock on the door, I grabbed her arm. "Uh, Jule."

"Yes?"

"You're going to do with me what—whatever you do with Margarite. Right?"

"If that's what you want."

"Yeah, yeah, I do." I was breathing too fast. Jule turned to knock and I grabbed her arm again.

"And what—what *exactly* do you do to Margarite at these parties?"

"Well, Margarite likes it when I blindfold her, bind her wrists and ankles in handcuffs that are attached to pulleys that come down from the ceiling—that's so I can get to any part of her body. When I have her bound, I open her clothes. Sometimes I use feathers, other times paddles. Occasionally I use a dildo with her. Ready?" She raised her hand to knock.

My mouth dropped open into fly-catching position and my heart thundered as we waited for the door to open. "In front of everybody?"

"Yes. Does that bother you?"

"Oh, no, no. I'm as sophisticated as she is. More. I'm more sophisticated."

"Then shall we?" She knocked.

The fear of that drunken guy instantly melted, Schuyler became a flimsy, ghost-like image. The immediacy of this party and what would happen to me on the other side of that door was all that enveloped me.

A maid let us in and took Juliana's wrap and my long coat. The man I'd seen with Juliana and Margarite in the Montmartre Church/Opera House appeared in the wide foyer to greet us. "Juliana," he exclaimed with utter joy at seeing her. Instantly, he and Juliana were giving each other those cheek kisses.

"Armand," Juliana said, "this is my good friend, Al. Al, this is Armando Vigolio, a brilliant impresario, but in France he is often Armand."

Armand kissed the back of my hand and said in his Italian accent, "Charmed, my dear." His goatee tickled. "Come in, come in. There are many here who die to see you, Julien. And to meet *you*, precious Al. Julien has told me much of you."

Juliana took Armand's offered arm while he took my hand and we strode into the next room together. "We worried it has been so long that you have not arrived that you became lost. Our roads are changed. Are they not?"

"We were accosted," Juliana announced.

"My dear. Are you all right?"

"Yes. Thanks to Al's quick thinking. My mind went blank. Al is a genuine heroine."

"Not really."

"Well, you must come in and tell us your story."

"A moment, Armand. There were people. People living in deplorable conditions. Not the slums. We weren't in the suburbs. Not the Algerians.

French men and women. What has happened to my France?"

"Nothing dear. We are the same and better. We are united; we are rebuilding what the war tore down. Now come, your friends await."

As we moved into the next room, Juliana was instantly surrounded by a gaggle of women wearing expensive dresses or suits and ties made of the finest fabrics. I backed away from the crowd to get a good view of the large parlor. The women chattered unfamiliar sounds with only an occasional English word popping out. I'd never seen so many women with short, slicked back hair all in one room before. Other women in dresses that flared around their legs clung to the arms of the mannish looking ones. They're smoking permeated the room making my eyes burn. There were colorful paintings on the walls and a broad fireplace with a gilded mirror above it. Some women, seemingly more interested in talking to their dates than hearing Juliana's story, were seated on thickly upholstered brightly colored furniture. All held glasses of something in their hands. Juliana sidled out of the circle to take my hand and introduce me. Since they were doing a lot of oohing and aahing and nodding at me, I figured she was repeating that ridiculous story about me saving her. It was embarrassing. What about the big guy who showed up? What would have happened if he *hadn't* come along?

Not being one for large gatherings, despite all the years I'd spent going to them in pursuit of my career, I gradually slipped from the circle and left Juliana to her friends and found the guy circulating around the room with the drinks. I lifted a reddish-pink thing in a champagne glass from his tray. It was garnished with a lemon peel. When I took my first sip, the thing practically knocked me down.

"Oui," Armand said, coming from behind me. "A strong kick. Yes?"

"You're not kidding. What is it?"

"Francais soixante quinze."

"I don't have a hope of ever pronouncing that."

"Being Italian, it took me a while to learn to say it too, but it is served in your country. The French 75, they call it. Named so because to drink it makes one feel that they have been shelled by a French 75 mm field gun. Be careful it may be lethal."

I thought it might be what I needed to get through this party, so I took another sip. My body became looser, freer, my head fuzzier. I took great pride in watching Juliana poised, conversing in three languages, and flirting. I'd sort of gotten used to her flirting; it was a part of who she was and it was good for business. Still, her flirting was usually reserved for men, and it was Richard who had to cope with his feelings about it. But tonight, she flirted with women. That's her job, I told myself. Those women will come to the show at the Lido. They'll get their husbands to write stories about her in the best French magazines. Perhaps they'll even be a source of investment money at some future time. I mean, she wasn't really going to do anything with any of them. Was she?

"This is a beautiful room, Armand."

"Merci. I enjoy it myself. I live alone. No paramour with which to share my days. At least, not at this time, but there have been a few, how do you Americans say, young bucks in my day."

"I imagine there have been. You're an attractive man."

"Madam, you make me blush. Have you tried the wine?" He held up his own wine glass. "Bordeaux, 1929. A superb year and much gentler than your francais soixante quinze. Delicate to the palate and the digestion."

"I'll be sure to try some before I leave."

"You must."

"That couch." I pointed. "A fine piece of furniture. It's an antique, isn't it?"

"You mean the settee. You have excellent taste."

"I share an apartment with a connoisseur of fine things."

"Then you must tell your friend you saw a genuine antique settee from the Italian Rococo period."

"I don't know anything about furniture. That's Max's department. Perhaps you've heard of Max's Mt. Olympus or The Haven. They're clubs in New York City. Max Harlington owns both.

"I know them. I love New York cabaret. I have been many times."

"Well, Max knows his furniture. And his wine. And his art. And I think he'd love that piece, because even in my ignorance I can see that it's special: the intricacy of the carved wood around the base, with the cushioning of the maroon velvet seat. Spectacular. Did you buy it or has it been in your family? I hope you don't mind my asking."

"No. Not at all. I appreciate a fellow lover of the finer things of this life. It has been in my family for generations."

"Really? I thought the Nazis ran off with all the art, but here in this room it all appears undisturbed."

"Uh . . . yes," Armand said, holding his glass to his lips and taking a big swallow, turning away from me.

I took another sip of my drink. "So, I guess you've known Juliana a long time," I said.

"Ever since the Conservertoire. She, I believe, was only sixteen, and I eighteen. I fancied myself the next great Caruso in those days. But I didn't have—how do you Americans call it—the chops. I didn't have the chops. I found I was much better on the business side of things, so for a while I had a business in which I collected and sold fine musical instruments—violins, violas, cellos, flutes. I met many people: composers, conductors, performers from all over the world. But my greatest love was the opera. Later I did well as an impresario to a number of successful French opera divas. Perhaps, you've heard of Monica Ramblay."

"No. Sorry. I go to the opera, of course, when I can, but I'm afraid I don't know much about it."

"Perhaps someday you will." He lit a Galoise. "I believe you are an impresario like me," Armand continued.

I laughed. "No, that's much too grand a title for what I do. I merely manage talent and organize the money to get the talent where people can see it."

"That's what I said. An impresario. You have done well with Juliana."

I debated quickly with myself whether to set him straight by giving Richard the credit. I decided to take the credit I'd earned. Who'd know at a secret sex party in Paris?

"There was a time that I thought I would put together an opera for Julien," Armand said. "Ah, but I was much too young and inexperienced, and she ran away from us. But Julien—she has a natural gift. She should never have ceased her opera. A voice like hers is a gift from God." He crossed himself. "It is a sin not to use it."

"She does use it. In the nightclubs."

"Ah, but that is not enough. She will not come to her true self until she shares her gift, her true gift, with the world. She must sing opera. It will be her salvation."

"Her salvation?"

"Do you think she is truly happy with half of her heart cut off?"

"She studies it."

"And that is enough?"

"She says she's too old to do anything with opera professionally now."

"Unfortunately, she's right about that if we're talking about singing in the Paris Opera or the Metropolitan in New York, but you're an ingenious soul. Surely you can come up with some way for her to share her opera with the public."

"*She* says she doesn't have what it takes. The chops."

"Ah, now that's her mother. Get her mother out of the way and voilá, there will be no one to stop her. Excuse me. I must mingle with my other guests or they will feel slighted. We will speak again soon, oui?"

"Uh, yeah, sure, oui. I'd like that."

The bulk of the guests stood in the center of the room. I heard someone say something in English about the war in Algeria. Some other guests got agitated and spoke in French and Italian with their hands flying all around.

My eyes wandered over the group looking for Juliana. She was gone. Panicked, I searched the unfamiliar faces making those unfamiliar sounds. She was nowhere. I drank down the last of my francais soixante quinze and spun around, looking for a hallway she might've gone down, and fell into a potted plant.

Armand set me upright. "I warned you to be careful of the francais soixante quinze. A wollop, no?"

"Juliana. Where is she?" My fingernails dug into the cloth on his shoulders.

"Answering nature's call, perhaps?" Armand said. "I doubt there is reason for such alarm. Let me help you to sit."

"Gotta find her." Still hanging onto him, I watched the room dip and sway.

"She perhaps has ended in the kitchen with Andy."

"Andy's here?"

"She came in a while ago. You know her?"

"Where's the kitchen?" I demanded, as if Armand was trying to keep its location a secret from me.

"Down that hallway on the left," he answered calmly.

My legs and arms flew in different directions, not quite under my control, as I slipped and slid down the hallway and knocked into the walls. I had gotten her away from Margarite—sort of—and now she was hidden in the kitchen with Andy? With me right here waiting to do that awful thing she wanted me to do.

I skidded into the kitchen, caught a glimpse of Juliana and Andy holding hands at the kitchen table, reached out for the back of Juliana's chair, missed, and landed on the floor.

"Al, what on earth are you doing?" Juliana asked.

I scrambled to my feet. "No. The question is—what are *you* doing?" I slurred. "I saw you two holding hands when I came in. Don't deny it. I saw it."

"You've been drinking," Juliana said. "I'd say you've been drinking a lot. Don't say anything more right now because it could get you into trouble."

"But you two . . . while I'm out there all by myself."

"Armand had you under his wing. I didn't know I had to hire you a babysitter."

"It's okay, Julie," Andy said, getting up. "I'll go."

"You're sure?" Juliana asked.

"Yeah. And Al, pal, I'm sorry I got you upset and I'm extra sorry about what I'm going to do now, but I'm going to do it anyway." She bent down and kissed Juliana full on the mouth.

"Hey! Stop that!" I squawked and slid back onto the floor. I sat there watching Andy give Juliana this long passionate kiss and Juliana loving it, her arms around Andy's neck. It seemed to go on and on. Finally, Andy straightened up and pulled on the edge of her suit jacket. "Thanks, Julie. And thank *you*, Al." She picked up her fedora from the table and left the room.

I scrambled to my feet and leaned heavily on the kitchen table so I didn't fall over. "How can you do that when I'm right here? We came to this place together to do, well, you know. How can you insult me like that? If you want to be with her, then—"

"Don't say anything more or I'm going to get angry. You've been drinking, so I'm giving you a little room. I'll tell you about it tomorrow."

I flopped into the chair Andy had vacated. "Tell me what?"

"Not here. Later."

"Julien, Al," Armand said, bursting into the kitchen. "Everyone has gone down. Come. We go to sing." He sprinted from the room.

"We're going to sing?" I asked Juliana.

"In a manner of speaking."

She led me down a staircase into a room lit only with candles and kerosene lanterns. A 33 rpm Glenn Miller album played on the record player and women danced with each other.

"Juliana," I said, as we entered the room, "why do the people here call you Julien? Margarite sometimes calls you that, too. Isn't that the male version of your name?"

"I often take a male role in these games."

"But you're so feminine."

She merely smiled.

I watched Armando lock the door to the room. My throat tightened. No way out. None of the men circulated with drinks—they weren't in this room—but there was plenty to drink. Bottles upon bottles of wine and gin and vodka were stacked high on tables as the women helped themselves. Juliana went to get us a drink.

Armando threw an arm around me. "You love her. I see it in your eyes. She is not easy to love. Oui?"

"Oui."

"I love her too. In a different way, of course. In a way that is easier for her to accept. Your love is harder for her, but that does not mean she does not feel it."

I looked up at him through a haze of drunkenness. "Do you think that maybe she . . . ?"

"Remember what I have said tonight. I know her."

He gave me a squeeze and pushed through the women to get his own drink.

"But . . ." I called, wanting him to tell me more about what he knew. I scurried after him. "Armand!" I stopped when I saw he stood near a naked woman on all fours, barking. She wore a dog collar around her neck and nuzzled another woman's tuxedo pants leg while that woman patted her rear. "Wag your tail for me, Lucy. Wag your tail." Lucy did. "That's a good girl." She patted Lucy again.

"Ginger ale," Juliana said, handing me a glass. "I think you've had enough alcohol."

Ordinarily I would have been insulted, but I was too sloshed to argue. I took the Ginger ale.

"Jule, there's, there's a woman over there with a leash on and . . ."

"Yes?"

"You won't do that to me, will you?"

"It never occurred to me. Do you want to observe first?"

"Uh, well, maybe that would be . . ."

We moved past a woman who was tied spread-eagled in a hammock. She still had her dress on, but the whole front of it was open and her underwear had been removed. A woman in pants with a loosened tie, her jacket gone, smoked a cigarette while she ran a big ostrich feather up and down the length of the woman's body and between her legs. The woman tied to the hammock wiggled and moaned. Others stood around watching. One lady stood near the hammock, dressed in what I was sure must've been a Schiaparelli original, not that I'm any kind of expert. She was fingering herself from outside her dress with no apparent concern that she could ruin that beautiful dress. It must've cost a fortune.

We passed another woman bent over a chair, her hands tied. She still wore what I was sure was an expensive dress, except a big hole had been cut out of the back of it so that her naked rear stuck out. Another woman, also in a fancy dress, was spanking her with a paddle. Glen Miller didn't seem to go with this scene.

"Uh, so, Julien." I was trying to get with it, but it was a struggle. "You and Margarite, you, uh . . ."

"You look cute tonight," Juliana said. "I love the suspenders." She ran her hand up and down them. "I wonder how they'd look hooked to your underpants if you weren't wearing anything else."

"Uh, well, I don't know, uh . . ."

She kissed me while undoing my bow tie and sliding it from my neck. "Let's take your jacket off."

"Okay," I said, starting to shuck it off.

"Let me do it." She slid my jacket off and pulled my shirttails out of my pants.

"I want to get this shirt off you, so I can bind you up," she whispered.

"And do whatever I want with you."

I giggled nervously. The alcohol swam through my head. She took off my shirt in front of all those strangers, but the alcohol kept me from caring. It all seemed terribly silly, and I laughed and laughed.

She kissed me while she backed me up against the wall and pulled down a set of pulleys with black metal cuffs on the end. She put my wrists into the cuffs and tugged on a rope that stretched my arms above my head so that I had to stand on tiptoe. I laughed. It was ridiculous. She ran her hand over my bra to the snap in back. She unsnapped my bra and pulled it away from my breasts. She lightly ran her hand over my breasts and kissed my face. Despite my vision being blurry, I thought I saw people pulling up chairs to watch like—like they were at the pictures.

She left my suspenders on me and ran a finger down the fly of my pants, which almost knocked me out, and I think I may have moaned some.

"I want to take *everything* off you," she whispered.

"You want to, uh, uh . . . sure, uh . . ."

As she unhooked my suspenders from my pants, a woman in the front row wearing large glasses with wings on them and smoking a long thin cigarette had her dress bunched up in her lap and her hand in her underpants, masturbating.

My pants suddenly fell around my ankles and I felt like I should cover myself with my arms, but since my hands were still tied up over my head, I couldn't. I laughed instead. I laughed harder as Juliana hooked my suspenders to my underpants. People in the circle of chairs watching joined me in laughing, and my laughing became more raucous, more out of control.

The crowd around us—I heard Armand's deep voice among them—shouted. "Take them off. Take them off her."

I too repeated rhythmically, "Take them off her. Take them off."

Jule put a blindfold over my eyes and unhooked one suspender. She slid her hand down past the waistband of my underpants, and I panted, and my panting became more desperate as she continued to touch me there. She had a finger on that place, and I was desperate for her to stop, desperate for her to go on, desperate to be rid of these weird people, desperate to go home, desperate to please her. I panted and laughed and panted and laughed.

She reached for the other suspender and I laughed harder and harder, and tears poured down my face and I was shouting, "No, Jule! Don't. No!"

"You're sure?"

"Get me out of here!" Tears flooded my mouth and my neck as she pulled up my pants and rehooked my suspenders to them. Voices rose in what sounded like protest.

She lifted the blindfold from my eyes and unhooked my hands. My unsnapped bra slipped off and I ran up the stairs without anything on top. Jule reached me on the stairs and helped me get into my shirt. I held my shirt closed, running the rest of the way up the stairs, not stopping to button it, and slammed right into the locked door.

"Is something wrong?" Armand asked among a chorus of French sounds.

Juliana wrapped me in her body, so I couldn't be seen by the others. "She's fine. Could you unlock the door, Armand? We need to go home. Too much to drink. I'll give you a call tomorrow."

"Certainement, ma cherie." He unlocked the door, and I flew out of that place with Juliana close behind. She collected our coats from the maid as we dashed into the night air. My tears flowed as we hurried to the car, Juliana's body still wrapped around mine again.

"I'm sorry, Jule, I'm sorry, I'm sorry." Tears poured in a steady stream as I got into the car. "I let you down. I let you down."

"No, you didn't, silly," she laughed. "Let me button your shirt. This is nothing to cry about. You've had too much to drink. I'll get you home and you'll sleep. Stop crying. It's nothing. A game. That's all."

"Margarite is better."

"Oh, stop. This wasn't a contest."

"I embarrassed you in front of your friends."

"They're too drunk to remember. Put your coat on. There's a chill." She helped me into my coat. "And stop crying. None of this matters."

I remember the sound of the ignition turning over and I remember my tears. I think I cried nonstop—at times almost hysterical—all the way back to the hotel. I remembered the sun's early rays peering into the window of my hotel room, but I didn't remember the drive through the streets or the walk through the lobby or even Juliana putting me into my nightgown and into bed.

CHAPTER EIGHTEEN

All was black. I couldn't see. I tried to raise myself up, but my arms were tied above my head. My nightgown was pushed to my neck. My breasts were lightly touched.

"Jule?" I called out. "Is that you?"

Slowly my underpants were slid down my legs, over my feet, and off. I pulled and thrashed at my bindings, unable to free myself. My legs were yanked apart, bindings placed on each ankle and tied to the bedposts. I struggled to move, but . . .

"Jule? Jule?"

A finger touched my clit and I felt mad with desire and yanked at my binding. The finger pressed deep inside me and then—something thicker going up and down, up and down, the weight of a body on top of me going up and down, up and down, waves of feeling rippling through me moving toward a crescendo. I was helpless to break away from it.

"My legs," I choked out. "Release them. I want to put them around you."

The bindings were slipped from my ankles and my knees caressed the gyrating ass on top of me.

"My arms. I want to hold you."

My hands were freed, and I held her as waves rippled through me, going higher and higher. Her mouth was on me and I was yelling, "More, more. Please, God, more." Then the quiet as I rested in her arms.

"Oh, gosh, Jule, that was, was . . . Wow."

She lifted the blindfold from my eyes and placed a kiss on each eyelid. "So, I see that you *do* like a bit of bondage. But the private kind, not public."

She slid off me, pulling out the dildo. We lay side by side.

"It was so—I mean with my eyes covered. I felt like everything was so focused. And I couldn't move my hands and my arms, and I couldn't see. It was kind of a helpless feeling and yet . . ."

She ran a nail down the center of my chest, past my breasts, to my stomach. "I was in complete control of you."

"It was a little scary, but a lot exciting. Part of me didn't like you being in control, but the other part—the other part of me did like it. At first I wasn't even sure it was you."

"Oh? And how many women do you usually have coming into your boudoir to tie you up and make love to you?"

"Not as many as you."

"I don't have women coming into my room."

"Margarite?"

"She's never been up here." She ran a finger around the nipple of one of my breasts. "I shouldn't have brought you to that party. It wasn't right for you. But you kept asking me about Margarite, so I thought . . . No, I knew I shouldn't have done it before I did it. It wasn't something you had to know about."

"But it's something you're able to do with Margarite."

"I wish you'd forget about what I might or might not do with Margarite. I've known her a long time."

"She's become a habit?"

"Sort of. You're so much smarter and more interesting than she is."

"And Andy? Is she a habit too?"

She turned onto her back and the dildo popped straight up.

"Oh, gees, Jule, will ya take that thing off?"

"I think it looks cute on me."

"I don't. I like what it does, but I think it looks better on me. You're too femme."

"And are you the butch? I don't like that low-class bar language."

"Well, whatever you call it, that thing doesn't suit you. I like your pussy the way it is."

She laughed and sat up, throwing her legs over the side of the bed. She unhitched the buckles of the belt. Together we pulled the belt down and off. She tossed it out of the bed onto the floor and lay on her side facing me.

"What's happened to my France?"

"What do you mean?"

"This is my home. I know this place as least as well as New York and yet... Well, I haven't been back for a long time. Those people. The anger in their faces. Did you see the sign that said 'Communists'?"

"Yeah, and 'Yankie Go Home.'"

"Scary. Paris was never like this. How did you know what to do to get us out of that?"

"Jule, I didn't do much of anything. There was that guy who showed up..."

"Yes, he helped a little, but..."

"A little?"

"You were so calm."

"I don't think I've ever heard you scream before."

"I don't think I ever *have* screamed before. How did you do that?"

"Do what?"

"Stay so calm."

"Believe me, Jule, I was not calm; I just knew I had to get you out of there."

"You had to get *me* out of there. All these years and I still don't understand you."

"There's nothing to understand. I love you. That's pretty simple."

"Yes, well... Everything seems strange now."

I wrapped my arms around her and pulled her body against mine, breast-to-breast, pussy-to-pussy. "Tell me. What seems so strange?"

"Changed. Everything seems changed."

She slipped from my arms and lay on her back. "I miss the Paris I once knew. When I was a child, there was no anger or poverty. I knew there were slums, but they were far from me. They never touched me. But this... Those people. Something seems so changed."

"Maybe it was always this way, but you were a child and didn't see it."

"No. Something is terribly different. Some deep wound has struck at the heart of us."

"How can I help you?" I ran my tongue over her nipple.

"Make love to me."

"With pleasure." And I did just that with the late morning sun streaming in through the open curtain and warming the bed. It was wonderful. It was exactly the way you'd plan it if you were dreaming of making love in a hotel room in Paris.

"Tell me about Andy," I said after we'd recovered. "She's in love with you, isn't she?"

"Yes."

"I knew it." I turned onto my back. "So, what does it mean for us?"

"Nothing. Get back here." She pulled me close. "It bothered you that Andy kissed me, didn't it?"

"You knew it would, but still you didn't stop. You made me stand there and watch."

"You could've left."

"Jule!"

"All right. I kind of enjoyed you watching and your jealousy, but there's nothing to be jealous about."

"A kiss like that?"

"It was a good-bye kiss. You're right; Andy says she's in love with me. You already know my view about two women loving each other in that way. Well, with Andy it's even more complicated. Andy loves me the way a *man* loves a woman."

"Well, isn't that sort of what we all—"

"Not in my view. Andy was telling me last night about an important decision she made. She gave me permission to tell you, but you can't speak to anyone else about it."

"What is it?"

"Andy's seriously considering—I don't know what you call it—you know Christine Jorgensen and what she did?"

"You don't mean... ?" I sat up. "Christine Jorgenson was a guy and Andy's a girl. Isn't she?"

"Yes, but Andy says she's always felt that inside she was a man. I don't know how any of this works. She said something about beginning to take male hormones next month."

"You can do that? You can take some pills and turn into another sex?"

"Apparently. She'll be under a doctor's supervision, of course."

"She's going to grow a beard?"

"I guess. She wasn't that specific."

"Wait. She can't grow a—a . . . I mean with Christine Jorgensen, they must've cut it off, but how is Andy going to get a—you know?"

"I have no idea."

"But they can do this? I thought only men could—"

"No. According to Andy, there's been at least one woman-to-man change. In Great Britain. It was before Jorgensen's change. Andy heard about it when she was traveling through Europe. She's going to Great Britain to consult with a doctor who's been doing this kind of work. She's excited about it. She was hoping that if she does make this change, that afterwards there might be a chance for her and I to be together, only she'd be a man."

"That's disgusting. It sounds like a creepy science fiction experiment. Like the monster in *Frankenstein*."

"I know. I wish I didn't feel that way, but . . . I want Andy to be happy and she's suffered for a long time because she hasn't feel right in her own skin. I don't understand it and . . . Oh, Al, it gives me the shivers. I would never want Andy to know that. I mean, she and I were once lovers."

"You think they'll sew on a phony penis? A rubber one like a dildo?"

We both cringed at the thought but when we pictured it we broke into wild laughter. Jule got serious again. "I don't want to laugh at Andy. But how can she do this? It seems so—so against God and nature. I'm nobody's saint, but . . ."

"You know that's what they say about people like us—that *our* love is against nature."

"I know."

All the time I was laughing and being disgusted by Andy, I wondered if somewhere inside me there was a man. I remembered that dream I used to have all the time. The one where I grew a beard. I hadn't had that dream in a long while, but still I wondered. Juliana would be disgusted by me if she knew about that dream. I shook the thought from my mind and wrapped my arms around her. "Let's forget about all this creepy stuff and call room service. We'll have breakfast in bed. Then I'll make love to you again. Or I'll make love to you first and then we'll have breakfast in bed."

"We can't call room service. Not like this. Or even with robes on. Two women ordering breakfast in bed? It'd be safer if we got washed and dressed first, but after we did all that . . ."

"The mood would be killed," I said. "Do you think there'll ever be a time when we'll be treated like everybody else?"

"Oh, there have been a few women like us who lived in Paris somewhat openly; women artists who were already considered odd like Gertrude Stein and Alice B. Toklas. They weren't really accepted by most, merely tolerated. Many others who came here to write or be artists kept their relationships secret. No. I don't think we'll ever be treated like everyone else."

"Then let's stay here all day and pretend the rest of the world doesn't exist."

She kissed me, and we made love again. Everything would have been perfect if I didn't have to keep shooing away Schuyler's face when it popped up in my mind.

CHAPTER NINETEEN

"**What do you** have planned for today?" Jule asked later as we sat down at a table at Le Chapeau, a rustic little bistro down a side street not far from the hotel. She took off the scarf she'd wrapped around her head, shook out her hair, and slipped the sunglasses into her purse. These were all part of her disguise. As a nightclub singer in the US, she didn't often get recognized, but in Paris there were times when she did, and it could cause an annoying ruckus and interfere with our time together. No one was likely to bother us here in this little out-of-the-way place frequented mostly by workers.

It was closer to lunch than breakfast by the time we left the room. The rows of tables were filling up fast with workers on their lunch break, dressed not unlike the men we saw when we took the wrong turn on our way to the party. But these men looked a lot less intimidating. There were a few women who probably worked in offices and another group of men in suits and ties. A young woman in a plain gray dress leaned against one of the poles that held the building up, playing the accordion and singing in French.

I remembered my father escaping to the cellar to play his accordion. I could hear the sounds coming up through the coal grate in the hallway. He wasn't good, all the songs sounded the same, but I think it made him happy and it got him away from Mom for a little while.

The garçon brought us a basket of French rolls, two baguettes, and two glasses of wine, which we knew he would refill frequently throughout our meal. It was a lovely Paris afternoon. Perfect, actually, except for . . .

"Well, I've got an appointment with some magazines to get you an interview or two. Then, I'm going to check the American Express office for our mail," I told Juliana, "and wire Max to tell him to get off his rear end and write to Scott. I have to follow through on some gigs I set up for my clients back in the States. Later tonight, I'm going to meet Scott for an early dinner and talk him into coming with me to hear a new French singer who's appearing in one of those little cellar clubs in the Latin Quarter. Maybe there's some possibility for me to expand into the French market, take on a French client or two." I tore off a piece from the baguette.

"You're forever the businesswoman, aren't you? Why don't you take a walk around Paris? See something. I wish I could take you, but with the radio interview and the extra rehearsal later . . ."

"No. You work. That's what I want you doing. That's why we're here. I'll be fine." I couldn't tell her that after our lunch I *would* be seeing a bit of Paris. Before any of my other tasks, I'd be taking the bus to see Schuyler.

Le garçon set a bowl of cassoulet, or bean stew, in front of us, the specialty dish of the house. Well, it was the *only* dish of the house. As we put our forks into the stew, a gruff French voice shouted, "Juliana!"

Everyone turned to look, including Juliana and me. A twentyish to thirtyish-year-old man in a cap with straggly hair peeking out marched toward us. He wore a filthy bandana around his neck and a black T-shirt with only a stump of an arm sticking out of one sleeve. He had a few days growth of beard and his blue jeans were streaked in dirt. Not the sort of person I'd expect to be calling for Juliana.

"Juliana," he repeated more softly as he leaned the knuckles of his existent hand on our table. He spoke to her in French, and she responded in French. The stump arm was facing me, and I didn't like watching it wiggle up and down as he talked. They had a few more words back and forth, and each time the sound of the words became more heated and the stump arm wiggled more viciously. Juliana was holding in her anger, but I could tell she was close to boiling over. Finally, she broke off the conversation, picked up her fork, and dug it into to her cassoulet as if the man wasn't still standing there. The man grabbed her arm and pulled the fork out of her hand.

I jumped up, "Hey! Leave her alone."

"No business to you," he growled and grabbed Juliana by the elbow. "Allez vous-en-bougez!" he said and pulled her across the room.

I ran after them. "Uh, uh, homme," I yelled at the men sitting at the tables as I searched for words. "Stop him." No one moved. I jumped up and down, pointing. "Uh, uh, arretez le."

A couple of Frenchmen stood and spoke to the man and to Juliana, then sat back down.

"What are you doing? Stop him. Arretez le!"

They kept eating their cassoulet. I punched the guy on the arm above his stump. "Leave her alone, goddammit."

"Go or I tell all which you are." He spat out in a harsh whisper, "Dyke!"

I backed away as if he was pointing a gun at me. No one had ever called me that filthy word before.

"It's okay, Al," Juliana said. "I'll be back. Wait for me. This is my brother."

I stepped aside as this bully, still holding her elbow, took her out of the room. When they'd gone, I scanned the place, suddenly feeling naked; had anyone heard him? Did that word in French sound the same as in English? I slunk back to our table.

I couldn't eat my cassoulet. I drank the wine and alternated between watching my watch and watching the door. Where was she? Where did that guy take her? I berated myself for not following them. What if she came back bloody? The accordion lady played something slow and easy, which helped a little.

After twenty minutes, Juliana came back—no blood—and sat down opposite me. Without explanation, she took her fork, speared some beans, and put them in her mouth. She took another bite of cassoulet, and another.

"Jule?"

She kept eating her cassoulet.

"Jule, what happened?"

"Sorry. I'm starved. You haven't touched yours."

"You think I could eat after some monster dragged you off to who knows where?"

"I told you. He's my brother. He's a little volatile, but—"

"A little?"

"I don't think he would hurt me."

"You don't think so, but you don't know? He's dangerous Jule, and you need to stay away from him. And how is it I've known you for fourteen years and you've never told me you even *had* a brother?"

"He's not easy to talk about."

"He's your brother. How hard can it be to tell me about him? At least that he exists."

"My family life is private."

"Oh?" She was putting another one of her knives into my heart.

"Or used to be. I don't want you getting the wrong idea about him. He wasn't always like you saw him today. He was such a sweet little boy, but life has been hard on him. Here, I think I have a picture." She reached inside her purse and took a wallet from a zippered compartment. She opened it to a picture— "Look."—and held it out to me.

I looked down at a little brown-haired boy about five years old with one tooth missing in the front. He could have been anybody's American kid. It was hard to believe this little boy was the same man who had just yanked Juliana out of the bistro. "Yeah? So?"

She took back the photo, admiring it. "Such a dear. Around the time of this picture, my cat ran away. I was about fifteen, before my adventures in Harlem. I loved that cat. It was the first pet I'd ever had because my mother was allergic. She finally let me get the cat if I promised to keep him in my room. I was a wreck when that cat ran away. Without saying anything, Christophe went out looking for him with his wagon. He was gone for hours. Much longer than any little boy should be out by himself. My mother was crazed with worry. She almost called the police. He didn't come home until after dark. He knocked on my door. When I opened it, he wasn't there, but I found his wagon with my cat sleeping inside. He never said a thing about it, never expected a reward or even a thank you. He did it out of love. That's how he does everything."

"Dragging you out of here was love?"

"I didn't say he was always wise in his approach to love. Only that he acts out of love."

"So, if he's so special how come you never told me about him?"

"Mother and Father made us both feel like he was a terrible black sheep. I loved him, but I was also ashamed of him because . . ." She looked down at her cassoulet, poking at it with her fork. "He was born out of wedlock. While my mother was married to my father."

"Oh." A shiver ran through me.

"When I was ten, my mother had one of her affairs and got caught—with my brother. She had had many affairs before but being pregnant with someone else's child was more than my father could bear. They separated as soon as my brother was born. My brother has had a difficult life as a result, and he isn't always the nicest person. The inscription on the rosary box. He thinks 'John' may be his father."

"And your mother's . . . murderer?"

"He didn't say that. I did."

"What did he want today?"

"Money."

"Doesn't he have any?"

"No. You saw the way he was dressed. My father, as you know, gave me the house and a handsome trust fund. Christophe didn't have a father to do that for him. Mother wouldn't say who Christophe's father was. And Mother, well, she left me most of what she had. Only a very little was left for him. That little bit I think he may have given to the French Resistance during the occupation. He's a passionate man with strict ideas about right and wrong. He fought with the Free French Army in North Africa. You saw his arm."

"He lost it in the war?"

"Yes. And what have I ever done for France except live here? And live here exceptionally well."

"But Jule, you're an American."

"So is he, technically, but he has no feeling for it. Well, you saw, he can barely speak his own language, which he doesn't claim as his own. French is the only language he wants to know, but he can never be a French citizen."

"But he was born here, wasn't he?"

"Yes, but to an American mother. The rules are different here. He needed a French father to come forward before he was eighteen to claim paternity. That didn't happen, so he must always remain a foreigner in his own country while being a citizen of a country he despises. Now, he's joined some group to support the French workers. He calls me a sycophant and I think he may be right. His friends fought and died for France, they stood up against tyranny. What did I do? I hid out in the United States safe and warm, worrying about my career. My career, Al. People were being crushed over here. How empty my dreams seem compared to his."

"You came over here to entertain the troops on the front lines. That was not an 'empty' thing to do. It was courageous."

"For a few weeks, and then I was evacuated when it got too hot. What is that?"

"Why are you belittling something you did that most people would not have even considered doing?"

"Because I was not a heroine, but all the PR about that time portrays me as if I had been. But these friends of Christophe—these heroes who saved France—Christophe tells me they now suffer in poverty; they are given starvation wages as they strive to rebuild France, while the people of my class benefit from their labor and contribute little. My friends congratulate themselves for the unity of France they have created, how they are all one, the rich, the workers, the poor. You heard Armando at the party. Blind to the workers' plight, and it was people like my friends, like Armando, who would have sold France to the Nazis for a few pieces of silver."

"He—he collaborated? But I—I like Armando."

"So do I. But I'm sure he made little compromises with the devil during that time. Compromises that my brother would not make. Look at all the fine things he still has, the antiques, the tapestries."

"No, that isn't possible. Armando is a kind, warmhearted man."

"Yes, he is. He truly is. That's not a ruse. But my brother, he is not kind, not warmhearted, but he quite literally gave an arm to free France from tyranny."

A sound deep inside me rose up, and I said softly, more to myself than Jule, "A certain man had two sons and he came to the first and said, 'Son, go work in the vineyard today.' The son answered, 'No, I won't,' but afterward he thought better of it and went. And the father came to his second son and said likewise, and this son answered, 'I go, sir,' but he didn't. Which of these two did the will of the father?"

"Exactly."

We were silent a moment, probably contemplating the meaning of right, wrong, good, bad. "And still," Jule said, "we don't know what Armando did or didn't do or if he did anything. I can't judge. I wasn't here. What would I have done if I'd been here? Do I know? I'd like to say I do, but . . . I guess I try to assuage my own conscience by sending Christophe money regularly, but he gives it away to the workers."

"If you already give him money, why is he coming around with all that desperation?"

"He wants more. A lot more. The reason I'm hesitating is because—

because this new group he's involved with . . ." She took a sip of her wine, looking around, and whispered, "I think these workers may belong to the Communist Party."

"Then you can't give him the money." I felt myself go pale.

"If only it were that simple. He's my brother."

"Half-brother."

"Yes. And no one ever lets him forget that. He has so much less than me."

"And he's playing on your guilt to get what he wants."

"I know. But you should have known him as a little boy."

"Juliana, listen to me. He's not that little boy who found your cat anymore. He's a grown man, a dangerous man. You can't give him that money. First, it would be immoral to give money to communists and I'm sure your church would not approve."

She nodded.

"Second. The HUAC hearings would be down on your head so fast you wouldn't have time take a breath before they threw you in jail as a traitor to your country. And they would also find out about . . . you know and tie them both together into a nice, tidy, little package. There's nothing more they'd like better than to publicly *prove* that we're all nothing but a bunch of commie traitors. They'll have you hanging in effigy as their poster child. You want that?"

"No!" Juliana said horrified. "Of course not, but—"

"And what about Christophe and that . . ." I whispered, "what he said about us. He knows. Would *he* use that against you?"

"I don't think so. He doesn't approve of it, but I don't think he'd make some public announcement. He doesn't want to destroy me. He simply wants to help his friends and his country. My mother couldn't give him comfort or look in his face without seeing the man who caused the breakup of her marriage. I want him to feel like he still has a sister, so that's why I thought—"

"No. You can't do this. I know you think that working on your career isn't much compared to what Christophe's done, but I've got to tell you, Jule, I've worked too damn hard for you to throw it all down the sewer now. Is that what you want to do? Give up everything we've ever worked for for some cause? What cause? A French cause? You're an American."

"Not completely. I'm French too. Maybe not by citizenship, but I was educated here, I have family here."

"And you left here when you were sixteen for the opportunities *America* offered you."

"I came back and forth. I didn't only stay in the States. You don't know what it is to belong to two countries."

"I can't believe you're talking like this about the United States. What did he do to you out there? Brainwash you? You are a citizen of the greatest country in the world. Are you now going to give that and everything else up for France? Do you *want* to go to prison?"

"Oh, dear God, no."

"Then don't give him one damn dime of your money. Not one damn dime." I was shaking. "I have to get to my appointment. I'll see you tonight." I walked out still shaking.

CHAPTER TWENTY

"Richard!" I choked out as I hurried into the hotel lobby to get the directions I'd forgotten on the desk in my room. "What on earth are you—?"

"Surprise! So, where's Julie?"

"A radio show, then rehearsal. A *long* one."

"We can go meet her. Where's she rehearsing? I can only stay a few days. My sister's looking after Mother as my birthday gift, but she can't stay long because of the kids. Take me to my wife." He smiled, slapping his hands together and marching toward the door; he stopped, seeing I wasn't beside him. "Al?" I was stuck to the lobby's highly polished, black-and-white checked floor. "Oh, Al, how thoughtless of me." He threw his arms around my shoulders, hugging me. "It's good to see you."

He left me standing there and hurried out the door. What's *he* doing here? I have to see Schuyler *today*.

"Well?" He came back inside. "Let's go. We'll surprise her. Then I thought you could take me to meet Dan Schuyler."

"No!" I screeched.

"What's the matter?" He fixed his fedora to his head.

"Well, uh, it's a closed rehearsal. You know how Juliana likes privacy when she's working." I could have added 'remember how she banned you from all the New York rehearsals?'.

"I guess it's just you and me until tonight. Let's go somewhere. We can talk about that script and then go to Dan Schuyler's place."

"Out of town."

"But I thought he said—"

"Nope. Out of town, unexpected, out of luck. Thoughtless guy. Let's go see Paris." I rushed ahead of him, my stomach turning and everything inside me sloshing around like lime Jell-O. I hated lime Jell-O.

"You know what I've always wanted to do?" Richard said, catching up with me. "I've always wanted to go boating on the Lac Daumesnil. I promised myself I'd do that the next time I came to Paris. And it's the perfect day. Sunny and warm."

* * *

"Nice here," Richard said, pulling the two oars toward his chest.

"Yes," I said, lying back in the boat making gruesome Schuyler pictures out of the clouds above. The one I liked best was the one with Schuyler's nose growing out of his forehead. "Are you sure you don't want me to take one of those oars?"

"No, I'm fine," he puffed, loosening his tie and continuing to huff-puff us through the water. His jacket looked a little tight, like he may have gained a few pounds since I last saw him. He was well into his forties now and some gray streaked the sides of his head. "I don't let the girl row my boat for me. When do you think Schuyler will be back?"

"Never!"

"What?"

We were surrounded by the beginnings of fall; the green foliage that floated overhead was beginning to be streaked with the slightest touches of orange and red, and the air was cool. It was a delight to be away from the heat that usually pressed in on me in the center of the city. I should have been enjoying it. "Look, Richard, I want you to stay away from Schuyler. The last thing we need is for you to ruin this deal. Juliana will never forgive you."

"I know you mean well, Al, but Schuyler and I hit it off on the phone and he understands the scope of Juliana's talent. I think he might rather talk business with me. You know, a man. That's how he sounded on the phone."

Schuyler was sure tightening those screws he had dug into my head.

"Getting together with Dan, you know, two men over a beer . . ."

Oh, brother, now he sounded like they both belonged to the Princeton club.

"We could come up with a plan to convince Julie what's best for her."

I wanted to jump out of my skin and smash something. *I should be sitting* with Schuyler now, but instead I was in this boat talking nonsense with this fool. "Richard, can we get out of this thing? I need to walk."

"Sure," Richard said, rowing the boat to the dock.

Always the gentlemen, he leant me his arm to help me from the boat. "May I say you look lovely in that dress? Much nicer than those dark suits you usually wear at the club."

I wore a simple, cotton, yellow shirtwaist decorated with little blue lollipops and a blue cardigan around my shoulders. "Thank you," I said as I stepped onto the dock.

We walked through skinny medieval roads sprinkled with odd shops and small cafes. "So, Richard, when were you last here?" I asked, desperate to keep him off the topic of Schuyler.

"Julie and I came here in '48. Kind of a second honeymoon to make up for the one we couldn't have in '40 when we first married. Europe was at war, as you know, so it was impossible to go abroad. Our first anniversary was in Niagara Falls. Quite a comedown from Europe. Not a proper honeymoon for a woman like Juliana. So, in '48 I wanted to give her something special for our anniversary, and she was missing her family. I guess you know her mother was—"

"Yes."

"I think missing her mother and the guilt she constantly carries around with her because she wasn't here to protect her and, well, the guilt she has over not fulfilling her mother's dreams—you know her mother wanted her to be a great opera diva—I think that guilt is something that kept Juliana from being the full-throttled singer she could be. Until you, of course. You seemed to get out of her what I couldn't."

We stood in front of the stone steps of a small church. "Sometimes I'm jealous of you, you know?" he said.

I think I stopped breathing then.

"Shall we go in?" he asked.

"Uh, yeah, okay."

"Do you have something to cover your head?"

"My head? Oh, yeah, sure. I think I have a clean handkerchief in my handbag." I pulled it out. "Will this do?"

"Fine. I know you're not Catholic, but it's only respectful, don't you think?

Of course, it seems a little silly that I have to take my hat off and you have to put one on. Where in the world did these rules come from?" He chuckled as we passed through the heavy doors.

It was dark inside, light coming only from the dusty stained-glass windows that lined the walls on the side and behind the altar. A large stone statue of the Virgin Mary stood on the altar with her arms outstretched like she was welcoming me into her. *Well, that's nuts.* I was raised to believe that making a big deal out of Mary was some kind of sin, but for Juliana, she was the Holy Mother. There was something soft about that, something to lie your head on. It would've been nice to have a Holy Mother to take the place of the mother who didn't work out so hot.

I waited as Richard genuflected toward the altar. Then we both slid into a pew. He bowed his head with his hands clasped in prayer. His shoulders shook; he hid his head in his tightly interwoven hands as his shoulders shook more. I saw that he was trying to hide that he was crying.

"Richard?" I whispered, not sure if I should do or say something. He didn't respond. Perhaps I should ignore it, I thought, make believe I didn't see what I was seeing.

After a few long, uncomfortable minutes, he wiped his eyes with his handkerchief and looked up at the altar and sighed. "I think she may be seeing someone else?"

I froze and stared at the Holy Mother, afraid to look at Richard. I prayed some message would float down on me, that maybe she'd overlook I wasn't Catholic and tell me what to say. He was crying again, and I felt sorry for him. He was in such pain. I wanted to comfort to him. *I* wanted to comfort him? Me. Could anything be more ridiculous?

"You want to get a glass of wine?" he whispered.

"Uh, yeah, sure."

We pushed through the heavy door. A burst of light as we stood on the stone steps again. Hard to see. "She's given me no reason to distrust her. It's my silly fear. You won't tell her what I said. I feel foolish. I know I can trust you."

We walked back over the cobblestones looking for the café we had passed a while back. We strolled by old women standing behind large wagons selling flowers, artists with easels wanting to paint our portraits, secondhand junk shops and a fortune-teller's trailer. The whole time we walked, my heart quaked with terror that he was about to tell me he knew about Juliana and me.

"Here, okay?" he asked when we reached the small café with a couple of inside tables and a couple outside. Colored leaves from the trees above us covered the ground and swished under our feet. Strange for it be so warm while surrounded by the beginnings of autumn. Some omen from the gods?

We sat outside at a small round table. A few feet from us there was a couple holding hands and speaking in a quiet French. Le garçon brought us two glasses of house wine. Richard lit a Marlboro. "I thought maybe if Juliana saw some of her relatives in France, you know when I brought her here for her anniversary... Well, maybe they'd know something about what happened to her mother that could soothe her feelings or maybe by reconnecting with these people, you know, maybe she'd feel less guilty. It didn't work. The relatives were cold to her. Except for her grandmother. She was a pleasant old coot. French, you know. Never approved of Julie's mother marrying that English earl or duke or—"

"Lord," I said.

"Oh, is that what Julie's father is? I can't keep that royalty nonsense straight. Anyway, Grandma never approved of her daughter, her ways. The way I've heard it, her mother was, well, she tended to like the gentlemen a little too much. I guess that's why I worry about Julie running off with some handsome..." His eyes looked into mine with intensity. "Is that sort of thing hereditary?"

"Uh... I don't think so."

"She'd never betray me. Would she?"

Sweat gathered around my neck as I tried not to look away from him. "No. Of course not."

He smiled and took a deep breath, "Well, you would be the one to know, wouldn't you?"

"Huh?"

"It's obvious that you're more to her than a manager."

"It is?" Had Schuyler told him? Is that what this was about?

"Anyway, the old woman doted on Julie. Let Julie do whatever she wanted. Bought her expensive gifts. And the way I heard it, Grannie had been quite the looker in her time and had lots of beaux herself. I guess that's where Julie's mother got it from. But once Grandma got married, she dropped the beaux and was loyal to her husband, whereas her daughter wasn't. That was the source of their conflict.

"Granny didn't know anything about the details of Juliana's mother's, well, uh, her demise as far as I could tell with my broken French and her highly damaged English. But, those other relatives? Those aunts, uncles, cousins, whatever, I think they knew something, but they weren't talking. I guess you've met that brother of hers."

"Well, I don't know if 'met' is the correct word, but I saw him from a distance."

"Yes, he's a difficult boy." Richard took a few puffs from his cigarette. "She sends him money, you know? Hoping he'll open some type of business and make a productive life. But those relatives . . . they talk like he doesn't even exist or that he *shouldn't* exist. They talk like that right in front of him. And they talk as if Juliana's mother never had all those affairs and the boy just magically popped into existence. I don't even want to think about that woman, her mother, but I can tell you *I* don't blame her father one bit from separating from her. I'll tell you if Juliana ever . . . with another. . ."

"What would you do?"

"Do? Well, I'd . . . Juliana would never do that. She's a good Catholic girl. But I still feel bad for her brother. I mean, it wasn't the kid's fault he was born . . . well, into that situation, uh, fatherless. Christ did teach forgiveness and non-judgment, but to hear them talk you'd think they were the holy apostles putting a curse on the poor kid's head. They acted like *he* planned his birth all by himself."

A man and woman in orange, red, and green shirts and pants stopped near our table to play their accordions. Their fingers sped along the keys making music that was bright, but desperate too.

"They never solved the case," Richard continued. "But I still think those relatives know something. I came back here in '52. By myself. Juliana doesn't know that. I'd appreciate you not telling her."

"No . . ."

"I was going to solve the case for her. I thought that might give her peace. Sometimes she seems filled with such a restlessness. Have you noticed that?"

"Yes."

"She's restless like she needs something. Something I can't give her. Do you have any idea what that could be?"

"No." Keep breathing, Al.

"I told her I had to go on another one of my business trips when I came here in '52. I hired a private detective."

"You did?"

"I was limited in who I could choose. I needed someone who spoke some amount of English. My French is pathetic. I studied it in prep school, but I was a poor language student. I stayed here a month hoping the guy would come up with something, anything, but . . ." He sighed deeply. "I think those relatives, well . . . I didn't know the culture, the shorthand communications between people. They could've paid him off or threatened him away from the trail or—maybe he was just a bad detective." He laughed and took a sip of his wine.

"Did you ever meet Juliana's Aunt Sally?"

"Yes, I did. Wonderful woman. Terribly British. I took the boat across the Channel and she met me on the English side. We had a pleasant luncheon in a fine restaurant. I had a feeling she didn't want Juliana's father knowing she was talking to me and that's why we didn't meet at her home. She has a place on Juliana's father's estate. She practically raised Juliana until she was six or seven. The parents were still married then, but Grace Masden, Julie's mother, was rarely there. You've met Julie's father?"

"Yes. Stiff."

"That's a polite way of putting it. I gather he farmed off his parental duties onto Aunt Sally, but Aunt Sally loved the job. Unfortunately, her mother showed up one day and whisked Julie away from Aunt Sally. That's when all the lessons began in earnest. Before that, I take it, Aunt Sally saw Julie's innate musical talent and was helping her to develop it, but in a fun, game-like way. When her mother took over, she had her practicing night and day: dancing, piano, singing. A grueling schedule according to Aunt Sally, and Aunt Sally was powerless to stop it. If she lectured Grace about the needs of children, Grace would become enraged and threaten to never let Julie visit her again. That pretty much shut up both Juliana and Aunt Sally. From Aunt Sally's point of view, Julie's mother was a tyrant when she wasn't bedding every man in Paris and New York. I don't think that woman ever gave Julie the kind of love she deserved, so I try to make up for it, but I . . ."

"Gosh, to hear Jule talk about her mother, it sounds like she was some kind of saint, but from what you're reporting . . ."

"A different story. I know. I think Julie remembers the mother she *wishes* she had. But Aunt Sally knew nothing about the murder. When the murder happened, she had long ago lost touch with Grace Masden and Julie was already in New York. I had reached another dead-end. I came home with nothing."

"I'm sorry, Richard. That must've been disappointing for you. You tried so hard. You must . . . love her very much."

He lit a cigarette and smiled as he released a stream of smoke. There was a sweet sadness in his eyes. "There are not enough words in the English language *or* in French, to express how much I . . ." He puffed on his cigarette. "I know what we should do. There's an old candy store not far from here. Julie loves Bourges Forestines, not that I'm pronouncing it correctly. Let's get her some. The sweet chocolate smell of the place will put us both in heaven." He threw some francs on the table and a few more in the accordion players' cup and we were off again.

CHAPTER TWENTY-ONE

I sat on a bus headed toward a Paris district called Belleville. Paris buses were the same color as New York buses—green and yellow—but some of them were open air, no glass in the windows to hold out the breezes of the moving bus. I wished New York had those kinds of buses. I loved whizzing through the streets with nothing obstructing my view as we passed cafes and Chez this and Chez that and bicyclists carrying long obscene-looking baguettes under their arms. With the heat wave still hanging on, the breeze coming in through the windows was a welcome respite.

Richard had stayed for three days. Juliana and he went off both nights to who knew where, and I didn't get any sleep pacing in my room until they got back. Once they got back, I still couldn't sleep because I'd be picturing them doing—you know—on the other side of my door. And I didn't like that picture. Thank God, he finally left and I could get back to the business of trying to see Schuyler without him tailing me.

Yet, after Richard had left, something had changed and it felt strange. I felt closer to Richard than I ever had. I found after all the years we'd worked together that I liked him. But oddly, I didn't feel guilty about my relationship with his wife. That was a thing apart from the closeness I felt for him. I would never want him to know about us. Oh my gosh, no! But I didn't feel guilty. Maybe I was a really awful person.

The conductor called out my stop and the bus pulled over in front of a bakery, une boulangerie. I yanked a ticket from my carnet, handed it to him, and got off. I followed the makeshift map the concierge at the hotel had put together for me. I walked down the sidewalk a little ways and crossed over the cobblestone street. The sky was turning an ominous gray. I had a flash of recall: I was alone in the house; I was twelve; lightning pierced the radio and it burst into flames. Ever since then, I was terrified of thunder and lightning. Please, God, I've got enough to handle today. No thunder and lightning.

Two nuns passed by and nodded in my direction. I nodded back. Maybe they were a sign my prayer was being considered in higher places. The buildings I passed were made of stone that was cracking and, like that so-called village that Juliana and I had stumbled upon in the car, there were balconies, many with laundry thrown over the railings. I made another turn and came to the street that the woman on the other end of the phone had spelled out for me when I'd called for Schuyler. I stood before a building, much like the others, stone cracking, a wooden door that lead into a courtyard.

I took a deep breath; the stillness of the hot air held me closer in its arms. Yes, I could go in there and convince or manipulate Schuyler—whichever it took—to change his mind about all this. A nearby tree's green branches flapped in the breeze that was beginning to pick up.

I pushed through the wooden door and walked across the cement floor, the sound of my steps clicking through the silence as I read my scribbled directions. There was no other sound in the courtyard but me looking for Staircase A. All the apartment doors were shut tight.

Hanging onto the rickety banister that shook under my grasp, I climbed upward toward the sixth floor, hoping that Schuyler was home and hoping he wasn't. Max's cablegram had arrived only minutes before I left; otherwise, I'd be going in there with nothing. Richard delaying my trip had turned out to be a good thing. The heat got thicker with each upward step I climbed, and what the hell did the French have against elevators? I remembered the elevator operator strike in New York back in 1945 and how that had practically shut down the whole city. It was as if we no longer knew how to walk up long flights of stairs. Maybe these flights were good for me.

A little winded, I arrived at the sixth-floor landing, which was really the seventh floor because the French never counted the first floor. I had news for them—the first floor counts. It was so hot up there I had to stop a moment, leaning against the wall practicing breathing. I wiped some sweat from my eyes with my handkerchief and returned the handkerchief to my purse. I pulled my dress into place and knocked on the door. An old woman, small and stooped over, with big breasts that flopped against her loose-fitting dress, opened the door. "Madame Desmarais?" I asked, hoping she was the woman from the phone.

She nodded, waiting for me to elaborate. As soon as I said, "Schuyler," she said, "Entrez, entrez s'il vous plait," and led the way into a small room painted blue with a table in the center and wooden chairs around it. It reminded me of a smaller version of Mrs. Minton's Christian Ladies of Hope House, where I'd lived when I first came to New York City. I figured this must be a French boardinghouse.

The woman skipped from the room, sprier than her years would predict, while I paced, looking over the bookshelves that lined the walls. Of course, they were all in French so they couldn't hold my interest for long. The woman returned and said, "Il est prët a vous recevoir maintenant." I kind of got the gist of what she was telling me—that he'd see me soon. I found that was happening sometimes. That I could understand some words, but I rarely had the words to answer back.

I walked toward her. "Je suis désolé mais je ne parle pas Francais," I pronounced distinctly, which meant, I'm sorry, but I don't speak French." Jule had taught me to say that. I practiced it over and over till my pronunciation got so good that French people didn't believe I couldn't speak French. As soon as I said my phrase to Madame Demarrias, she spoke to me excitedly as if I were her long-lost French friend. She took my hand, sat me down at the table, and buzzed around the room making coffee while she chattered on. I smiled as a wash of French sounds poured over me like love music; if only I could understand.

While she waited for the coffee to percolate, she skipped over to the birdcage that sat above the sink facing the window. She sprinkled bird food into the cage as the two canaries happily sang. An orange and white cat sat on the ledge studying them until Madame Desmarais lay her wrinkled hand gently on top of his head. He purred with what seemed to be extreme pleasure, turning onto his back so she could pet his belly. She pulled the cat into her arms, holding him close and rubbing his head as she walked back to me. She leaned on one of the chairs by the table and said something that sounded warm and sincere. Her voice made me want to turn over on *my* back, so she'd pet my belly. Still petting the cat's head, she bent over and laid him gently on the floor. His claws clicked against the linoleum as he headed for his plate of food. She whispered something in my ear, and I wondered if she were talking about the cat or telling me something useful about Dan Schuyler. I so much wanted to respond in some kind way to those gentle eyes that peered out of that wrinkled face. Instead, I said, "Je suis désolé mais je ne parle pas Francais."

The wrinkles on her forehead sunk deeper. "Oui?"

"Oui," I repeated. "Schuyler?"

She shook her head, giggled to herself, and said, "Si vous voulez bien me suivre, mademoiselle." I followed her into a hallway and we passed by a few doors. She knocked on one of them and my stomach flip-flopped as I waited for it to open. I had to remain calm. I couldn't let him think he rattled me, even though he did. I pulled myself up to my tallest height.

The door opened and there he stood, looking a little more tired than I remembered, but still impeccably dressed in tie and suit.

"Merci, Madame Desmarais," he said, bowing to the old woman.

They had words. Madame Desmarais sounded firm. Finally, she grabbed some knitting from a table that stood against the wall and marched into the tiny room. She planted herself onto a straight back chair in the corner.

"Well, Mr. Schuyler," I said, removing my gloves and placing them in my purse.

"I like the hat, Miss Huffman. Dior?"

"Schiaparelli. Dior would never work in straw. Now can we get down to business and cut the crap?"

He took in a barely perceptible breath. "I see you've found me out. I don't know a thing about women's hats. Won't you sit down? I was so pleased when Madame Desmarais told me you phoned. I've looked forward to your visit."

"I am not here for a social visit, Mr. Schuyler, and you know it."

I looked over at the exposed toilet sticking out of the wall, not far from the fold-out bed with the thin hard tack mattress. An ugly purple and green cloth was thrown over it as a makeshift bedspread, but it was too small to cover the whole bed. The air was stale with cigarette smoke and lack of ventilation. There was only one tiny closed window at the peak of this attic apartment. It was streaked with city muck.

Schuyler sat on the bed. I was about to sit on the only chair left when something bubbled up in me and I forgot all about being calm and sophisticated. "How dare you call Juliana's husband and involve him in your scheme. Who do you think you are? I told you *I* would work on it."

"But you haven't, have you? I keep waiting to see that signed contract in my hand, but alas . . ." He held out his palm. "It's still not there. It's nearly a month since we arrived in Paris. I needed some assurances. I also feel badly for the poor man, two women making a fool of him behind his back. Shameful." He leaned toward me. "If you do not produce that contract and soon, I will take great joy in telling the papers, French *and* American, everything I know about you and watch you both squirm like worms stuck on my hook." He leaned back, a pleasant smile creasing his face. "However, I am a gentleman and I have not broken our agreement. I haven't involved Mr. Styles in my 'scheme' as you so inelegantly put it. I merely let him read the play. After all, *he* is Juliana's true manager, is he not?"

"Yes." I wanted to strangle this man.

"Yes," he repeated. "Yes, he is. You have done most of the work, but Richard Styles is Juliana's true manager." He grinned. "*And* her husband. You have hardly claim on her at all, Miss Huffman."

I looked over at Madame Desmarais who calmly knit as we spoke. "You're sure she doesn't speak English?" She was giving me a kind of Madame DeFarge feeling.

"Yes, I am."

"Still, I'd like more privacy with this topic. Could you please ask her to leave us alone?"

"Oh, but Miss Huffman, she would never do that. She is here for *your* benefit, not mine. She has developed motherly feelings toward you and is here to make certain that I do not compromise your virtue. She is your chaperone."

"Oh?" I looked over at her clicking knitting needles.

She lifted her eyes to meet mine and smiled. I smiled back.

"She has no idea you could not be tempted by me. If she knew the reason for that, she would spit on you and throw you down her steps. Won't you have a seat?"

I sat on the chair near the toilet. It smelled. It was bound to smell in such close quarters.

"I gather you do not have Juliana's signature on the papers. When may I expect that signature, Miss Huffman?"

"It must have been difficult for you to have been locked up. A whole ten years? That's a long time."

"Brava, Miss Huffman." He clapped and Madame Desmarais looked in our direction, her wrinkled brow wrinkling more. "You have done your research. I would not expect less from you. I knew you would be a worthy opponent. But no, it was not difficult. It gave me time to reflect, to read, to plan a renewed life."

"Let's cut the bull. How many investors do you think would invest with a producer who did six years in the jug for embezzlement? I think we're at one of those Mexican standoffs. Can we call it a draw?"

"Five years, ten months. A crime in my tormented youth. It was found that I, a mere boy of twenty-two, had been led astray by an older, more experienced criminal. The court saw promise in me and cut down my original ten-year sentence, especially when I told them where they could locate said older, more experienced criminal. I have never been in trouble since, Miss Huffman. Americans are an awfully forgiving lot."

A yellow zigzag of lightning sliced through the sky and sped across the small window behind Schuyler's head. Then a crash like a bomb. I gripped the chair with my nails as if it were about to be whisked off into the air like Dorothy's house.

"It's your turn, Miss Huffman."

Concentrate, Al, hang on. Forget the lightning. You can't let this guy . . . Another crash. My heart jumped into my throat.

"Miss Huffman, certainly *you* are not speechless."

"No one will—no one will care how young—twenty-two is not a child. You were convicted of stealing—stealing *money*. What investor would—" Repeating bombs of thunder circled the splintery wooden upstairs apartment. Wind battered the glass and the room shook. He was saying, saying something, but I couldn't, couldn't . . . *Snap out of it, Al.*

". . . a matter of public record. I haven't tried to hide . . . to India . . . rehabilitated . . . penance . . . giving to worthy causes like the Red Cross and the March of Dimes. This also is a matter of public record. And do you think anyone is going to care a twit about my dull background once the scandal sheets start tossing around Juliana's secret life as a baritone babe? The *New York Times* might even get into the act. They have a penchant for writing about '*perverts.*' Every day they seem to have some juicy article about perverts endangering our national security."

Everything was spinning. This couldn't be happening. Why didn't that damn thunder shut up and leave me alone?

"Oh, by the way, did you enjoy my gift?"

"What—what are you talking about?"

"The book for your office. *Female Homosexuality*. Didn't you find it entertaining?"

Madame Desmarais looked up, concern on her face.

"Oops! That word is the same in French. Sounds a little different, of course. We must be careful." He oozed French words at her and she went back to her knitting.

"You? How did *you* get into my office?"

His lips curled into a self-satisfied grin and he crossed his arms over his chest. "I didn't. I had a friend. A most accommodating friend. A friend of yours too. We have something in common. This friend, I believe, left it in the center of your desk so you wouldn't miss it. Those were my instructions. Be sure to deliver that signed contract to my office—not here, my office, the address is on the envelope I gave you—no later than Thursday, or I will have no choice but to act."

"Thursday? But that's only two days away."

"I know. But you're a talented woman and I know you can—"

A triple blast of thunder trilled through the air and I charged out his door, down the stairs, and through the courtyard with no plan except escape. I ran into the street as if I were being chased by the devil himself. The sky, dark with no sun, opened up and poured cold buckets of water onto my new Schiaparelli hat.

CHAPTER TWENTY-TWO

Was there any way I could have handled that worse? I sat in the back of the Lido nursing the last of my scotch. The house was packed, and I wanted to hide from it all. Max would've been so disappointed in me. Juliana sat on a stool center stage singing *Pourquoi M'Avoir Tant Donne*, a romantic ballad. I drained my glass and signaled the waiter to bring another. I had taken to drinking scotch recently, prompted, I suppose, by my survival instinct. I hadn't had a sidecar since I left the States. I missed it, and it made me angry that some anonymous "they" could make me drink something other than what I wanted. Le garçon gracelessly dropped my scotch on the rocks in front of me. Despite my having sat there alone all month, he still didn't approve of a woman sitting unescorted at a table, not even Juliana's manager.

Max, in his cablegram, had wanted to know why I was asking about Schuyler, but how could I tell him without telling the guy who took down the cablegram message? Somehow, I had to solve this myself. I'd make it go away, so why upset him? I would tell him about it when it was over, and he'd be proud of me. Except—I wasn't going to solve it. I was going to have to tell her. I was going to have to tell her the worst thing she could ever hear. I drank down the last of my scotch.

I'd suspected it'd been me all along. Me who gave us away. Maybe I did it by how I walked. I didn't take delicate little steps like I was supposed to. Maybe I gave us away because my hands were too big. I looked at them lying on the table. Were they? Or maybe it was how I pushed my hair out of my eyes, so I could see. It could've been the way I ran the club. Too tough. But I hadn't been tough today. Maybe I let my feelings for Juliana show in some wrong place.

Schuyler got into my office because had a "friend." A friend that had posed as my friend and betrayed me. But who? Bertha? Bertha, the hatcheck girl? She's not my friend, but how would Schuyler know that? It must be her. None of my real friends would've done Schuyler's bidding. Bertha was a weird girl, always following me, always wanting to do something for me. Whenever I turned around, there she was staring at me. I was always falling into her, all that phony embarrassing fawning. Yes, it must've been Bertha. But is she too much of a simpleton to—

Bart. That's who. Of course. Bartholomew Montadeus Honeywell the Fourth. He had a reason to betray me. First, I don't think he ever liked me. Plus, I fired him. He said I'd regret it. Was this his revenge? Yes. Bart had done it. He fit so well with Schuyler; he was just like him. Why didn't I see it sooner? But would he put Max in such jeopardy to get back at me? It was Max who told me to fire him. Could Bart know that? I'm sure they were once lovers.

No. No, it was Lillian Wadwacker. Of course! No, not Lillian. She and I have become close. Still, she'd been part of that trap with her friend, Ethel. And she came begging for the job at the club. A sadness filled me. It must be Lillian. How could I have been so stupid to fall for her innocence routine? Believing she didn't know what Ethel had been up to. Believing she thought Ethel was a terrible person for doing that striptease dance for me. That little traitor. She plotted against me from the beginning. So she could spy on me. And I even promoted her. What an ass I'd been. Yes, it's Lillian. But . . . what would she get out of it? What would any of them get out of it?

Money? Bart was the only one who seemed willing to do about anything for money. But Schuyler didn't have money. Look where he was living. That toilet in his living room. He wanted Juliana for his show to build his career as a producer by pleasing that secret investor. He didn't have the money himself.

Should I cablegram Max again? Max had told me he'd call if he found out anything more about Schuyler, so before coming to the Lido, I sat on a chair in the hotel lobby staring at the phone. I was trying to send thought messages to Max, so he'd call. He didn't. Max could survive this mess. He'd fire me and announce to the world that he didn't know I was like that.

But Juliana. My beautiful Juliana. I looked up from my scotch long enough to see her dancing, singing and flirting to "Coax Me a Little Bit" in English. It was a samba and oh, so sexy. She was dancing all over the stage with the male dancers. She danced in high heels and a black gown with a slit going up her left leg. She was gorgeous. And she could be such a delicious flirt both onstage and off. I couldn't stand watching her. I had to tell her. If I didn't act right away, it could hit the papers and everyone would know before she did. Two days. I'd tell her tomorrow. I couldn't wait until the last minute; it would kill me.

I walked back to the hotel along the Seine, the ever present, always steady, always there, Seine. It flowed out to sea unperturbed by things like Schuyler, scandal, shame, or loss.

Back at the hotel, I thought I might achieve unconsciousness by falling into a deep sleep, so that I'd forget all that was happening and all that I must tell Juliana. But I soon realized sleep was impossible. My stomach was a tight ball of anguish. There would be no sleep tonight.

I walked into the hotel lounge where the stage was lit with a floorshow of dancing girls prancing around, bare-breasted except for the pasties they'd glued to their nipples. Those glued tassels looked painful. I was getting more used to watching women on stage with their breasts hanging out. Actually, it was getting boring. Juliana was ever so much sexier in her heels with that slit on the side of her dress than any of those boob girls could ever hope to be.

I sat at a back table. The waiter came over and I ordered, "un baby scotch les rocks." The hotel staff was getting more used to seeing me sitting in the back by myself. I can't say their opinion ever moved up to approval, but I think I was tolerated, an unescorted woman.

I kept running the two scenes over and over in my mind. The one I'd botched up with Schuyler that afternoon and the one I knew I had to have with Juliana in a few hours when she awoke to what she thought would be a bright new day. How would I tell her? How would I get it past my lips?

The floor show ended and I recognized the sound of polite applause that I guess surrounded me, but it seemed distant and fuzzy. I didn't know where I'd go next, but I knew I couldn't go up to my room. I needed to be around people but not talk to them.

As I stepped out of the lounge, an exhausted Juliana smiled at me. "No drink tonight," she said. "I'm beat. I'm going right up. See you tomorrow for breakfast?"

"Uh, yeah, sure," I said as the bellman guided her toward the elevator. I watched the elevator lift her in the air toward our floor, clanging and shaking all the way.

"What's going on, Al?"

I jumped to the sound of Scott's voice behind me. He leaned against the wall smoking a cigarette. He wore his custom-made, tan, cashmere jacket. "And don't say it's nothing, because I know it's something. Talk to me."

"Will you walk with me? I can't talk right now. It's too hard. Just walk."

I started out ahead of him, shoving myself against the hotel door. How indelicate. No wonder people could tell about me.

Lights blinked at me from across the Seine and I followed them, watching the water ripple as I moved along the quay. Scott caught up. I was walking fast; I needed to walk fast, to walk out the pain, the confusion and fear inside me. I'll tell her on Thursday. Two days would give me time to think of a good way to tell her. But what if Schuyler put the word out tomorrow and didn't wait till Thursday? *Don't think about it. Keep walking.* But I had to think about it. I had to tell her tomorrow, which was really today.

"Al, where are we rushing off to?" Scott asked.

"I don't know."

We wandered into a shadowy corner of the city where there were clubs and dimly lit late-night cafes. The haunting sound of a saxophone drifted into the air. "Let's go there," I said to Scott. "I think I could use some jazz right now."

We went down a series of dimly lit cement steps and found ourselves in one of those cellar boîtes that were cropping up around Paris.

We took seats at a table that was pushed up against a brick wall. The place was mostly empty except for the jazz band and a sprinkling of patrons. The band, composed of a saxophone player, a piano player, and a drummer were perched on a small stage in front of us. The sax player, whose haunting sound had called to me from the outside, was a young Negro man dressed in a brown suit with a tie pulled slightly away from his throat. His eyes were closed as he played, and he seemed oblivious to anything but the music that poured from him. The other two band members were white.

A woman—I guess the waitress, though she showed no signs of it— passed by our table and dropped off two glasses of wine.

"Al," Scott began. "Can we talk now?"

"Shh, I'm listening to the music. These guys are good, especially that sax player."

After a few more numbers, the band took a break and most of the other patrons left. It was Scott, me, and one guy who looked like he'd had a few too many glasses of wine. "Are you ready to tell me what's going on with you now?" Scott asked.

I got up. "I've never managed a sax player before. I wonder . . ."

"You have no experience with that. Stop this, Al, and talk to me."

"Later. I'm going to talk to the sax now."

Scott sighed and slumped down in his chair, drinking his wine.

"Hi," I said, approaching the sax player who sat on the edge of the low stage; he lit a Gitanes. "I'm Al Huffman."

"I know who you are, Miss Huffman. We met briefly at an after-hours party at the Vanguard a few years back. I wouldn't expect you to remember me. I was a nobody. Still am."

"But I'm sure you have a name."

"Willie Washington. What do you want?"

"Well, Mr. Washington, I was hoping you'd join my friend and I for a drink. I haven't often had an opportunity to speak to many American musicians since I've arrived in Paris. Except, of course, the ones I came with."

"Then you consider me an 'American'?"

"Well, aren't you?"

"Let's go. Introduce me to your boyfriend." He headed for the table before me.

"This is Scott Elkins," I said as Scott rose. "And he's not my boyfriend. He's my musical director. He also expertly plays the piano for Juliana at Le Lido."

"I'm supposed to be impressed, I suppose."

"Not if you don't want to be. Won't you have a seat?"

"Al, what are you doing?" Scott asked as the Negro man sat down.

"Mr. Washington . . ." I began.

"Willie," he corrected. "Mr. Washington was my father."

"All right then, Willie, and please call *me* Al. Scott, why don't you ask the waitress to bring Willie a glass of wine."

"If you're paying, I'd rather have a scotch. Neat."

"Could you ask her to bring me a scotch too?" I said. "But I want it on the rocks."

"Sure," Scott said, his eyes boring into mine like he wanted to punch me.

"Well, Willie, I enjoyed your playing. Since you know who I am, you know that I manage talent. I do have a reputation for recognizing talent in others, and I—" I heard Schuyler's voice saying 'exploit it'—"I support it. So, Willie, how long have you been away from home?"

"Away from home? I'm not."

"But—surely . . . You're an American."

"And you decided that by the color of my skin?"

"Your accent."

"Do you have any idea what it's like to be on tour in the US, cross the Mason-Dixon line, and be told you have to use a separate washroom, one set aside for 'colored,' like you're some kind of alien species?"

"No. I don't. And I'm sorry those terrible things happened to you, but in the North—"

"The North? You Northern white folks love to congratulate yourselves about how liberal you are. You take such pride in how you're so much more 'open-minded' than Southerners. But at least in the South I knew where I stood. You Northerners are a lot sneakier bunch. You broadcast how free and equal we are, but tell me, Miss Huffman, could you and I sit together like this in a club in the North? Would they even let me in?"

"Things are changing, Willie. Granted it's slow, but . . . The club I run, for instance, The Haven, now admits Negroes as customers, not only as entertainers."

"Well, aren't you a nice white lady. I bet you even give to the NAACP too. Maybe you and I should go and get coffee together at Schrafft's when I'm in town. Talk business. Wouldn't that be fun?"

"Well . . ."

"Oh, that's right, Schrafft's doesn't serve Negroes. Now, *you* tell me where my home is."

Scott returned with the scotch. I immediately started drinking mine.

"No one cares what I look like here," Willie went on. "They don't see me as different from them. All they care about is my music. The US is *not* my home. A home is a place that when you go there, they welcome you. I was *welcomed* here. And you wanting to manage my career or whatever you want doesn't matter one bit to me if it means going back there. I'll never go back. I found my home. Here. In Paris where I can be me and it's okay." He picked up his scotch glass. "Thanks for the scotch. I have to get back to work." He strode back to the stage.

"I gotta go," I told Scott, hurrying to gather up my gloves and my purse. "I gotta get out of here."

"What is it Al?" Scott asked. "Tell me."

A terror ripped through me and propelled me up the steps like I was trying to outrun it. Scott chased after me.

"Al, what is it? What'd he say?"

I paced back and forth over the cobblestone. "Queers. Queers," I mumbled, hitting my fists together. The sound of Willie's saxophone drifted into the night air.

Scott grabbed my arms. "Stop it! You can't say that in the street. What's the matter?"

"The matter? The matter?" I laughed. "Queers, that's what. Queers." He crushed my face into his chest. "You gotta stop saying that."

I looked up at him. "But don't you get it?" I screamed at him. "We have no place. No place in this whole goddamn fucking world. That Negro man found a place, a place where *he* can be. *We* don't have that. *Nothing's* safe for us."

"What are you talking about?"

"Queers!" I shouted, pulling myself out of his arms. "Queers! Dykes! Faggots!"

"Al, stop it! You're going to get us killed." He grabbed me back into his arms.

"You see? You see?"

"What!"

"We have no place, dammit! Not one damn place in this whole goddamn world. Why don't you get it? *Everyone* hates us. Even God and the French."

CHAPTER TWENTY-THREE

The sun streamed into my room and my eyes. Too bright. I squinted at the clock on the end table next to my bed. Seven. I'd had a sum total of three hours' sleep. It'd be hours before Juliana woke up.

Juliana and I had become so much closer over the last few weeks, and now everything was about to dissolve into ashes. I hid my head under my pillow, trying to return to unconsciousness, but I couldn't get back there and it was too early for a scotch.

I kicked off the covers and headed for the bathroom. I'd taken to wearing nightshirts lately, the way my father used to. I'd bought a couple in a little shop near the hotel. Only I didn't wear the little cap on my head like he did. I liked the less frilly feel of them. More me. And Juliana liked me in them, too. I bent over the basin and splashed water on my face and reached for the tin of tooth powder on the shelf. Colgate Ammoniated. Ammoniated? What did that mean? I supposed the morning I was to be guillotined I'd still be reaching for the tooth powder, ammoniated or not. Can't have my head chopped off if my teeth aren't clean. This morning felt very much like one of those head chopping days.

I wandered back into my room and stared out the window. People walked by the hotel down there. What were *they* scared about? Anything? Did any of them feel like today was the last day of their lives? I had to tell her today. A knot formed in my stomach. I couldn't wait till tomorrow.

"Good morning," Juliana said from behind me. "You were out late last night."

"Yeah. Business." My stomach tied itself into a great knot. She was up earlier than I expected. I should tell her now. Get it over with. Then tomorrow morning I could bring Schuyler the papers and . . . Juliana would hate me for the rest of my life. I took a deep breath and turned toward her, "Juliana . . ."

"Al?" she said at the same moment.

We giggled at the timing. "You go," she said.

"No, that's okay. You."

"Well . . . This is hard . . ."

Did she know? Did Schuyler . . . ?

"I . . ." She hesitated. "Uh, well . . ."

"Yes?"

She sat down on my unmade bed. "Do you mind?"

"No."

"This is hard for me. Asking you this, but . . ."

She knew. She suspected me.

She looked down at the wrinkled bedspread and held one of its tassels between her fingers. "I was wondering . . . There's something . . ."

Oh, god, just say it. "Yes?" You know about Schuyler and you want nothing more to do with me. I closed my eyes waiting.

"Uh, my mother's grave . . ."

"What?" I opened my eyes.

"I've never been. Would you go with me?"

"Oh, Jule." I ran to sit beside her. "Of course."

She sighed a deep deflating sigh and took my hand in hers; she kissed my fingers. "Thank you."

*　*　*

She didn't ask Richard to go with her when he was here. She asked *me*. The first time to her mother's grave and she asked *me* to be with her. I felt elated and like shit all at the same time. How could I tell her now?

Notre Dame peered through the clouds up ahead. Juliana looked lovely in her crisp red dress cinched with a belt. The skirt's flare formed a circle around her legs. She wore a new hat she'd bought a few days ago. It sat at the back of her head, a feather poking out of one side. "Your mother is buried in Notre Dame?" I asked as we passed the bookstalls lining the banks of the Seine.

"No, my mother isn't buried at Notre Dame," she laughed. "I thought that before we went there, I'd take you to see this beautiful church. There's been no time for sightseeing."

"Oh." I tried to smile, but my stomach was turning over and I thought I might throw up. "There's a line to get in," I moaned when we walked onto the grounds of the church.

"Well, we're not in a hurry, are we?"

"Uh, I guess not." I got in line behind her. The air was crisp, but I felt warm. I needed this to be done.

"It's so dirty," Juliana remarked, looking over the face of the church. "I don't remember it being this dirty." She reached into her purse. "I brought these." She handed me a pair of binoculars. "You simply must look at the outer wall through these. There is nothing like the outer walls of this church."

I held the binoculars to my eyes and the strange gargoyles came into clear view. One guy, the devil, I guess, had a mouth that seemed to be saying, "You suckers." There wasn't one spot not covered by individual sculptures of Biblical characters or scenes with the most minute details. There was John the Baptist, the Virgin Mary with the Baby Jesus, only that baby looked to be about fifty years old. I could see Adam and Eve and the sly flirty look in Eve's eyes as she offered the apple to Adam. The men who did this had to have a fierce love for what they were doing to make such exacting sculptures, ones that mostly looked like shapeless stone if you didn't have a good set of binoculars. They did all this work and then sunk into obscurity. What do our lives mean that we live, we struggle with horrors like Schuyler or we create great beauty like the sculptures that crowd the outside of this Cathedral and then we die. None of it matters anymore. What sense does that make? But this church *does* matter even if we don't know the names of those who made it. As I lowered the binoculars I kept looking up, trying to touch those anonymous artists who left behind the grandness of their souls. A few tears of gratitude slid out of the corners of both eyes.

"We're moving," Juliana said as we followed the others toward the entrance. "This is good."

"What's good?"

"That I can show you a bit of my Paris."

A smile formed in my heart and for a second there was no Schuyler.

We entered the church. It was dark and quiet, like everyone was afraid to breathe in this holy space. Juliana immediately genuflected in the direction of a gold cross surrounded by a large sculpture of the Virgin Mary with the dying Christ lying across her lap. Behind the sculptures were three huge stained-glass windows—the Rose Windows—and along the side walls there were more stained-glass windows and paintings, and more sculptures. Numerous small candles in red glass holders, their flames dancing in the air, stood on stands throughout the church. Those must've been the candles they lit when praying for some special favor. I wished I could secretly slip over to one without Juliana noticing. Maybe if I lit one of those candles and said a little prayer telling Mary about Schuyler, things wouldn't go so bad. Maybe it'd even turn out good. *Come on, Al, that's going a little too far, don't you think? I'm sure Mary doesn't like queers any more than anyone else.*

Juliana slid into a pew and I slid in beside her. She took out her rosary and gripped them between her fingers as if trying to squeeze something out. Perhaps her mother? My eyes wandered over the high vaulted ceilings and the statues of saints that surrounded me. I figured if you were going to worship, you might as well do it in a place where you were surrounded by great art, and I was a sucker for the tormented Jesus stuff.

Juliana kissed her beads and raised her head.

"You okay?" I asked.

"Yes." She nodded. "Let's go."

As we rose to go, the deep sound of a bell rang out. I stopped in the aisle to listen. Juliana saw me stop and backed up to stand beside me. She knew how much I loved the sound of church bells. I breathed in the deep vibrations. Oh, how I loved that sound. They called you—they called you to—something—I couldn't find the word. When the deep bong stopped, I felt Quasimodo, the Hunchback of Notre Dame, standing beside me. How could I not feel him when I stood in his church? Of course, most people would say Quasimodo was never truly here and he never truly rang the bells in the bell tower. They'd say he was only a story, a creature made up in Victor Hugo's mind. But is that all he is? Is that all any of us are? Creatures made up in God's mind? Quasimodo is as real to me as I am to myself. He became real the moment I picked up Victor Hugo's book and began reading his story; I was only a kid, living in the country. Quasimodo lived in a faraway, exotic land, centuries away from me, inside an old church I thought I'd never visit, but still we belonged to each other. He lived in me now. His love for Esmerelda, the woman he knew he could never possess—I looked over at Juliana, standing patiently beside me—Esmerelda, the beautiful gypsy girl. She alone gave him solace when he cried out from his prison of aloneness. I knew him as well as anyone who I might put out my hand to touch. Didn't that make him real? As real as me? As real as Juliana?

We stepped into the daylight once more. "What do you get out of that?" I asked her when we stood again in the courtyard.

"Out of what?"

"That. Praying. The rosary. Does it comfort you?"

"I think I get out of it what you get from listening to the ringing of the bells. Let's go look at the books. Maybe you can find some hard-to-find book you've always wanted. Something rare. Expensive." She practically sprinted toward the booksellers with me running to catch up, but I wasn't ready to hurry yet. I was still mired in stained-glass windows, holy sculpture, bells, candles, and Quasimodo.

I caught up with Juliana at one of the stalls where she was merrily talking in French to the bouquiniste. "Look," she said to me. "He has lots to choose from. Pick something out. I'll get it for you."

I so wished I was in the mood for being a carefree sightseer. "No, Jule. Thanks for the thought, but I don't want anything right now."

"No?" She sounded disappointed, which made me feel worse, but I couldn't take anything from her. Not now.

"I thought we were going to your mother's, uh . . ."

"Let's go down that street over there." And she took off with me chasing after her.

"I love these little streets, don't you?" she said. "Tres mediéval." I followed her as she wandered through the shops, gaily chatting with shopkeepers.

"Let's get your hair cut."

"What? No."

"I know a little place near here. A salon. Off the beaten track, but the owner is so talented. We'll have *him* do it. No one but the boss will do for you." She charged down the street again.

"Jule, no!" I called as I ran after her. "I hate beauty parlor stuff."

"Oh, but you would look so cute in one of those new Parisian short styles.

You like my hair, don't you?" She trotted past a leather shop and a bakery. She was moving so fast it felt like me getting my hair cut had suddenly become an emergency.

"Yes," I said, catching my breath. "It's terrific for you, but nothing looks good on me, so let's skip it."

"That's because it's not styled properly. By an expert."

"Max sends me to the best."

"But Max doesn't understand what you need." She pointed down the street. "It's down there."

She almost ran the rest of the way with me running alongside her. "Jule, are you all right?"

"I'm fine. Couldn't be better. We're going to get your hair cut." She stopped in front of a small door.

"But Jule—"

"Let me do this for you. Please."

"Okay," I sighed.

We walked into a dark little shop where two women hairdressers were working on their customers' hair.

Juliana asked something of one of the women and the woman pointed to a curtain, yelling, "Marco!"

Marco, a brown-skinned man with thick gray hair, tossed the curtain out of his way with great joy. "Bonjour, mon amie." They fell into each other's arms and immediately bubbled back and forth with French. She pointed to me and Marco came close, studying me, walking around me, looking at me from every angle. It felt creepy. I was pushed into one of the chairs.

Juliana hovered over Marco the whole time while he worked. I was mostly in a daze. I couldn't unlock my thinking from Schuyler and Juliana was making it so much harder for me to tell her.

"Well?" Juliana said, waking me from my stupor. "What do you think?"

"It looks—good. But—you don't mind it this way?"

"Why would I?"

"Because uh . . ." I looked over at Marco who leaned against the mirror, smoking a cigarette and staring at me, apparently enjoying his masterpiece.

"You can say it," she whispered. "He knows. They all know."

"Yeah?" I looked over at Marco who was grinning at me.

"You're afraid it might be a little masculine?" she whispered. "I like that. This is a salon where women come who want to express themselves differently."

Now I look like what they think I am, I thought. What will that mean in the real world? But it felt so right. No more stupid curls hugging my neck. This style swept back from my forehead and ended before my neck. It was loose and free.

"And," Juliana said, "when you need to add a feminine touch for your job, you can—" She ran her finger lightly over my lips— "add a little lipstick, or—" She ran the same finger over my eye lids. It was heavenly. "—eye shadow here. And you know what? Adding a pair of small earrings—" Her finger played with one of my earlobes and I didn't care who was watching. I was slipping into heaven. "—would be perfect for this style. Voila, a girl! Yes, Marco?"

He nodded.

"Marco's one of us. So are those two ladies and their customers." They waved at me and I waved back. "Of course, like in the States, we never talk about this place to outsiders."

"Of course." I stared at myself in the mirror. "I love it, Jule. I look like me."

"Yes, you do. Let's go." She thanked Marco as she paid him.

It was getting to be afternoon, and I thought for sure she'd want to take off to her mother's grave, but . . .

"Oh look, a café! You wouldn't have a true Parisian day if you didn't stop at a café." She was off again.

"Jule, I've been to cafes. I didn't come here to have a Parisian day. I came here because—"

"I know. I know. But mixing it with a little fun can't hurt." She sat at a table and I joined her.

"Wine?"

"It's kind of early in the day."

"Not for a Frenchman. And you seem to be a little low in energy. Lack of sleep. The wine will perk you up."

"Or knock me out."

"Garçon, garçon." She waved her gloves in his direction.

Maybe I should tell her now, I thought. Over wine. No. Then she might never be able to go to her mother's grave. I can't do that to her.

The garçon brought two glasses of wine.

"Such a lovely day, isn't it?" Juliana said, leaning back in her chair and taking a sip of her wine. "I think autumn has finally arrived."

"Are you all right?"

"Couldn't be better. Enjoying my wine. Why don't you enjoy yours? That hair style is perfect for you."

"Jule, I don't have time to—"

"To be with me? To enjoy the weather and a glass of wine with me? You don't have time for that?" There was an edge in her voice. I couldn't tell if it was anger or sadness or both.

"No. Of course, I have time to spend with you. I'm just worried about you because you're . . ."

Her attention wandered from me to a man playing an accordion for a young couple holding hands a few tables over.

"They look very much in love. Don't they?" she asked.

"Yes. Are you all right, Jule?"

"Why do you keep asking me that? I'm fine, the weather is fine, we're in Paris, I'm a hit at the Lido. What could possibly be wrong?"

"You're afraid, aren't you?"

She looked away from me. "Have you—ever been to the grave of someone you cared about?"

"My grandmother."

"Tell me."

"Well, I had two grandmothers, but we didn't go to the one who was my father's mother because my mother had a fight with her before she died. But my grandmother on my mother's side . . . I loved her a lot. She was the one I told you about. The one where I jumped in the leaves. Oh, you don't remember that story."

"Yes, I do. That story means a great deal to me. I feel like it's almost my story."

"That's nice. I like my story being your story, too. Anyway, she had a heart attack when I was sixteen. I never expected her to . . . I mean, she was always strong and then one day she wasn't there anymore."

"It was hard for you to get over it?"

"Very."

"But you got over it."

"I don't know. I still think of her a lot. And sometimes when I'm by myself, I cry because I miss her."

"I didn't know that. I should know these things about you. I—I've been avoiding thinking of my mother being gone ever since I learned of it. For a long time, I told myself it never happened, that she was safe, living in Marseille. And sometimes I could even make myself believe it. I can't do that anymore. I should have been with her, Al. I could've stopped it."

"Oh, Jule, I've heard you say that before, but you must see how silly that is. No one even knows who did it."

"I do."

"You think you do. You have a hypothesis. But you don't know."

"Yes, I do. I saw him."

"What? But you weren't even in France when it happened."

"No one knows this. I never told anyone."

"What do you mean?"

She took a sip of her wine and looked in the direction of the graveyard.

"I won't tell anyone," I assured her.

"I know." She took a breath. "I saw him push her. He pushed her into a wall in our house. She probably was expecting my brother at the time. Maybe she'd told him about being pregnant. I don't know. But I do know he pushed her. I saw him. They didn't see me. He pushed her hard. Her head. There was blood. I never said anything. Why didn't I say something? Why didn't I say, 'Mama, you can't stay with him. He's going to hurt you bad.' Why didn't I say that much to her? It would have been so simple."

She looked at me as if I could give her the answer. Her face was lined with the pain she felt. I wanted to help her, but I didn't know how. "How old were you when this happened?"

"What difference does it make? I don't know. Around ten."

"It makes a difference. How could such a little girl be expected to take care of her mother?"

"I was busy with my damn career and all my lessons."

"Like your mother wanted you to be. You did exactly what she wanted.

Did that creep live with you, then?"

"No. After he pushed her that day, he was never around. She was still seeing him, though. Sometimes, in an evening, he'd pick her up for dates. Sometimes, she didn't come home all night. I think she was protecting me from him. He moved in the year I left for the States. She was so happy. She told me in a letter. 'He was the one,' she said. The special one she'd been waiting for. I could have stopped it, Al, but instead I dropped out of the Conservatoire. She was so proud I got accepted into that. Then, I quit to go to the other side of the world for my own selfish pleasure and let that man kill her." Some tears bubbled up, but she wiped them away with her handkerchief.

"Did you ever think you left to come to the US because you knew staying would be dangerous for *you*? Maybe it wasn't selfish; maybe it was survival."

"No, I was selfish. You more than anyone else knows that's how I am. Thanks for trying to make me feel better, but no, I was plain selfish and thoughtless. I can't prove it and no one knows where he is, but I know *that* man who would not claim his son and give him peace was the one who . . . He bashed . . . he used a hammer and he . . ." Her throat seemed to clog and she could barely speak for a few seconds. "She gave up everything for me. She could've been a great opera diva, but because of me she didn't reach those heights. And I didn't either. That's what she hoped I would do, that's what she prepared me for, that I would take my place among the greats. I'm a nightclub singer, Al. She must look down from the heavens with such disappointment. How can I ever face her?"

"You're one *helluva* nightclub singer and I betcha she's proud."

"I'm—I'm afraid—to go there. To the grave."

"I know. I'm going to be there with you." I wanted so badly to take her hand in mine and for us to walk to the grave together hand in hand. But we didn't dare.

In the distance, I saw a young man and woman sitting under a tree at the side of the stone pathway that led to the cemetery. They were kissing and groping each other.

"Flowers! I should bring flowers, shouldn't I?"

"If you want."

"I saw a woman selling flowers by the side of the road over there. You wait here."

She paid the waiter and dashed to the road where a woman sold flowers from her wagon.

Once she had her flowers, Juliana signaled me to follow her. We walked up the stone pathway that led to her mother's grave. She had a piece of paper with a map to the site that her brother had given her. The walkway was lined on both sides with the last of September's flowers. Down the sloping green hillsides were a few trees whose leaves were beginning to change color, but mostly the lawn was sprinkled with headstones. Juliana clutched a bouquet of daffodils. "Oh, I got this for you." She held out a lavender rose. "The old woman said it means enchantment."

"Enchantment, heh?" I took the rose in my hand.

She checked that no one was on the road with us and touched the side of my face with her fingertips, "Mon cherie. I wish I could . . . Oh well," she sighed. "There's tonight."

Juliana started again on the road, moving ahead of me. I watched how beautiful she looked in her new dress, the way she stepped between the stones with such feminine ease. Everything I ever hoped for was happening that day right alongside everything I ever dreaded.

"Coming?" She turned around, waiting for me.

We walked up the hill side by side, periodically consulting the map. "I think it's right over there," I said.

She stopped.

"Come on, Jule, it's only a few more steps away."

"Could you—could you go and make certain?"

"Sure. You wait here. I'll go ahead."

I walked the short distance to the top of the hill and turned onto a small tributary where there were grand headstones with cement crosses of Mary or an apostle or Jesus. Next to one of these grand monstrosities sat a small gray headstone peering out of a knot of grass. I squatted down close to read the name. "Grace Masden." That was Juliana's mother. I stood up and waved my hand to signal her.

Juliana took the last few steps to her mother's grave and we stood side by side.

"Hi, Mama. I brought you these." She bent down and laid the flowers on her mother's grave. Together we kneeled near the headstone, our hands interwoven into each other's like we'd become one stone sculpture created from two stones. Juliana freely cried, probably for the first time, not stopping the tears.

CHAPTER TWENTY-FOUR

I lay on my stomach on top of the mussed sheets trying to get unconsciousness back. I don't know how much time ticked by, but at some point, soft hands and prickling nails ran down my back under my nightshirt and lingered a moment at the waistband of my underpants. I stretched out on my stomach, making it easier for her to get them off me. I might as well enjoy this one more time before all our time was gone. She tugged at the leg holes of my underpants, slowly pulling them down to my ankles. I always loved the feeling of that last moment before she took them off. That whoosh of freedom. She slipped my underpants over my feet and off. Oh, yes! There was the whoosh. She pulled my nightshirt up to my waist and nibbled on my rear while she reached around to the front and put her fingers between my legs, letting them slowly walk up my thighs to my clit. I let out a deep sigh. She turned me over and pulled my nightshirt above my chest. Her tongue circled a nipple while her fingers played between my legs. I wanted this, and I didn't want this. In only a short time, I was going to lower the worst possible boom on her. How could I let her do this for me? I grabbed her by the shoulders and crushed her into me, kissing her. I tore off my nightshirt. There was nothing so wonderful as being naked with Juliana when she was naked too. Soon I was going to lose this. So, I would have it now. I *will* have it. I *will* have it. We kissed and touched in desperation. Forget tomorrow. Forget the next damn minute. Be one inside me now. Now! Now! Only now! Oh, God, Oh God, Juliana . . .

"Oh God, Al, Oh God, Oh . . ."

Our voices, our bodies melting into each other. Take me, take me, possess every inch of me. And we shot high into the air and met each other there. We slowly came down. A moment of silent gazing on the pillow turned into laughter. And more laughter. And tears. I cried and cried and she held me against her breasts.

"Al?"

"I'm fine," I said, sliding out of bed. "We got there at the same time, didn't we?"

"I think so."

"It was one of those firsts, wasn't it?"

"Uh, huh. It was beautiful."

"I know."

Now, how was I going to tell her about Schuyler? I stood there in the middle of the room naked, crying.

She got up and put an arm around me. "Are you still held in the thrall of our orgasm or is it something else?"

I went to my bureau and pulled on underwear. *Our orgasm*, she'd said. "Nothing. I mean . . ." I put on my shirt and turned to her.

"Yes?"

"Wait. I can't do this without pants on."

I put on a pair of pants, not a skirt this time, pants. I needed the security that pants would give me. "There's something I have to tell you, Juliana."

She must have detected the seriousness in my voice because after I said it, she pulled on her nightgown and sat back down on the bed ready to listen.

"I . . There's something, uh. . ."

"Just say it, please. You're scaring me."

"Schuyler. Dan Schuyler."

"Who?"

"You met him on the ship. You danced with him a few times."

"I danced with lots of men."

"Medium height. Dark hair, thirtyish."

"You just described more than half the ship. Who is he? Why are we talking about him?"

"Remember I told you about a musical that I thought would be good for you?"

"Yes. And I told you no. So . . .?"

"Schuyler, he . . . he knows . . ."

"Knows?"

"About us."

I waited for her to say something, but she didn't. She just sat there looking at me, her expression frozen, unreadable.

"That musical is his property. He wants you to play the lead and if you don't, he's going to the press with . . . with what he knows." She still wasn't saying anything. She seemed to be waiting for me to come to some punch line, something to give this horror a happy ending. "I sent a cablegram to Max with all the latest details. I had to talk in code because I didn't want the cablegram guy to know what— I expected to hear from him by now with some great advice but—nothing. Schuyler wants your signature on the contract today or else he'll—"

"Where's the contract?"

"Here." I pulled it out of the bedside drawer. "I tried to stop him, Jule. This might be my fault." I wouldn't let myself cry.

"I don't understand."

"One of the people I hired at The Haven may have helped Schuyler. I'm so sorry."

"You had no way of knowing that any of them would do such a thing."

"But, Jule, you're going to be great in that part. It's perfect for you."

The house phone rang.

"Do you think so? Under a threat like this?"

"Well . . .?"

The house phone continued to ring. To shut it up I figured I had to answer it. "What? What do you want?"

"Max!" I screamed into the phone, breaking all those politeness rules. "We'll be right there, Girard. Don't let him hang up."

"Jule, get dressed." She'd already dashed into her room.

I thought about changing out of my pants, but I was too jumpy. So what if they stared at me. I hopped into my shoes. I don't think Juliana ever got dressed so fast in her life or ever looked so sloppy; her dress was wrinkled, her hair a frazzled mess, no earrings, no makeup.

We didn't bother with their pokey elevator. We flew down the three flights of stairs. I grabbed the receiver. Max! Oh, gosh, Max, I knew you'd come through."

Monsieur Girard Fournier stood uncomfortably close to me, whispering something in my free ear. I moved away from him. "*You* can fix that lousy dirty rat Schuyler," I said into the phone. "What are you gonna do, Max? Oh.

She's right here." I held the phone out for Juliana. Monsieur Fournier was now leaning over Jule, anxiously talking to her in French. She shooed him away. "Take the phone Jule. He wants *you*."

Jule hesitantly stood. Getting help from Max in this desperate circumstance had to be hard for her after all the years of not speaking to him. I hoped Max didn't rub it in and make her feel worse.

I handed her the receiver and stood listening. She didn't say anything. She was focused on Max's words with every muscle in her face. Girard stood practically on top of my feet. "Madam, Madam, you cannot stay in the lobby in those clothes."

"Shh. Please. I have to hear this," I said.

"You cannot." He gestured wildly. "Trousers are not . . ."

I moved closer to Juliana.

She said quietly, "I understand. If that's what you think is best. Thank you."

Her hand still on the phone, she stared at the back wall, past Girard who was pacing and jabbering in English and French about pants. She hung up the phone.

"Well?" I said. "I know he's got a plan to get you out of this."

She headed back up the steps to our rooms, slower this time. I followed, wondering what in the world Max had said.

"Well?" I asked once inside my room again. "What'd he say?"

She spoke with no expression. "He told me to sign the contract."

"What?"

She sat down on my bed, her fingers dug deep into the edge of the mattress. "He said there isn't much he can do from the States, but when we get home he'll get Schuyler off my ass—his words, not mine—so Schuyler can't keep me prisoner forever. He said that if you think this property is good for me, I should listen to you and pretend there is no Schuyler for now. He said you know what you're doing."

"Oh, gosh, Jule, I'm sorry."

"The contract." She held out her hand.

I handed it to her with a ballpoint pen.

"I can't use a ballpoint for this. My fountain pen. On top of the vanity."

I ran into her room and snatched the fountain pen, inkwell, and gold-plated blotter from the top of her vanity and dashed back into my room. I placed the ink and blotter on the bedside table close to where she sat and held the pen out for her. She dipped it into the ink.

"You know we'll have to be even more careful when we get back," she said. "You and me. More careful than we've ever been."

"I know."

She signed her name in a flourish.

Juliana

End of Book 3

Get a FREE full-length play, Why'd Ya Make Me Wear This, Joe?

This play was the beginning inspiration for the Juliana Series and it was my most produced play.

https://dl.bookfunnel.com/ecgczdzuw9

Some Fun Facts

Al complains that Billy (Juliana's director) takes TWA to Paris instead of the ship with the rest of them. She has a good reason for being angry. In 1956, a first-class ticket on the *SS United States* cost about $365. This amount had the spending power of $2,097 in 2016. However, a TWA flight from New York to Paris cost $711, which had the spending power of $9,240.

When Al and Richard are boating in the Lac Daumesnil, Richard speaks of the phone conversation he had with Dan Schuyler. He tells Al that he and Schuyler should meet because "... you know, two men over a beer..." Al thinks to herself, *Oh brother now he sounded like they both belonged to the Princeton Club*. No women were admitted to Princeton University until 1967; therefore, women did not have an important college club to join, one that gave men important business connections. In that moment, Al's feeling her lack of access to resources that men easily had available to them.

The story Al relates to Juliana on the deck of the *SS United States* about the lesbian who bashes her husband's head in with a hammer, and then dashes off to a bridge party comes from F.S. Caprio's book: *Female Homosexuality: A Psychodynamic Study of Lesbians*, 1954, p. 148. It seems important to note that Caprio was an M.D. To give a flavor to exactly what Juliana and Al are up against and why they are so afraid, I've listed a few quotes from Dr. Caprio's book.

"Lesbianism is capable of influencing the stability of our social structure." (p. viii)

"Crime is intimately associated with female sexual inversion (lesbianism). Many crimes committed by women, upon investigation, reveal that the women were either confirmed lesbians who killed because of jealousy or were latent homosexuals with a strong aggressive masculine drive." (p.302)

"Some lesbians manifest pronounced sadistic and psychopathic trends. Kleptomaniac tendencies, for example, are not uncommon among them." (p. 302)

REVIEWS

Dear Reader,

Your opinion about my book matters. It matters to me, it matters to Amazon and it matters to other customers. The more reviews I get the greater opportunity I will have to spread the story of LGBT history.

Won't you please help spread the story of the LGBT culture and history by writing a review? Your review can be long and detailed or short and simple. It's up to you.

Whether you're gay, lesbian, bi, transgender, you choose no gender, are questioning, straight, or something else I want to hear what you have to say about my books and this series.

Where to leave a review:

US: https://amzn.to/2I8Wn5K

Canada: http://bit.ly/2KjfNWd

UK: http://vandawriter.com/UK

Australia: http://vandawriter.com/AUSamazon

Goodreads:
https://www.goodreads.com/series/215717-juliana

Hey, It's Still the 1950s

There are times when readers have contacted me and written wonderful letters about my characters and their relationship to them. This thrills me because these characters are part of my soul, so when a reader believes in them too, I'm in heaven. One such letter came from Sallie Castillo.

Sallie said: "I have a love affair with historical lesbian fiction, so when I discovered your *Juliana* I couldn't wait to read it. I was not disappointed. The time period, the focus on the fear of discovery in the 40s, all brought to life, for me, our history and the fascinating world of Gay New York in the war and postwar years. I also fell in love with your characters, the complex Juliana and the sweet young naive Al. Max, Shirl, and Virginia Sales, I loved getting to know them and learning of their lives. But it is your protagonist "Al whom I most related to." She goes on to explain why she relates to Al so much and then she came to the "but. . ."

She said, "I became disappointed in Al. How could she not move on (from Juliana)? How could she not have other love stories and adventures!?"

I'm sure others have had some of these same thoughts, so with Sallie's permission I'm going to reprint my response back to her.

Certainly, Juliana is no easy woman for Al to be in love with. I've worried about this myself. Still, I need to remind you and myself that we are still in the 1950s; it is not even the 1970s. No one's consciousness has been raised yet.

We in our modern world, are highly sensitive to "abusive" relationships. We don't put up with them and we try to not let others put up with them, either; if they do, we get mad. Our culture has been through a lot to get us to this point, but this all occurred long after the 1950s, Al's world. As a child in the fifties, I remember a woman who lived down the block, a mother with three kids. She was badly beaten regularly by her husband. Occasionally, the cops would come and take him away to cool off for the night, but they always drove him back in the squad car each morning. She, of course, did not press charges. No woman would in those days. No cop would have taken her seriously; it was only a husband-wife spat. There were no laws on the books that made any of this illegal or even terribly shocking. I was young and I liked the husband a lot. He used to give me soda to drink, which my mother would never allow. The neighbors would whisper about the wife and say things like "Isn't it awful," but they all knew there was nothing to be done because she was Catholic and would never leave him; even if she hadn't been Catholic, divorce was pretty much frowned upon by every religion back then. Everyone knew what a divorced woman was truly like, wink, wink. No neighbor thought it was appropriate to speak to the woman about this situation because the norm at that time was no one had a right to interfere with another's family, no matter what was going on. It wasn't our business. There weren't even any outside agencies who could guide or protect her. When the decade turned into the 1960s and ideas were changing, this woman left her husband.

We are greatly influenced by the times we live in. At this point, I don't think Al would know how to be with another woman. She's gotten somewhat comfortable with Juliana, I doubt she could even picture herself with someone else. She has no close gay women friends at this point (Yes, there are Shirl and Mercy, but they are mimicking a heterosexual marriage, which was common in those days; this isn't something Al would seek.) The gay men too (Max and Scott) are struggling during this decade to figure out how to be a couple. Al hasn't gone to the bars. Yet. She might've met other gay women there, but the bars were looked at as a place for low class women. Given Al's background, she would be sensitive about being in a place for "low-class women." Also, the fear of being arrested and exposed was very real. Al has a career she is trying to protect.

In the 1950s, many women didn't want anyone to know they were gay. It was dangerous to reveal yourself. During this time, some women were giving up on living with another woman because they feared being fired from their job. (Faderman, 1991) Al works in a straight club. Even Bertha and Lillian can't know that she, Max, and Marty are gay, because if it were discovered that "immoral persons" were running their nightclub, they could be closed. It's hard to imagine, but during the forties and fifties even the lone beat cop could close down a club. Remember, Max gives the cops money to keep them away. (Book 2)

Another reason I think Al hangs on is because she knows intuitively more about Juliana than Juliana knows about herself. Juliana says she can't leave Richard because of religion and that's true, but I think it also serves as a convenient excuse. She's just plain terrified of being publicly gay. With good reason. If she were found out—good-bye career.

Have you ever read about some of the female actors who were gay in the 1940s and 50s? Women like Judith Anderson, Dorothy Arzner (feminist director), Gertrude Lawrence (married to a man), Mary Martin (married to a gay man)? Have you heard of Hildegarde, the highest paid supper club singer in the 1930s and 40s? She was mentioned in my series a few times. She died at ninety-nine years old in 2005, denying being gay. I met a cabaret singer, KT Sullivan, who knew Hildegarde and knew a male friend of Hildegarde's. He was in his eighties. He had had affairs with Hollywood stars like Rock Hudson. KT introduced him to me on the telephone and asked him if I could call him at another time to ask questions about Hildegarde. He eagerly said yes. However, when I called him a week later, he had forgotten I was going to call. (Well, he *was* old). Not remembering who I was, he became extremely upset and told me not to write a single word about Hildegarde being gay or I would be sued. I pointed out that she was dead. He said Hildegarde had hired lawyers who would sue anyone, even after her death, that mentioned she was homosexual. He was desperate to shoo me away. This was a man who had had affairs in Hollywood with famous actors, who had hidden in literal closets when the star got an unfriendly visitor. On the phone with me, he was terrified and he was still protecting his friend. The Seattle Times said that the glamorous Hildegarde often described herself to reporters as "an incurable romantic . . . I traveled all my life, met a lot of men, had a lot of romances, but it never worked out. It was always hello and goodbye. (Dellair, 2005) She leaves out any reference to Ana Sosenko, who managed her career, wrote some of her songs, and with whom she lived in a huge apartment in the Plaza Hotel for twenty years. (Nemy, Aug 1, 2005). When Faderman (1991) looked for lesbians to interview for her book, *Odd Girls and Twilight Lovers*, many insisted on anonymity and others simply refused to participate. Faderman wrote her book in the nineties, but people were still terrified of revealing themselves; they'd been that scarred by the times they grew up in. I think it would be impossible for us in our world today to fully grasp the threat these people were under.

France Was Not The Haven For Gays Often Thought

It is popularly believed that France was more accepting of homosexuality during the mid-twentieth century than other countries such as the United States. In the US during the fifties, homosexuals were persecuted daily in the *New York Times* and other newspapers. They were accused of being dangerous to children and likely to be blackmailed into helping the communist cause. Also, during that decade, the police were raiding gay and lesbian bars and occasionally arresting these patrons. Some lesbians stopped moving in with lovers for fear that their orientation would be discovered and they would lose their jobs. Other lesbians made hasty marriages, maybe some believing the pop psychology hype that marriage could cure them. Others dashed into convents. (Faderman, 1991)

It is true the French had rid their country of anti-sodomy laws way back in 1791 (Jackson, 2009, p.20), while the US did not eradicate these laws in all fifty states until 2003. However, France's legalizing of sodomy in the eighteenth century should not be taken to mean approval or even acceptance. Like the U.S and all other countries in the 1950s, France considered homosexuality to be "an abhorrent vice." (Merrick & Ragan, 1996, p. 8), "a milieu favorable to delinquency, a breeding ground for criminal viruses." (Sideris, 2001, p. 22) French moralists condemned both male and female homosexuality as the "worst of sins." All lesbians were considered to be prostitutes, and in 1843, a law was passed that specifically prohibited streetwalkers from living in the same apartment with other streetwalkers. (Jackson, 2009, p. 20) I gather so they couldn't engage in the "sin" of lesbianism.

France's motivation for repealing the sodomy laws at that time had more to do with the spirit of their revolution than it did with any "love" of homosexuals. The repeal of sodomy came at a time when the French were striving to secularize their government, disallowing all laws having anything to do with religious dictates or the Bible. Therefore, laws against heresy, blasphemy, *and* sodomy were repealed. (Jackson, 2009, 20) At the same time as sodomy was being taken off the books, there was an increase in the number of men being arrested for same-sex behaviors such as "public immorality" or "unruly behavior." (Jackson, 2009, p.21), code phrases for homosexuality.

The myth of French society being a free one for homosexuals may have originated with Oscar Wilde. Before Wilde was to stand trial in Great Britain for sodomy and gross indecency, his friends encouraged him to escape to France where these were not crimes. If Wilde had followed his friends' advice, he would not have been imprisoned; however, neither would he have been embraced. He most likely would have been ostracized and forced to take a false name as he ultimately did after completing his two years of incarceration in Great Britain. (Belford, 2000)

Another reason we, in the US, may think homosexuals were accepted in mid-twentieth century France is because of the literary and artistic figures who clustered together in the Latin Quarter in Paris from 1920 to 1950. Women like Gertrude Stein, Romaine Brooks, Natalie Barney, Janet Flanner, Colette, Sylvia Beach and others came to Paris for the relative freedom it would give them to create. (Belford, 2000) Most of these literary and artistic women were lesbians, but they did not make a cause out of their same-sex relations. Except for Natalie Barney, who was open about her sexuality, most of these women kept it to themselves, leaving that part of their lives dark to the world. (Benstock, 1988, p.10) Gertrude Stein explored the meaning of her sexuality through her writing; however, these often sexually explicit works were not published until after her death. Stein considered "serious" writing to be the province of men; therefore, the primary point of taking on the male role was to allow her to write.

In 1942, a sharp legal distinction was made between homosexuals and heterosexuals with the changing of the age of consent law. Prior to 1942, the age of consent for all French citizens was thirteen. With the passing of the new law, the age of consent was changed to twenty-one for homosexuals, but it remained thirteen for heterosexuals.

In 1950s France, there were often police raids on bars, just like in the United States. However, this was true only for the gay men's bars, unlike in the US. The French did look down on lesbians but didn't consider them important enough to raid their bars. Raids on men's bars were especially common in the Saint Germaine-des-Prés district, where gay bars and cafes were beginning to proliferate. Although sodomy was legal, other homosexual behavior was not; for instance, two men dancing with each other was illegal.

In the 1950s, the US mainstream culture was finding parallels between homosexuals and communists (both were considered immoral and of weak character); during this same postwar period, France saw homosexuals as Nazi collaborators. (Jackson, 2009, p41) They even went so far as to blame Andre Gide, for holding values that caused the fall of France in 1940 at the beginning of World War II.

A film that can be found on you-tube, "Lesbians and Gays of the 1950s," about French gay men and lesbians makes 1950s French attitudes toward gays clear. The first part of this short documentary-like film shows a nightclub with a group of rather sleepy-looking women dancing with each other; some wear dresses, others wear men's suits and ties. There is absolutely zero sexual energy in this club and everyone looks rather bored. An old woman with gray hair plays a violin in the background. "The narrator gravely asks, "What deep rooted emotions have removed them so completely from the company of men but cause them to emulate the masculine appearance with such *pathetic* results? Despite their blasé attitude one is aware of their underlying sadness." And so, we witness first-hand the 'if you're a lesbian you must be sick' hypothesis. No different from the US in the 1950s.

The film moves on to a gay men's club where we see equally bored men dancing with each other. The narrator, attempting to sound scientific says, "while literature and tradition condones the weakness of woman, man receives only the heavy weight of ridicule. No matter how hard man tries to negate woman she's forever present inside of him. The more he tries to deny her, the more womanish he becomes. Yes, woman is apparent in hermits, eunuchs, the chaste and more than ever in *them.*(meaning the gay men dancing on the film)" It is difficult to communicate by written word the venom with which this man says. '*them.*'

It seems that in the 1950s and beyond, France was as restrictive and hateful toward gays as the United States. It was not the haven that it is often claimed to be. France had to go through an arduous learning process similar to what we in the United States have been going through to arrive at a more accepting view of differences in sexual orientation.

REFERENCES

Belford, Barbara. 2000. *Oscar Wilde: A Certain Genius*. New York, NY: Random House.

Benstock, Shari. 1988. *Women of the Left Bank: Paris, 1900 1940*. Austin, TX: University of Texas.

Jackson, Julian. 2009. *Living in Arcadia*. Chicago, IL: University of Chicago Press.

Faderman, Lillian. 1991. *Odd Girls and Twilight Lovers*. New York, NY: Penguin.

Merrick, Jeffrey, and Michael Sibalis. (Eds.) (2001) *Homosexuality in French History and Culture*. The Haworth Press.

BEHIND THE SCENES
WELL-DESERVED THANK YOUS

First, I have to thank all of you who have become fans of the Juliana series and have told me in your reviews and your letters that Al, Juliana, Max, and the rest have become a part of your lives. This fills me with such humility and gratitude.

A very special thank you goes to Karin de la Penha Collison who did all my French translations. I'm sure I drove her mad with my quick emails asking: "How do you say . . . ?" But she never complained. As a working actor, she's a busy woman so

I'm grateful she could spare a little of her time for me.

I also must thank my Street Team who were the first to read *Olympus Nights on the Square, Book 2* and left reviews. Reviews make such a difference. I want to especially thank the Street Team members who volunteered to be my beta readers and/or my proofreaders for this book. These were (alphabetized by first name): Amanda Beilfuss, Catherine, Tejal Johnson, Nicole Person, Katrina Schmidt, Laura Huff, Tanya Marie Wheeler. These women read all of *Paris, Adrift, Book 3* and gave me helpful feedback and I am grateful to them.

My editor, Deborah Dove at Polgarus Studio, did such a great job helping with all the finer points of grammar and putting the commas where they're supposed to be. Thanks, Debi.

Once again, my writers' group, The Oracles, gave me useful feedback as I was writing *Paris, Adrift*. The Oracles are some of the best writers in the country, so their feedback proved invaluable. Thank you: Liz Amberly, Edgar Chisholm, Bill Cosgriff, Stuart D'vers, Elana Gartner, Nicole Greevy, March Goldsmith, Nancy Hamada, Olga Humphrey, Penny Jackson, Robin Rice, Donna Specter and Mike Vogel

ABOUT THE AUTHOR

I was born and raised in Huntington Station, New York. This town shouldn't be confused with Al's hometown of Huntington. They are two different places, and it's too long a story to explain the significance of that difference. Now, I live in New York City, and I have for some time. I've been a professor at Metropolitan College of New York for twenty-four years, but I don't teach writing like many people guess. I teach psychology because my advanced training was in psychology, and I am a licensed psychologist.

I was a writer long before I was a psychologist. I wrote my first novel in eighth grade, with encouragement from my teacher, Mr. James Evers, who would meet me before school every week to discuss the latest pages I had penned. He wrote in my junior high yearbook, "My children will read your words." Unfortunately, others were not so encouraging, and I wandered away from my writing. I spent a lot of years going from job to job because the work-a-day world could not satisfy the restlessness in my mind. Along the way, I found playwriting and was a playwright for about twenty years. The desire to tell the story of LGBT history with fictional characters who live through that history brought me back to my original form, the novel, but I learned a lot about dialogue from playwriting.

I'd love to hear from you. My online home is www.vandawriter.com. Come sign up for my mailing list there and get info about new releases and forthcoming events. You can also connect with me on Goodreads at https://www.goodreads.com/drvanda and Facebook at www.facebook.com/vandawriter or twitter at www.twitter.com/vandawriter. You can contact me directly at vanda@vandawriter.com.

Happy Reading

Made in the USA
Middletown, DE
13 August 2018